WILL CAIN

THE REBEL

WILL CAIN
THE REBEL

By
William B. Parker

TATE PUBLISHING
AND ENTERPRISES, LLC

WILL CAIN THE REBEL

Published by Tate Publishing & Enterprises, LLC
127 E. Trade Center Terrace | Mustang, Oklahoma 73064 USA
1.888.361.9473 | www.tatepublishing.com

Tate Publishing is committed to excellence in the publishing industry. The company reflects the philosophy established by the founders, based on Psalm 68:11,
"The Lord gave the word and great was the company of those who published it."

Published in the United States of America

ISBN: 978-1-62854-069-7
1. Fiction/Christian/Western
2. History/United States/Civil War Period 1850-1877
13.09.26

Dedication

This book is dedicated to my oldest son, Thomas Keith Parker, who left us too soon at the young age of fifty. He read the original draft and said, "Dad this is good." He was the first one to encourage me to continue on this journey. Tom was an outstanding athlete in football and wrestling in high school and continued to wrestle in the Coast Guard Academy. He enjoyed horseback riding as a child in Oregon. In Hawaii he became the spear fishing champion for two years. Tom was a courageous fireman in Kona, Hawaii. He was well respected by his family, friends, and fellow firemen. I love and miss him dearly.

CHAPTER 1

His shock of red hair soaked with sweat, young Will Cain took his ax and whacked with all his might at the resinous log, nearly as big as a calf. His papa had dragged it out of the canebrake that morning with the family mule. In twenty minutes, the lad had managed to extract a half-dozen good-sized splinters and numerous giblets from the heart pine, rich in resin but hard as a rock, for use as fatwood kindling. Exhausted, he plopped down on the small pile of oak firewood he had split earlier. He reckoned it was too warm in south Alabama for a fire, even if it was February. The day had been mild and the night promised to be just as pleasant, and chopping wood and kindling was the last thing he wanted to be doing as the sun set over the Cain farm. Surely, the family had enough quilts to get them through the night, he thought, as he stood up and aimed another blow at the unyielding stump.

A familiar nicker interrupted Will's chore. Grinning, he tossed the ax onto the woodpile, ambled into the barn, and offered a handful of hay to the line-backed buckskin mare that had lately become the apple of his eye. She was a beauty, with a dark dorsal mane, a black stripe down her back, and dark points on her legs from her hooves to her knees. Will thought she was uncommonly smart too, an opinion shared by his papa who knew a thing or two about horses. The family had called the filly Nellie since Chickasaw, her dam, foaled her three years earlier, but lately Will had been experimenting with another name he thought best suited the horse's great speed.

“Hey, Cat, old girl,” said Will. “Cat, you like that name?”

“Boo!”

Will jumped in mock fright “Polly, you sneaky little varmint! What do you want trying to scare me out of my skin?”

A triumphant smile bloomed on the girl’s face. She was a young girl a year or so shy of Will’s twelve years, with glossy raven hair, a beautiful tawny complexion, and green eyes that danced with mischief.

“Papa says for you to hurry up with that firewood,” she said. “He said it’s going to be cold tonight.”

“I doubt that,” said Will. He nudged past her, scooped up an armload of wood and kindling, and stalked away toward the front porch.

“Nathan and I want some, too!” Polly called after him. “We’re roasting the sausages we stuffed and cured last fall.”

“Get it yourself, then!” Will said crossly, in jest.

He stepped onto the porch, breezed past his parents who were sitting together on the swing, and unceremoniously dumped the wood in the box next to the river rock fireplace in the snug little living room. When he came back outside, he saw Polly dragging two oak logs out to the fire pit his father had built when Will was a little boy. His brother, Nathan, was squatting down in front of the pit, blowing on a pile of twigs and leaves to get a fire going. Rattler, the grizzled old dog that had been a top-notch cattle herder and watchdog in his day, sat alongside him waiting patiently for some scraps of sausage. Will fetched another armload of firewood and then sat down in a chair alongside his parents, who were deep in yet another discussion of the war. He knew little about the war, other than Alabama had seceded the previous month and that the Confederacy had entered into it courtesy of a $500,000 loan from the state. His papa was always bringing up this fact, which, as a proud son of Alabama, pleased him no end. Will couldn't wrap his mind around that much money, and the reasons behind the dissension between the North and the South were just as cloudy to him, despite his dad's nightly harping on them. He only cared that his papa might be going off to join something called “the cause,” and the specter of his doing so frightened the family to death.

The Cain's of Coffee County, Alabama had done their share of soldiering in the Revolutionary War, the War of 1812, and the Creek War of 1836, but Bob Cain had never thought much about joining anyone’s army until Alabama seceded from the Union on January 11, 1861. The Cain's owned no slaves, believing that slavery was not in line with the New Testament. Furthermore, Bob was firm in his belief that a central government had no right to tell the individual states what they could do. The Northern tariffs on Southern cotton were horrendous. Bob had had about all he was going to take on the behavior of what he called uppity Yankees.

Will got up and sidled close to his papa as he cleaned with great care the old T. W. Tignor .36 caliber rifle his daddy had carried in the Creek War, Bob all the while doing his best to ignore his wife’s usual arguments. Will had long coveted the half-stock rifle with double-set triggers and silver mountings, but as it was his papa's favorite gun—he had even painstakingly carved his name in the stock—he knew he would take it with him to the war, when he went.

"Why do we keep having this conversation, Bob?" Said Ellen in her slow, low voice, "I don't know how you could even consider marching off to war. Others that don't have three children to care for like we do—let them go plenty in your stead. Don't you understand? Why, you could be disabled or killed. What would happen to our family then? Don't you love us? Don't you care no more?"

"Ellen, yes I do."

"Ain't we getting by, even with all the Yankee tariffs laid on us? Lay down that damned Scottish pride of yours, Bob Cain! Forget those Scottish tunes you like so well that glorify war, and stay home where you belong."

"Ellender, many years ago my family was oppressed in Scotland and we had to take a stand," Bob replied, a mild note of irritation creeping into his pleasant drawl. "That is why we are here in Alabama today. I have heard my grandfather go on about the inequities in the old country. Well, it must stop here, too, and it's my duty to help do something about it. We don't agree with slavery. The British sent many white slaves to America because they were just poor Scots, Irish or poor Englishmen, and putting an end to that kind of treatment of no common voices in the government is only one of the many fine reasons I can think of justifying this war. The only thing I fear about secession is we could end up just like Europe."

"How could we ever be like the old country?" Ellen clucked. "We don't have a king."

"We could become a country of many little nations, and every time something happens we don't like, someone will cry secession." Bob shook his head vigorously. "Naw, that isn't what the folks wanted back in 1775. We are supposed to be one nation, founded on God's principles. I don't want to let the government get so big it forgets about regular farm folks like us. No sir, the South must take a stand for what is right. I've made up my mind. I'm leaving tomorrow morning."

Ellen was aghast. “Tomorrow morning, Bob? But I figured you’d be around a few more days, at least.”

“I did too, Ellen, but I heard tell from Uncle James that the 29th Alabama is picking up a load of recruits from this part of Alabama. His own boys are going. I can’t very well sit idle and let my cousins do my fighting.”

“If you must go, papa, can I go with you?” Will said. “I am big enough to be a soldier,” he added proudly and puffed his chest out.

Bob smiled and tousled the boy’s hair. “Son, I reckon you are just about big enough, but you are not old enough. I am going to go and do my duty the way I see I must do it. Way down deep, I don’t want to go, but I had to make a choice. I cannot stay here and let the rights of my state be trampled on. Everything we do in life is the result of the choices we make good or bad, and we have to live with the consequences. Can you understand that, son?”

“Yes, papa,” said Will quietly.

Nathan and Polly had overheard Bob’s announcement and came up on the porch.

They listened respectfully as their father continued to address Will.

"I'm sorry, son, that the farm will have to fall on your young shoulders, but I believe you are man enough to take care of yourself and the children," said Bob, looking Will hard in the eye. "Y'all will have to share the work, but you are the man while I am gone, you'll have to do most of the work." Bob jerked his head toward the dim lights of a farmhouse looming in the near distance. "If you get in a real bind your Grandsir Garrison is a stone's throw away and, if he is too busy, he will send one of his hired hands over to help. Make sure y'all get to church on Sundays, for your Grandsir don't like it if his family ain't there when he gets all het up to preach."

Will was feeling guilty for not being diligent about his chore. Hadn't his father come right out and called him a man? He had never done that before. Will resolved then and there not to let him down again ever.

"Yes sir, papa," replied Will. "I will do everything that I see needs doing and whatever else momma or a family friend tells me to do, and I will try to take care of this place just like you would."

"I know you will, son," said Bob solemnly. "Now, I figure me and Grandsir have about three hundred cows plus calves running around in the canebrake. Bring them in occasionally, gentle 'em down, and keep them branded up, if you can. You can get help from Grandsir or Uncle Tootsie when you brand. Oh, and have Tootsie breed any mares to our stud horse, as we can use the colts later."

Will's face lit up at the thought of working with Uncle Tootsie Westbrook. A free black man, he and his wife, Winnie, farmed forty acres of land adjacent to his grandpa's place and were as close as family to the Cain's. Moreover, Tootsie was a horseman par excellent and a patient teacher to anyone wanting to learn about horsemanship, and Will certainly had that desire.

"You can count on me, sir," He said with assurance. He hesitated a moment and posed the question that had been preying on his mind. "Papa, that buckskin filly I have been riding is a real corker. Can I have her for my own?"

Bob breathed on the rifle stock and rubbed it with his rag. “Tell you what, son. She will be your wages for minding the farm. You get that mare broke real good now, don’t jaw her around and ruin her mouth. It will take a lot of wet saddle blankets to break her right. Do you understand? If you need help with her, ask Tootsie.”

“I will, papa,” said Will. He added shyly, “I’ve decided to call her Cat ’stead of Nellie on account of she’s quick as one.”

“Cat exclaimed Nathan. He was a husky boy, about ten, with red hair like his father and Will, and had a heavily freckled moon face. “That’s a silly name for a horse.”

“You just be quiet, baby brother,” said Will hotly. “Papa says she’s mine and I’ll call her whatever I want.”

“I think it’s a fine name,” said Polly diplomatically.

“I do, too, princess,” said Bob, poking both her and Nathan in the ribs and setting them to giggle.

“Bob,” said Ellen softly, “it’s getting late. Could you and I go for a walk together? I have wanted to be alone with you for a while."

Bob rose and leaned his rifle against the doorjamb. "Sure, sweetheart," he said and taking Ellen's hand, they strolled around the yard and the outbuildings, clinging to each other as if they wished their fleeting moments together could last forever. At length, Bob led Ellen over to the handsome pine bench he had built when they were newly married. It was well dark now, and he kissed her with all the feeling he had and she responded in kind.

"Oh, Ellen, I wish this was all a bad dream," Bob whispered. "I am not fearful of going to war, but I don't want to leave you."

Ellen's eyes smoldered. "Let's go in the house, Bob. I want to lay with you before you go. I want to feel your hands and body all over me. That may sound wanton Bob, but I want you so much. Like a young bride."

"I have a more romantic idea," said Bob with a gleam in his eye as he led her down to the barn.

"But Bob, it's starting to get cold—we'll catch our death," Ellen protested, but she followed him eagerly after snatching a quilt off the clothesline.

He made their bed in the hay with a wagon sheet and covered Ellen's tender skin with the quilt, and they came to each other not as young lovers, but as folks that knew the joy of being a long time together. They gloried in each other and every movement was sensuous, until the joyous cascade washed over them.

"If I was to get pregnant again, I think it would be nice to be from this, time."

When the rooster crowed before dawn the next morning, they rose and walked hand in hand to the house. Ellen set about making breakfast and Bob called for the children to rise and shine.

"What do you want for breakfast, Bob?" Ellen asked cheerfully as she puttered around the kitchen. Her cheeks glowed readily and a secret smile played upon her lips.

"Well, after the fine time you gave me last night, bacon, biskits, and white cream gravy will top this morning off to a farewell," said Bob as he swatted her behind lustily.

"William Robert Cain, you should be ashamed of yourself!" Said Ellen as the children gathered about them, tittering in unknown mirth at their parents.

An hour later, Bob had his gear ready. Aside from the Tignor rifle, he was taking a Bowie knife (another keepsake from his father) from the Creek War, a powder horn, a cap box, and a bullet mold. A flour sack bulged with clothes, toiletries, tobacco, his Bible and the bottle of Scotch whiskey he thought he kept hidden from Ellen in the oat barrel in the barn. The family had gathered around the oak tree in the yard and everyone was crying loudly.

Bob stood in front of them solemnly with his hands clasped at his waist and his head bowed. He cleared his throat and said, "I reckon war is harder on those that stay than those that go. Y'all be good, take care of one another, and I will try to get home whenever the army will let me. And don't forget to keep me in your prayers, along with our kinfolk who are going off, too."

After a moment of prayer, Bob formed his family into a circle and walked around it, hugging and kissing each loved one in their turn.

"If I don't make it through this war, I want y'all to go on with life and not spend a lot of time crying for me," he said, his own eyes welling with tears, "since I will be in a better place, and someday we will be in a circle around God's throne. So don't weep for me—spend your time helping each other. I love each of you."

Ellen and the children watched him walk toward the crossroads to catch the army wagon that was scheduled to pick up a load of recruits for the 29th Alabama Infantry. The old dog, Rattler, trotted behind his master for a few paces before Will called him back. Just before he faded from sight around the bend, Bob turned around, danced a little jig, and waved to them one last time.

For the next few days, Ellen went through all the motions of being a strong Christian mother, but inside she was sick with worry and longed for her Bob. She did her best to hide her misery from the children, but they guessed her inner turmoil and were all the kinder toward her because of it.

She prayed nightly, “Please, dear God, help me find the strength to carry this through to the very end and help me be a person of wisdom and strength to my children. I know you did not ordain this war, but you know the end of a thing from the beginning, so no matter what happens, help me keep the faith. The Bible says our footsteps are ordered by the Lord. Please help me to see your hand in this.”

Will settled into his new responsibilities as the man of the family with conviction and enthusiasm. Polly and Nathan took their chores seriously and Ellen, of course, did more than her fair share. Young Will took charge of the farm doing exactly like his daddy asked. That first spring after Bob’s departure, the family put in cotton, sweet potatoes, and wheat on the hundred-acre parcel that adjoined the farm of Ellen’s parents. Grandsir (Grandpa) and Nanny Garrison had eighty acres, which were well tended by the two families of free blacks in their employ.

At twelve, Will was a strong, lithe lad, tall for his age, broad in the shoulders, and mature beyond his years. Among his friends at church, he was one of the biggest and strongest, even counting boys several years older. His wiry body belied his great strength and he excelled at wrestling due to his upper body strength. He wasn't the fastest runner when they had races, but he always placed in the top three. Racing horses against the other young boys was a favorite pastime, and he and Cat made a formidable team, seldom losing a race. Will doted on the filly, and they rode off together often to hunt deer, turkey, possum, raccoon, and wild pigs. Being an excellent shot, he didn't waste ammunition and never came home empty-handed. The life of a farm boy agreed with his easygoing nature, and he liked to plow and feel the fresh turned, sweet smelling earth under his feet.

Will worked with the mare whenever possible, even riding her after dark just so she got used to the wet saddle blankets his papa had recommended. One afternoon in late March, he rode the mare over to Uncle Tootsie's forty-acre farm near Grandsir's place. It was balmy for the time of year and the promise of spring was on the breeze.

“Howdy, Uncle Tootsie,” Will sang out. “I brought the mare over for you to look at.”

The stooped old black man removed his straw hat and wiped the sweat from his brow. He had small, deep-set yellowed eyes that looked lonely and out of place on the wide, friendly face. The corded muscles in his forearms stood out like ropes against his purplish-black skin as he rolled a decrepit old wagon wheel toward the barn for repair. He rose up painfully and smiled at Will, showing a mouthful of brilliantly white but jagged teeth, like the shards of a broken teacup.

“Ah is doing’ tolerable, Mars Will,” he drawled as he patted Cat’s flank with affection. “How y’all doin’ wid de mare? She sho looks good. I notice she don’t slang her head none. Dat show me you got a light hand on the reins and dat is a sign of a real good horseman.”

“I am doing pretty well, I believe,” said Will, beaming at the compliment, for Tootsie’s skill with horses had earned his renown in Coffee and surrounding counties. “Uncle Tootsie, would you mind riding the mare and telling me what you think about her, and see if there ain't something I should be doing differently?"

"Well, now dat you mentions it, der' is one or two thangs," said Tootsie. "Lets' me gib you uh demonstration."

Tootsie climbed on the mare and loped her off down the road. In about ten minutes he returned at a good run, set the little mare up, and slid to a stop.

"Mars Will, y'all need to wuk on dat stoppin' her jess like I did, and y'all need to wuk on dat lead change," he said. "Mak her do dat figga eight so she has to change dat lead foots and wuk on her neck reinin' some mo ever day. She is a fine filly, sho 'nough."

"Where'd you learn so much about horses, Uncle?" Will prompted him. He knew well the story of Tootsie's early horse-trading adventures, but he never tired of hearing his "uncle" say it in that deep, rumbling voice that sounded like thunder trapped in a cave.

Uncle Tootsie scratched thoughtfully at his woolly pate. "Well, suh, Mistah Will, me an yore gram'pa Cain and yore great-grandpappy Cauley did a lot of hoss-tradin' long time ago, all ober Alabama,

Jawge, duh Carolinas, and Virginny. We won lot's money on racin'. Ize was a powerful lot smaller dem ole days, so Ize was da jockey. Ize din't belong to Mr. Cain, doh, he just rent me. Ize belong to a Mr. Carpenter, and wid some of dat money Ize got from winnin', Ize buy myself from Mr. Carpenter, and Ize able to buy dis heah foety acre and buy my wife Winnie, too. Da Lord been good to this ole darky, yes suh, He sho has.

"Now me and Mr. Cain, we allus had us a powerful good time. Ah declare, ah can 'member goin' to Virginny with him when yore papa was about nine year old and gettin' a bunch of dem hosses offen dem Chawktaw Indins. Dis heah filly ub yorn is a gran'daughter of dem same hoss. I got two of dem myself. Dat reminds me, Mars Will, Ize needs to fix up one ub my mares with yore daddy's stalyun, ole Dan."

"Sure thing, Uncle," said Will. "We'll need your help with breeding our own mares, for ole Dan can be contrary. Well, I'd best be runnin' along. I will come back sometime and let you see how I'm doing with Cat."

“You do dat! Say, Mistah Will, if’n y’all need hep on yo farm while yo daddy gone, jess lemme know.”

“I will, Uncle,” said Will. He cocked his head wistfully and added, “Sure hated to see Papa go off. I don’t know anything about war. What do you know about it, Uncle?”

“Not turrible much, Mars Will,” Uncle Tootsie allowed. “Ize followed yore gram’pa Cain off after them Creek Indins back in ’36. Didn’t do no fightin’ mysef, but yore grandpappy got in the middle of it. I just drove mule teams.” He cackled and added, “White folks didn’t know what to do with a free darky.”

“I hope you’re not filling this boy’s head with romantic notions of war,” said Aunt Winnie, who had come up silently from the house bearing a basket of blackberry muffins, made from last year’s preserves.

“No ma’am,” said Tootsie sheepishly.

“See that you don’t,” said Winnie.

She was a well-spoken woman of dignified bearing with smiling, reddish-brown eyes and graying hair that peeked out from underneath a Shaker-style bonnet. It was said of Winnie Westbrook that she always looked like she was dressed for Sunday. True, her homespun dresses looked well on her willowy frame, but she worked no less hard than any other woman in the community. She was kind and wise and Will loved her like a second mother.

She turned to Will. "Mister Will, don't listen to him. He's got cotton between his ears and lives in the past. Now, have a muffin while they're hot."

An outstanding cook by any measure, Aunt Winnie's baked goods were second to none. Gingerly, Will took a muffin from the basket, popped it whole into his mouth, and chewed with delirious pleasure.

"You, too," she said, thrusting the basket at Tootsie. He took two muffins, sticking one in his overalls pocket and taking a huge bite of the other.

"Sure is good," said Will, taking another muffin and devouring it whole.

Winnie clucked her tongue. "Child, you eat like Jonah's whale," she said, shaking her head. "If the Confederacy does get a hold of you, you will eat them out of business."

"Yes ma'am," mumbled Will. "I am too young to join just yet, but if the war goes on long enough, maybe I'll get the chance—"

"Bite your tongue, Will!" said Winnie. "Long enough, you say. Child, you had best be beseeching the Lord for an early end to this nonsense. I hold with beating swords into plowshares, not the other way around. Men and war, two stupid things that deserve each other if you ask me!"

She stuck another muffin in Will's hand and stalked off.

"Feisty little lady, ain't she, Uncle Tootsie?" said Will.

"She sho is," said Tootsie. "But she be a smart woman. She jest don't wan' see you all git kilt, Mars Will."

Will had a fleeting vision of himself as an invincible knight, swept up in a mighty gray tide, its thousand members screaming like banshees as the juggernaut overwhelmed and destroyed its puny blue foes.

"That could never happen to me," he said as if he really believed it.

That spring and summer, Will worked shirtless most of the time and his body was tanned bronze from the hot Alabama sun. He heeded his father's advice to raid the canebrake occasionally for stray cattle, but it was hard work, even with the Hope saddles he and Nathan were outfitted with. Bob had brought the saddles back with him from down along the Brazos River in Texas, after a visit to see his parents and brother, who had migrated west several years before the war. The brothers were grateful for the Hope's outsized horn, which stuck up like a sore thumb. Holding onto the thing saved their necks time after time when the going got hairy. Cat proved to be a real winner at cattle work, being able to anticipate a cow's move before the critter made it. Rattler pitched in, too, but the dog was just too old to be much help. Will turned thirteen in August and by the end of the month, they had caught thirty head, which Grandsir, who was not one to lavish praise, pronounced an impressive feat, considering their age and inexperience. With Uncle Tootsie's help, they branded and castrated ten steers and branded twenty heifers.

"Not bad for a couple of greenhorns," said Will with satisfaction when the work was finished. "But I'd hate to think what a chore it would be to bring in much more than we did. Let's save those two brindle steers back for meat and keep that young red and white calf back, also—we can butcher him early next spring."

"Maybe we should keep back that black and white heifer for Uncle Tootsie as payment for his help," Nathan suggested.

"That's a fine idea, Nate," Polly chimed in. "We don't need to be tight-fisted with what Providence has given us."

Will gave her a big grin. Polly had turned into a real hand. She was petite, but she rode like an Indian and had an easy hand on her horse's mouth. Her role in the roundups had been primarily that of a scout, but even at that, she excelled beyond Will's expectations. His affection for her was boundless. She was slim and supple, with big green eyes with flecks of brown, and a good sense of humor. She was fond of Indian wrestling, mumblety-peg, and roughhousing in general, and Will enjoyed her company every bit as much as that of the boys he knew.

Will and Nathan called Polly a tomboy, and she took it as a compliment, but she had an intellectual side, as well. She learned to read quickly under Ellen's tutelage and devoured the few books the Cain's owned Noah Webster's The American Spelling Book, two volumes of McGuffey Readers, a mammoth volume of Shakespeare that had come down through Ellen's family, and the Bible. She quoted freely and accurately from the latter, which made Ellen, who called her "a hungry fool for learning," proud as a peacock. While Will and Nathan didn't share Polly's enthusiasm for book learning and were deliriously glad of the fact there was yet no schoolhouse in the community, they sat dutifully alongside Polly for Ellen's lessons in arithmetic, English, and science, and were smart, attentive, well-mannered boys.

Polly had come into their lives in a most unusual way. Will remembered well the day his papa had come home from Elba with a letter he had received from a lawyer in Arkansas, where Bob's maternal grandfather, Bartholomew Cauley, had moved to from Alabama some years earlier, taking his family and slaves with him. The letter, written in a formalized language Bob and Ellen could scarcely understand, said the old man had died and bequeathed to one of his favorite grandsons a slave girl and sundry personal belongings. She was an octoroon, the daughter of unknown father and a quadroon slave mother, and being one-eighth black by descent and the child of a slave, she was black and a slave under the law. The unhappy circumstances of the girl's life had touched the old man's heart and he had granted the child her freedom in his will. Bob made arrangements by return post to pick up the child and the other items at Montgomery, where she was to arrive by train.

Finally, the day came to leave. Will was all of eight at the time. The long buggy ride was a thrilling, eye-opening experience for him. He thought they would never get there and once they actually had, he doubted they would ever find their way home again. The train station was hot, noisy, and alive with the hurly-burly of more people than Will had ever seen in his life, all of them in a tremendous hurry. Arriving much the same as baggage, and looking frightened beyond belief, the child was a mere slip of a girl—a year or two younger than Will, but this was uncertain, owing to imprecise slave records. All agreed she was a pretty thing, and Will and Nathan likened her lovely tawny coloring to buckskin. When Ellen saw the waif, she burst into tears and clutched her to her bosom, and all the way home she sat in the back seat of the buggy and talked soft and low to the girl to reassure her everything was going to be fine.

Bob and Ellen named the child Polly Ellender Cain and in no time at all, she became like a sister to Will and Nathan.

From the beginning, the fact that Polly was black had bothered Will, because she had to sit with the colored members in the back of his grandsir's church. More often than not, he sat with them, as Polly was part of his family. The black parishioners welcomed Will with open arms and he felt no discomfort sitting among them. Will knew this segregated arrangement was not Grandsir's idea but one imposed on him by the largely white congregation, many of whom resented the presence of blacks in "their church," period. Pastor Garrison, as he was known outside of the immediate family and church, fought the good fight for a church of all colors, but he ruffled many feathers in the process.

This unhappy circumstance often played through Will's mind as the family worked together, brothers and sister in the field, or when they were all together at mealtime. Why must they as a family, have to see one of their own mistreated so? Now that he was the man of the house, the unfairness tormented his young mind more than ever, and he sought out his grandfather for words of comfort.

"Grandsir, I don't like it that Polly has to sit in the back of the church," he announced boldly. "In fact, I don't like it that any of the colored folks have to sit way in the back. Uncle Tootsie and Aunt Winnie are just as good as gold. Most of the other blacks, too. Why does it have to be this way?"

"Well, son," Grandsir explained, "in the beginning God made one race, that was the human race, and white, black, Indian and Oriental are all part of it.

Somewhere along the line, the white man decided that black folk were less than human, so they could be treated as inferior and enslaved just like other uneducated poor folk. To our society's depraved reasoning, a person need only a little bit of black in their makeup in order to set them apart and shun them. In Polly's case, her having that smidgen of black blood makes her black under the law, her tawny complexion notwithstanding, and inferior in the eyes of ignorant people for that reason alone. Man always seems to need to be better than the next man, and therein lays the root of all prejudice. The Garrisons and the Cain's are more progressive in their thinking about the issue of race than most, and I don't need to remind you that this fact has caused some friction in the community.

"We in the family all love Polly and we see her for the beautiful human being she is," he went on. "That is just how it is supposed to be, for Jesus said love your neighbor as yourself. So you go on and sit with Polly and the black folks and don't fret yourself about it."

Will did fret about it and spent many a restless night wrestling with the injustice of it all.

It was a warm September day in 1862 and Corner Creek Church, which David Garrison had founded and was pastor of, for thirty-five years, had a full house. With his shoulder-length silver hair, great stature (an inch or so over six feet), and shoulders wide as an ox yoke (as Bob Cain often said), Pastor Garrison cut a striking figure behind the pulpit. He was not ordinarily a fire and brimstone preacher, but if the mood took him, he could be motivated to theatrical movements that brought the congregation to the edge of their pews.

This day, however, his mood was pensive and most of the congregation, fidgeting and drowsing in the close-packed pews, found his sermon insufferably dry. Will, on the other hand, was wide-awake and thoroughly captivated. With Polly's head resting on his shoulder, he perked up his ears as his grandpa droned on.

"A wise man surrounds him-self with a multitude of counselors," Pastor Garrison was saying. “Proverbs 11: 14 says: ‘Humility leads one to seek counsel from others in matters of importance.’ It is entirely possible that if all sides in this present conflict had applied this and other scriptures, our lives would be different today. However, they have only sought counsel of like-minded men, ones who would agree with their thinking. The lesson is clear: A humble man will seek counsel from those like-minded and also those with opposing views then weigh the different views to make a sound decision.”

Seeing that half of his congregation was asleep, Pastor Garrison slapped the pulpit with the flat of his hand. The resounding boom brought every drowsy head to attention and made Will jump. He listened as his Grandsir’s voice rose to an impassioned crescendo, and the words he heard would stay with him all his life.

“I challenge you, for the rest of your life,” he declaimed, pacing behind the pulpit, “to seek counsel from all people, not just your cronies, amen. Y’all have a good week in the Lord, go home dust off those Bibles and read the good news of Jesus Christ and what he did for us all when we get saved. The Bible isn't to hug and kiss on it is the instruction book of life."

"Grandsir, please tell me more about counselors," Will beseeched him after the service.

"Well, son, most of the time a man gets by on his own with the help of God," the old man said. Will liked the way his grandfather's snowy mustache twitched when he spoke and the merry twinkle in his blue-gray eyes. "Sometimes, however, things come into a man's life that are above the ordinary. About seventy years ago, for instance, a brilliant man made a remark about the Revolutionary times. His name was Thomas Paine. 'These are the times that try men's souls' was what he said, and it was a statement just as true now as then. When perplexing times come along, a man has to rely on himself and hope he has folk he knows and trusts that can help him make important decisions. That is the counsel, getting all sides of a situation and putting the information into a useful conclusion, and going on to face your situation. Son, there aren't many things that you will face that someone else has not faced before, so ask for help, King Solomon says in Proverbs.

"There is nothing new under the sun, King Solomon said—be humble and not stubborn, thinking you have all the answers. There are many other things Mr. Paine ascribed to that I don't find worth the effort to discuss, I will say beware of Paine's doctrines."

Grandsir stuck a chaw of tobacco in his cheek. He had gotten het up, Bob Cain would say, and Will was obliged to listen.

"As for the times that try men's soul statement, at that time it was about America and England," the old man went on. "These men were mostly Englishmen and to go to war against their king was a foreign idea to them. They had always had a king to make decisions for them, you see, but now they wanted the king to leave them alone. The choices were clear stay with a king and have taxes and no say in government, or leave the kingdom and establish their own country with liberty for all. America's situation today is not so different. The North is industrialized and needs our cotton, but they don't really give the South anything in return unless you count tariffs. Now, slavery is another matter entirely. Some say it's at the root of this conflict, but I suspect we'll be contemplating that and a hogshead of questions just as deeply about this thing forever and a day. The industrialized North doesn't need slaves, whereas the Southern cotton and tobacco farmer feels he needs slaves as laborers. I don't hold in slavery. Jesus teaches against it and so do I.

"One more thing to consider son, don't let yourself become a narrow-minded yokel! Develop your body and your mind. Study the Bible first. You'll find the answers to all of life's questions there. Then read the classics, starting with Scott and Shakespeare."

Seeing the vacant look in Will's eyes, Grandsir smiled benevolently at him. "You got all that, young man?"

"I think so, Grandsir," said Will dubiously. "If I ever need any counsel, I'll come see you—after I talk to momma first."

"That's good, son," said the old man, laughing. "Your mother is a woman that uses her head. Listen to her every chance you get. If most men would counsel with their womenfolk first, they wouldn't have as many problems. You remember that when you get married."

Will made a sour face. "Aw, shucks, Grandsir, I ain't never getting married."

Grandsir was a warmhearted and demonstrative man. He enveloped Will in a tight embrace, saying, "How I love you, boy! You were my first grandchild. God said in Deuteronomy Chapter 28 'Blessed will be the fruit of my body.' That is you, and as such, you have a special place in my heart."

Will thought about this conversation quite a bit as the days turned to weeks and the weeks rolled into months and the years followed after. He never appreciated until he was an old man just how much he had learned from his preacher grandpa.

CHAPTER 2

As Bob was literate and but not one to put pen to paper, the family received just a handful of letters from their patriarch those first three years of the war and they saw him only once, in March of 1863, when he was granted a brief furlough upon his reenlistment. He looked thin and pale and none too gallant in his ragbag uniform, but he was no less jolly than ever and regaled the family with rousing war stories that often took a ribald turn, much to Ellen's indignation. Bob tried to put a brave face on the South's chances for victory, but even in their remote environs, Ellen and the children had heard the rumblings of doubt about the Confederacy's vaunted supremacy and whisperings of defeat were on every chatty neighbor's tongue. The fact Bob had seen fit to reenlist, when he might have let a young man take his place, only served to confirm the rumor's accuracy in the family's eyes.

Bob heaped praise on Will for the outstanding job he had done with the homestead and farm, in particular, his efforts at bringing in cattle from the canebrake. After their first go at it in 1861, Will and Nathan had again forayed into the brake the next summer with middling success. They still counted themselves as rank amateurs when it came to herding cattle and much to their chagrin, the cows they collected were apt to stray from the pasture not soon after they were caught. Bob shrugged off this fact, and commended both boys' efforts, as well as Polly's.

Will was fifteen now, with a birthday coming up in August, and had grown into an impressive physical specimen. At five feet nine, he was now about five inches shorter than his papa. The previous Fall Will weighed an even 160 pounds on the scale at the cotton gin. Ellen reckoned Bob weighed about the same now, although he had left home fifteen pounds heavier than that, and she resolved with a vengeance to fatten him up in the two weeks he was to be at home.

After Bob had said farewell, Will was more than ever convinced in his mind that the Confederacy needed him. His papa hinted that casualties, disease, and desertions were taking a devastating toll on the South's war effort, causing Will to feel a powerful twinge of guilt that an able-bodied boy like himself wasn't in there giving the Yankees hell. Sure, he was needed at home, but with Nathan himself grown into a stout young fellow and Uncle Tootsie and Grandsir and his hired men available to help out when needed, he reckoned the farm was in good hands and he just couldn't justify his staying home when there was a greater cause at stake.

His few reservations about enlisting were sorely put to the test when a neighbor boy, Jeremiah Bacon, came home that August on a hardship furlough when his father, thrown from a skittish horse and trampled, had died. Jerry, as he liked to be called, was three years Will's senior and had enlisted in a local unit, the 53rd Alabama Calvary Regiment, that spring. Jerry looked so spruce in his single-breasted gray shell jacket with yellow stand-up collar and cuffs, and carried himself with such dignity and self-assurance, that he nearly took Will's breath away. A kepi worn at a rakish angle completed the dashing portrait, but it was the roundabout, as Jerry called the jacket, that Will coveted, and he told Jerry so.

"Jerry, I sure would like to have me a smart gray jacket like that."

"You can, kid," Jerry replied airily. "If you've got a horse and saddle, you can ride back with me to Tennessee. The cavalry will make a man out of you."

That was all Will wanted to hear, but he felt in his heart of hearts he should seek counsel first. He went to Grandsir with his arguments and was not surprised at his candor.

"Boy, you are taking a big chance to go and join the war," said the old man. "The Confederacy's about licked! War's a tough scene, fuller of more horrors than hell. It amounts to little more than a pissing contest on a grand scale, and it's the worst thing man has come up with to waste lives and money. You will see men become animals and do wicked things, men maimed by cannon shot, arms and legs amputated by the basketful. It will turn your stomach, and I pray it don't ruin you. Nor Leans was not a picnic, I can tell you for a gospel truth. Nanny and I covenant to pray for you daily, just like we do for your daddy. We trust that God has some great thing for you to do later in life and put your life in His hands. If you change your mind, God bless you, and if you don't, may God protect you."

That same evening, just before twilight, Will went to the corral, caught up Cat, and led her out into the pasture. He brushed the mare down well and then lay down to look at the fleecy clouds scudding across the baby blue sky. He mulled over the questions that had tormented his mind the last few days Was he doing right by joining the cause, which so many were saying was lost, or should he stay home, where his family needed him? Could they make it without his strong back? What would his papa do in the same situation?

These thoughts and more like these were preying upon him when he heard the squeaky screen door swing shut and the distinctive clip-clop of his mother's hard leather shoes stamping along the porch boards. He did not reply when she called to him repeatedly that supper was ready, and continued to reflect on the monumental decision he had to make.

"Will, what in heaven's name are you doing, lying on the ground with that mare standing right atop of you, just like a watchdog?" clucked Ellen as she advanced toward him, arms akimbo. "Didn't you hear me say supper's ready? Come in the house this instant, boy. Polly has put the coffee on and there is a fresh pea-con pie cooling."

Will smacked his lips at the thought of his favorite dessert. "I've got to talk to you before we go inside," he said boldly. "I want to join the 53rd Alabama Cavalry and go do my part, like papa."

Ellen hesitated a moment before replying. "You've been talking to that Bacon boy, haven't you?"

"Yes, I'm needed for the cause."

"The cause, the cause, I'm so sick of hearing about the cause," Ellen echoed bitterly. She bit her lip to stop her tears and looked heavenward for strength. "What are you trying to do to me, Will? It was hard enough to see your pa go away to war, but you are just a boy! It would kill me if something happened to you. How can we care for the farm with you gone? Oh, Will, I won't have it—you're just a baby."

"I am not a baby, mother," said Will coldly. "I've made up my mind. I'm riding back to Tennessee with Jerry at the end of the week. I must go. You'll just have to understand."

That was the end of it. On August 11, Will said his bittersweet goodbyes to the family and rode off on Cat to join the war.

When Will enlisted, the 53rd Alabama was enlisted in Gen. Philip D. Roddey's Brigade, Wheeler's Cavalry Corps, of the Confederate Army of Tennessee. The captain who drew up the enlistment papers considered that Will was still wet behind the ears despite his size and assigned him to the commissary detail, where he predicted he would see the least action. He was directed to Sgt. McKenzie Renfro's tent and came to attention before a burly man smoking a corncob pipe, his feet crossed atop a rickety desk.

"Private William R. Cain reports for duty, Sergeant," He announced and saluted awkwardly

Sgt. Renfro looked him up and down then reared forward and snatched Will's papers out of his hand.

"Boy, how old are you?" He sneered.

"I am almost sixteen, sir," Will replied.

"Fifteen!" the sergeant drawled sarcastically. "You should be home sucking at your momma's breast. Well, we'll take 'em just about any age these days, hair on their chest or not. Do you know anything about war, boy?"

"Sir, I don't know a thing except my papa is out there with the 29th Alabama Infantry."

"Huh! Well, at least you admit it," said the sergeant, puffing earnestly at his pipe. "When I get through with you, you'll be able to soldier with the finest we got and make your family proud. Aside from teaching you about handling supplies, I will see you learn close order drill, military courtesy, marksmanship—the whole shebang. Your primary task will be to move livestock around to be food for the fighting men. Contrary to what the esteemed captain probably told you, the commissary ain't the softest lot in the army and you'll see your share of mayhem. With any luck, maybe you'll get home with your mind intact—but don't count on it."

Sgt. Renfro sprang to his feet with an agility that surprised Will and went over to the supply closet. Even more surprising was his stature. He was as short and stout as a pickle barrel but he carried himself with the swagger of a prizefighter. He rummaged for a moment in the closet and unceremoniously threw a wad of clothes at Will, which he failed to catch.

"That's your uniform, kid," the sergeant barked. "Now skedaddle over to the commissary tent and then introduce yourself around."

Will looked down at the rumpled heap at his feet and picked up the wrinkled jacket. It was a single-breasted roundabout like his friend Jerry's, but tinted a yellowish-brown. The pants were the same unbecoming color. A gray slouch hat and a pair of severely straight-cut brogans completed the ensemble.

"But I wanted a gray coat," said Will, holding the jacket to his chest with distaste, "and a butternut brown kepi to go with it."

"I don't give a damn what you wanted, soldier!" Sgt. Renfro howled. "They have to use dye made out of walnut hulls these days on account of the blockades, and this turd brown is the result of it. It's good enough for the other new recruits and it's good enough for you! You'll be a butternut brown and like it! The Yankees know you ain't on their side because you're brown, now get out of my sight!"

Will gathered up the rest of the uniform and bolted like a shot. He reported to the ordnance officer where and he was issued a Sharp's carbine, a pair of Griswold and Gunnison pistols—serviceable Reb copies of the northern-make 1851 Colt Navy revolver—and a saber. Afterwards, he sought out Jerry and expressed his disappointment in the uniform.

"Well, I guess you'll never look as trim and handsome as me, old boy," Jerry laughed, "but I tell you what, if anything ever happens to me—not that it ever will, mind you—you can have my jacket."

"That a Promise?" asked Will.

"Promise, Butternut!"

The friends shook on it and laughed.

Their bargain became a running joke between them as Will underwent his basic training in the weeks that followed. Sgt. Renfro proved to be equal part mother hen and a vicious taskmaster. His bellicosity overshadowed a deep solicitude for the well-being of his troops and the men all liked him, though they would never give him the satisfaction of saying so to his face. Will made friends among his fellow troopers and earned their respect and admiration in the off hours by riding Cat to victory in races and ring tournaments. Gambling was rife in the camp, and Will become a skilled and often a lucky participant at chuck-a-luck and faro. Will tried whiskey for the first time in his life and while he liked it well enough, he judged it to be an acquired taste and could take or leave it. For a time, he had a pet raccoon, a young orphan he had found in the woods. The critter's antics were a great source of amusement to Will and his friends and they were sad when it wandered away.

At the end of September, Will experienced his baptism of fire at the Battle of Chickamauga, Georgia. The taste of mayhem Sgt. Renfro promised proved an understatement, as Will and his fellow commissary workers were sent to fight alongside the main force of infantry troops. He hated leaving Cat behind, but a sick friend said he would see to her keep. Nothing could have prepared him for the savagery and the carnage he both witnessed and eagerly participated in. Will killed his first Yankee on the first day of the battle, shooting a freckle-faced youth in the gut and sending him sprawling from his horse to a watery grave in Chickamauga Creek. He was troubled that night and tried in vain to reconcile his bloodthirsty actions with his Christian faith. However, in the tumult of battle the next morning, he forgot his pangs of guilt and shot three more Blue Bellies. After that, the bloodlust was upon Will and he never again thought twice about shooting a Yankee.

In the months that followed, Will became very sure of himself. He was an excellent shot with both pistol and rifle, but he had so much disdain for the cavalry saber that he abandoned his in a gully. He perfected a blood curdling Rebel yell, which startled even his own comrades. Sgt. Renfro begrudgingly praised both his horsemanship and his marksmanship and admonished him not to grow too prideful, lest his head swell too large for his butternut cap.

While he was far more literate than his father, Will wrote home only seldom and always enclosed most of his monthly pay of $12.00. What little he kept back he used to buy some trinket from the sutlers, whose rare appearances at camp were more welcome than Santa Claus. He received correspondence from home regularly, both Ellen and Polly writing him separately and Nathan sometimes adding a line or two. Rarely, a letter would come from Grandsir, and these were always lengthy missives replete with scripture. Will welcomed each and every letter and the news from home they imparted, although reading them made him homesick.

In April of 1864, the 53rd Alabama became to be part of Gen. M. W. Hannon's Brigade and saw constant action in the Atlanta campaign. Will and his comrades were forever driving cattle around the Yankees to get food to the Confederate troops and in doing so, they found themselves being attacked by Yanks and forced to abandon the cattle and wagons to launch attacks of their own. Actually, the commissary unit spent far more time fighting than they did delivering rations and developed into a hard-hitting guerrilla outfit that asked for and gave no quarter.

As a commissary man, Will ate better than most soldiers and thanked his lucky stars for that. The job came with other added benefits that were beyond the knowledge of the average soldier. Taking food, money, and goods from the Yank troops they captured or killed, Will and his merry band began to see themselves as latter-day Robin Hoods and his saddlebags bulged with more money than he had ever dreamed of. He was finally obliged to cut the stitching around his saddle skirts and sew in the skirts of his Hope saddle, stitching it together with thin leather strings so it would not be so noticeable. He soon realized that the value of Federal green backs was an acceptable substitute so he kept the paper and gave silver and gold in exchange knowing if he made it home, the money would provide comfort for his family against the advent of the hard times that surely were to come should Dixie not prevail. His swag also included two authentic, almost new .36 caliber Navy Colts, courtesy of an unlucky Union captain whose patrol the 53rd had waylaid. Will took to wearing these in his twin saddle holsters instead of the Griswold and Gunnison copies he had been issued.

The 53rd Alabama saw bloody duty at Resaca, Georgia in May and nipped ferociously at Sherman's heels as the siege of Atlanta commenced. In July, Will was on the go most of the time. He was tired, worked ragged, and sometimes felt he was in a waking nightmare. He put great store in the wise words of the South's beloved Gen. R. E. Lee, particularly his remark at Fredericksburg. 'It is well that war is so terrible, otherwise we would grow too fond of it.' Will had had his fill of war and fond of it he knew he would never be. Miraculously, he had not been hurt other than a shoulder wound at Atlanta, which healed quickly but left a big scar other than that not so much as a scratch. Jerry, who lorded it over Will that he was a regular trooper and not a lowly commissary grunt, had been just as lucky. He kept his gray roundabout in immaculate condition, brushing and spot cleaning it as soon as possible after every skirmish.

"Yo Butternut!" He often teased Will. "You should be glad I'm such a dandy and like to keep this jacket looking bran-span new."

"I'm much obliged," was Will's retort. "When the time comes, it will look a heap better on me than it does on you."

In late August, the men of the 53rd Alabama found themselves en route to the rural hamlet of Jonesborough, south of Atlanta. There, unbeknownst to the

Confederate command, Sherman had gathered his vast forces in a bold gambit to cut the Rebels' supply lines and force the Army of Tennessee's evacuation of the Gateway City, which had doggedly refused to fall despite heavy bombardment. The 53rd was among the Rebel host charged with aiding the defense of the all-important Macon and Western Railroad.

It was the afternoon of August 31 and the men of the 53rd were making small talk to calm their nerves before the battle. Will looked out over the placid fields, so much like those at home, feeling his guts tighten like they always did.

"Hey, Jerry, what did the captain say the name of this burg was?" He asked.

"Jonesboro, I think," Jerry replied. "Looks like the backend of nowhere for me, but I reckon the railroad's got strategic importance."

"What don't have importance these days," said Will. "Heard tell the Yanks have put up some good breastworks and got more cannon than you can shake a stick at. Heard tell if we don't win this one, Atlanta's a goner. Heard tell anyway."

Jerry grunted. “Don’t be such a scaredy-cat, we’ll take ’em,” he said and punched Will hard on his arm.

“Ow!” said Will, wincing. “You just be sure and keep my coat from harm, you hear?”

“I always do,” said Jerry with a wry grin.

At just after two o’clock, the Battle of Jonesborough started with 60,000 Yankee troops defending the town. The attacking Rebels were turned back all down the line and suffered heavy losses. When the smoke had cleared several hours later, less than 200 Yankees lay dead, compared to nearly 2,000 Rebel fatalities. It was the first day of the last battle of the Atlanta campaign. The next day, September 1, the action would move down the road apiece to Lovejoy Station, where the Yanks would seal their victory. The rail line effectively severed, Gen. John Bell Hood would have no choice but to abandon Atlanta and leave it in Union hands. The coup almost assured Lincoln of reelection and paved the way for Sherman’s march to the sea. For those with the vision to see it, the end of the war was in sight.

Even if Will could have known these facts, they would have been unimportant to him. He had fought like the devil, same as always, and all he cared about was that he was still alive. He thanked the Lord for delivering him. The main fighting over, the dead and wounded lay between the lines as light skirmish fire whizzed overhead. It occurred to Will he hadn't seen Jerry in hours.

"Anybody seen Jerry?" he asked generally.

Several sooty, haggard faces turned toward him but no-one spoke, and they quickly looked away.

Laughing nervously, he spoke louder. "I said, any y'all seen Jerry? I just want to see if my jacket's all right."

"I seen him," a boy named Hastings spoke up. "He was badly hurt. I give him some water. That's about all I could do he has lost most of his leg."

Will's color went ashen. "Where, Jim? Tell me where!"

"You can't go out there, Will. Anyways, he's probably dead by now the way he was bleeding. I made a tourniquet for him and told the medics where he was."

"Don't say that! Where is he? Tell me where he is."

Hastings pointed in the direction of a stand of sweet gum trees about 200 yards away. "He's over there. It's ugly, Will. I wouldn't go if I was you."

He did anyway after stripping the saddle off Cat. Will leaped onto Cat's back and raced toward the grove, his head down and his back nearly parallel to the horse's back. They skittered across the broad field, dodging corpses, heedless of the skirmish fire from the Yanks. He wasn't alone. There were other Rebs dragging and carrying the wounded to safety. By the time Will reached the grove, the assault had ceased. He would later say a begrudging prayer for the Yanks because they had apparently ceased fire out of respect for the rescue mission. Right now, all he could think about was Jerry.

He found him straight away, propped against the bole of a sweet gum. His right leg was utterly gone. A host of flies buzzed around. Jerry sat in a thick gelatin of blood, which had leaked from the leg. As Will knelt by his side, Jerry opened his eyes.

"Well, Will," he said in a hoarse whisper, "your jacket's fine, wish I could say the same for me."

Will felt his gorge rise up and he nearly threw up. This was not just a casual acquaintance, it was his friend. What happened?

Jerry smiled weakly. "A bouncing cannonball, you've heard people say 'blown to smithereens'? That's what my leg was."

"Quit talking, Jerry. They've stopped shooting. I can get you back to camp."

"No."

Will moved to raise Jerry's body, saying, "Come on, and let me get you back to camp."

"No! It's too late. Take the jacket."

"No, Jerry, it has been just a game. I never really wanted it."

"Please take my jacket, Will, in honor of me every time you wear it."

Gently, he unfastened the roundabout and eased if off. By the time he was through, Jerry was dead. He kissed the boy's forehead, took off his butternut jacket, and laid it over the boy's face. Mechanically, he put on the gray roundabout and didn't notice it was a perfect fit.

CHAPTER 3

It was in the aftermath of the Atlanta campaign in early September that Will chanced to meet members of the Eighth Texas Cavalry, better known as Terry's Texas Rangers and John Bell Hood's men. Their superb horsemanship, colorful array of weaponry, and fearlessness in battle had earned the devil-may-care regiment admiration on both sides of the war. The Rangers had distinguished themselves at Shiloh, Murfreesboro, and Chickamauga, as well as Atlanta, and their formidable reputation as a "shock troop" preceded them.

The 53rd Alabama and the Rangers shared the same route for a short time. Will quickly fell under their spell and their boisterous company helped to ease his pain over Jerry's death. He became particularly close to a young fellow named Clement Patterson. Five years older than Will, Clem had come off a cattle ranch down on the Nueces River in Texas. Will could listen for hours to Clem's tall Texas tales and he learned a great deal from him about the art of roping cattle, something that Will was particularly keen to know about, owing to his earlier stabs at raiding the canebrake. Will was an apt pupil and quickly caught on to the finer points. Clem told him he had the makings of a real cowboy, which pleased Will greatly, as he had already caught the Texas fever in a big way.

On the night before the regiments were set to go their separate ways, Clem produced a bottle of bust head whiskey. The two of them shared it around the campfire with a trio of Clem's rough and ready cohorts with whom Will had also become friendly Robert McWilliams, Tom Wolfe, and a half-Cherokee named Manfred Porcher, whose long, jet-black hair, aquiline nose, and bright, feral eyes fascinated Will.

"What y'all gonna do when this thing is over?" asked Will. "Anyone with a lick of sense can see we are whipped. I can see it in the eyes of the soldiers, it's in the way they walk, like dead folks come to life. Yet they won't quit and give these damn Yankees any satisfaction. They get up every morning and go on and fight some more."

"I am going back to Oklahoma and get me a wife and raise a passel of kids," said Manfred. "Before the war, my folks had a nice place down along the Arkansas River by Red Bird. If it's still there I'm going back and either ranch or farm where I don't have to see no Bluecoats ever again."

"Amen to that," said Tom, who allowed he might go up to New Mexico. "I had been over there early in the war and thought that it would be far enough from civilization to suit me. Find myself a young bonito Mexican lady and just settle down to see what the hell happens. Get me some land along a river or creek and raise some good horses, kinda like the one ole' Will owns. Say, Will, tell me again where you got that horse."

"My Grandpa Cain got them from the Chickasaw and Choctaw Indians over in Virginia many years ago," replied Will, who was always in the mood for good horse talk. "Tell you what, Tom, after the dust settles over this mess, you get a-holt of me in Elba, Alabama and I'll see you get a stud colt, how 'bout that?"

"Yore on, pilgrim!" said Tom as he pulled Will's slouch hat down over his eyes.

"I'm goin' back to Texas and see if they still got the real Texas Rangers," said Robert, yawning. "If they do, I want to be one. Gonna try and get a parcel of land around Cuero, Texas have some cows after a while of rangerin' and marry a redheaded woman I know from Victoria, if she ain't been spoken for. Then I want to be so peaceable I don't ever say a cross word, and join the church. We McWilliams boys have always settled down after the last hurrah is over. My grandpa says it's been that way since we got run out of Scotland."

"Clem, you're being awfully quiet," observed Will.

Clem had been toasting the end of a long stick in the fire. Now he took it out and began drawing in the dirt with it. "Boys, I don't know what I wanna do," he sighed. "I've got a little four-year-old boy livin' with my ma and pa. My wife died from childbirth fever, you see. I really want to see him grow up better than me. My folks have been real good about takin' the boy in. I have tried to send money when I could I don't know if it ever got through, though. I got some Yankee money socked away, and I'll take that home myself. My pa is like ever'body else down on the Nueces River jest as poor as a church mouse. We have a big house and raise lots of cows. Although I am shore they ain't been much brandin' and markin' since I left—kindly the same boat you're in, Will. Them darn Mesican bandits may have stole all his stock by now anyway, so when I get home there will be some gunpowder burnt to make amends.

"It's a rough country, but God knows I love it! My family's been in Texas since General Houston brought the first settlers in. We have been fightin' Mesicans and Indjuns ever since we got there. I am sure we gonna have some trouble with the winners of this mess, too. It pains me to admit it, but that's likely gonna be the Yanks." Clem made this statement with great bitterness and he spat into the fire to emphasize the point.

"What about you, Will?" inquired Robert. "Goin' home to Alabammy with a banjer on your knee?"

Will laughed. "Well, the first thing I'd like to do is go home and find my papa waiting for me. Might be too much to ask of the Lord though, for I hear tell his outfit, the 29th Alabama, caught pure-dee hell around New Hope Church. Tried to find him a couple times toward the end of the Atlanta business, but it was no use, in all that bedlam. Reckon, I'll help my folks get the farm back in shape and round up some of them cows and hogs, then who knows? I might follow my nose to Texas."

Clem stood up and stretched. "Fellers, we'd better get back to camp," he said, and turned to Will. “Kid, if you ever do get over to Texas, hunt me up in Uvalde. I’ve taken a real shine to you, and I whutn’t kiddin' when I said you’d make a fine cowboy.” He kicked the bottoms of Manfred’s boots. “Get up, Manny, if you can, and prove to this boy that Injuns can hold their firewater.”

The Rangers lurched over to their horses. Getting on them in their liquored condition was tricky and not a pretty site for a cavalry outfit, and Will had to laugh.

“You’re mountin’ that nag like you don’t know yore right foot from yore left foot, Porcher,” Robert teased.

“You ain’t got any room to talk!” The Cherokee retorted good-naturedly.

“So long, Will!” Clem called out. “Come see us!”

As the Rangers disappeared in the gloom, Will felt a tear trickle down his cheek. He doubted he would ever again know such a fine bunch of fellows as long as he lived.

He only wished Jerry could have met them.

Before he knew it, April 1865 came around. The month had been eventful. On the second, Richmond, the Confederate capital, fell. On the ninth, Palm Sunday, Lee surrendered to Grant at Appomattox Court House in Virginia. On the fourteenth, Lincoln was shot and died the next day. On the twenty-sixth of April 1865, two important things would occur, Lincoln's assassin would be found in a burning tobacco shed in Virginia and shot, and Gen. Joseph E. Johnston would surrender to Gen. William T. Sherman in James Bennett's farm house near Durham Station in North Carolina.

That same date, the 53rd Alabama, having done its part in the Carolinas campaign, waited for the last hurrah near Greensboro, North Carolina, at a little bump in the road called Jamestown. There were but a few left in the regiment to celebrate, and the end could not come soon enough for Will. In the waning months of the war, he had grown rather surly and taciturn and had made a point not to grow too fond of his comrades, lest their deaths affect him as Jerry's had. Sgt. Renfro had noted the change in his disposition and had advised him to snap out of it. Will privately thought the old slave driver was himself different, seeming slightly less gruff at times now that the war was winding down, but it could have been his imagination.

Sgt. Renfro had assigned Will one last detail. He was to drive the handful of scrawny cows that remained down the road five miles or so, where they were to be slaughtered for a coterie of officers' consolation barbecue. It was an easy job and Will was glad to have it for the opportunity to be alone and think. It was too warm to be wearing his roundabout, so he stowed it in his haversack. He still thought about Jerry every time he put it on.

As he traveled along, he wondered what would become of all those brave Southern men that would now hobble homeward, so many of them maimed by grapeshot and crude amputations. How would they provide for their families? It was funny, when they all started out, they were foolhardy and fearless and invincible, believing that nothing could possibly happen to them. It was always "someone else" who was hurt or killed. Will knew just how they had felt, because he had shared their reckless regard, until Jerry had died. After that, he began to fear for his own precious mortality, even though he fought as hard as ever.

The cows delivered, he turned the mare around and headed back to camp. His thoughts dwelled on his papa, as they so often did those days. Had he made it home? He prayed nightly that the Lord had seen fit to make it so, but his spirit was plagued by the awful fear that his pa would never see his beloved Ellen again, nor dote on his children, nor play his bagpipes it wasn't fair if he was dead, but war wasn't fair. War didn't care what a man had done when he was a civilian and cared even less what deeds he might do, great or small, when it was done with him and spit him back out into the world.

He was conscious of a hot flame in his gut that symbolized how the war had changed him from a peaceable boy to a hard young man. There was a chip on his shoulder now, and he wouldn't take any abuse, verbal or physical, from any man. Following the atrocities he had seen in the Atlanta siege, he was consumed with a loathing for Blue Coats and would sooner shoot one than spit in his eye. He had prayed about it, but the heavens seemed made of impenetrable stone, and his hatred only deepened.

As he rode along, the words of a favorite hymn went through his head and he sang aloud in a clear tenor voice, heedless of whoever might hear him, “Amazing grace, how sweet the sound, that saved a wretch like me! I once was lost, but now am found, was blind—”

In keeping with the common soldier’s eternal knowledge, Will didn’t hear the shot that hit him. He fell sprawling from his horse and the burning pain in his side was intense. He couldn’t see the damned Yankee either, but he knew he must be close by. Unperturbed, Cat had moved away after the shot and was leisurely cropping a tuft of grass. She was dog gentle, having been cared for by Will from a colt, and had long since learned not to shy around gunplay.

Will knew he must move quickly before the Yankee shooter reloaded. Fatefully, he had landed in a little depression, and he used that as cover to crawl toward the mare. Cat just kept on eating as he moved toward her. Will reached up, got his hand on the stirrup, and spoke to the mare to move ahead. Cat obliged and slowly drug Will toward a patch of brush. The brush wasn't thick and it didn't take long for the horse to get through to the other side.

Spying a larger stand of brush about five yards away, Will urged the mare on. The pain in his side was almost unbearable, but he knew he must hold on a little longer. At length, he halted Cat underneath a Chinquapin tree, which provided him with ample cover, and almost in a faint, he released his hold on the stirrup.

"How bad are you hurt, lad?" rang out a voice from the other side of the tree. "I'll crawl over and take a look."

In his delirium, Will failed to notice the voice was Southern and friendly. "You won't find me easy pickings, Yank!" He warned, cocking his pistol. But seeing that the figure that crawled up to him had on the tattered gray uniform of a Confederate cavalry sergeant, he un-cocked the Colt and allowed the man to examine him.

“Lemme take a look at that bloody mess and see how good a shot Mr. Blue Belly was,” the sergeant said as he explored the wound with practiced care. “My company’s already disbanded for the most part and I was just taking my leisure when I heard the shot and ducked behind this here tree. Right fortuitous that you should land where you did. I’ve become an old hand at treating injuries, medics being scarcer than hen’s teeth.”

“I’m all right, I think,” said Will, wincing oh my sweet Jesus, how it hurts! I am not afraid of dying I just don’t think it is my time. I’ve gone through this whole damn war with only one wound and nary a pimple or a cold and now some fool Yank shoots me on surrender day!”

“Guess some Yankee sniper just wanted to plug one more Rebel before he slunk back north,” mused the sergeant as he scrutinized his patient’s face. “Why, you’re just a sprout! ’Course, with the war going on like it has, the men coming up are boys and those boys quickly become men or die. ’Tis a grand irony you should get shot today of all days. What were you doing, lad, riding around by your lonesome like that?"

Will gazed up at the bearded, dirty face of the sergeant. Despite the grime and the haunted aspect of the eyes, it was a kind jovial face, and the smile it bore reassured him. He judged his caretaker to be in his mid-thirties, about the same as his father.

Will explained his errand and confided weakly, "I was afraid you were a Yankee and I had my pistol ready to send you to hell with the rest of 'em." His head was spinning and he was vaguely aware he was slipping into darkness.

The sergeant eased Will's head back against the tree and spoke gently to him. "You rest now laddie and don't go fighting the war in your dreams."

It was late afternoon when Will at last came to himself again.

"Good thing you passed out for awhile, lad," the sergeant said. He sat cross-legged at Will's side, savoring a smoke from a corncob pipe. "I was able to dress up that wound while you were out. It's not serious, but you lost a lot of blood. Here, have a drink of water—it's warm but wet," he said, proffering a canteen. “You’re a lucky fellow. The mini ball passed through the muscle in your flank and didn’t appear to have hit anything important. The trouble with these big bore rifles even a near miss is scary. You’d best take another swig, son. Don’t know when we will find water that isn’t fouled, because there are dead men, horses, and mules all around, and any local water’s bound to be dirty, unless we find a clean well.”

Will gulped the water gratefully and gave the sergeant back his canteen. “I’m getting chills,” he said with a shiver. “Could you get my blanket off my horse, please, sir?”

“Certainly I can, lad.” said the sergeant. He sprang to his feet, retrieved the blanket from Will’s saddle, and covered him gently with it. “What they call shock is setting in on you, and that makes you cold, even though ’tis springtime here in North Carolina and rather balmy.”

Will looked around, the dappled sunshine piercing the dense canopy of leafed out trees warmed his face. He breathed deeply, savoring the loamy smell of the leaf mold and the sweet fragrances on the light breeze. For a moment, he fancied he was home again, but with a jolt, he came back to earth.

"Sergeant, do you know if we're surrendered?" asked Will.

"Yes, lad, it's done and done," the sergeant replied. "Word is Johnston surrendered to Sherman at a little place east of here called Durham Station. The war in the Carolinas, Georgia, and Florida is officially over. We Rebels are to muster out to Greensboro, which isn't too far from here, turn in our arms, and get our paroles."

"Paroles?" said Will. "Like what they give prisoners?"

The sergeant chuckled, "something liken' to that. We Southerners have been naughty children as far as the Yanks are concerned. We have to turn in our weapons and sign a piece of paper giving our pledge not to take up arms against the government again. In return, we'll be permitted to return to our homes and get on with our lives."

"Well, dog bite a rabbit!" Will exclaimed. "All this mayhem and bloodshed and it finally come down to a

3x7 piece of paper. I can't believe it! We outfought them Yankees seven ways from Sunday. Now we're expected to slink home with our tails between our legs and just behave ourselves like nothing ever happened!"

"Easy, son," the sergeant said. "We outfought 'em, true enough. In the end, though, we were out-supplied, outnumbered, and outgunned. You must realize that there is, or were, two million Blue Coats, and the most we could muster were about seven hundred thousand. As good as we Johnny Rebs are, that's a three to one advantage in the Yanks' favor. Yes sir, it's all over but the shouting now."

Twilight was settling in among the trees. Feeling safe and warm under the blanket, Will harkened to the chorus of night bugs, taking up their monotonous songs. The face of his new friend was but a ghostly outline in the gloom.

"Damn, damn, damn those Yankees," he murmured as sleep claimed him again. "We coulda licked 'em, we coulda licked 'em."

CHAPTER 4

They were yet in the scrub brush when the sun awoke him the next morning. The sergeant was cooking something over a small fire. The heavenly aroma stirred Will's appetite as he sat up and stretched.

"Think we can get out of here today?" said Will, yawning loudly. He got up shakily and limped a little distance away to relieve himself in the bushes. The wound in his gut still throbbed but the pain was tolerable now.

"That depends on you, lad," said the sergeant. "How do you feel?"

Will had returned to his blanket. "It pained me a little when I took a leak just now, but I think I'm fit enough to ride."

"Well, we'll have to see about that," said the sergeant, coming over with four pieces of bacon in a small iron skillet. "It's a little rancid but it won't hurt two old iron-gutted Rebels like us, will it, lad?"

"Shoot no, I'm so hungry I could eat soup made with an old boot," said Will as he plucked two slices from the hot skillet.

"Glad to hear you got an appetite," said the sergeant. "I've got a little coffee going, too. It should be ready before too long. By the way, my name is Angus MacDonald from Enterprise, Alabama and lately, with the 26th Alabama Cavalry."

The sergeant stuck out his hand, big as an oven mitt. Will shook it firmly and said, "My name is Will Cain, sir. I'm from Coffee County myself, up around Elba."

"Are you, now?" said Angus. "'Tis a small world, as my dad always said. What regiment were you with, lad?"

"The 53rd Alabama Cavalry, and there ain't many of us left to surrender," Will replied. "I worked in the commissary, herding skinny beef cattle around for food. It wasn't a bad detail, but sure got lots of attention from them Blue Bellies. Those cattle were skinny to start with, but after we all got run around by the Yankees, the cattle were all horns and had flat ribs that you could play a tune on like a xylophone."

Angus chuckled and said, "Well, now that it's daylight let me have a look at that wound." Will pulled up his shirt, stiff with blood. "Hmm, looks better since I cleaned it up," Angus observed. "I poured some whiskey in the hole last night, and you never made a bobble. It will be sore for a while, but young like you are, you may never notice or miss a step."

"I'm much obliged to you, Sgt. MacDonald," said Will. "I hope you didn't use all your whiskey on me last night."

Angus winked and fetched Will a little coffee in a tin cup and sat down with his own cup.

"No, lad, I've still got enough for your needs and mine besides," he said. "Good Lord willing, we may find some more. A shot a day sure does a fellow some good, I believe. They say every man has a vice, and I guess whiskey is mine. These are going to be good days for us, lad. We're alive and we are going home, by Jiminy! So many of my friends in the 26th aren't around anymore, but they may have been the lucky ones, for I've heard some terrible stories of those boys that went north as prisoners. Heard Lee tried to get a prisoner swap with the Yanks, but Sherman wouldn't hear of it. I try not to harbor hatred in my heart, but I just can't find a single good word for that sadistic Yank. I'm willing to forgive and forget as far as the rest of it goes, but if I could get Uncle Billy in a room, just me and him, I'd gut-shoot him and feed him to the hogs."

"Yeah, I know all about Bloody Billy," said Will with distaste. "The 53rd tried to keep him out of Atlanta but couldn't do it. We hocked his heels all the time. The North had us outnumbered and their supplies were rolling right along. It was nip and tuck for us. I have done a lot of praying the last year or so, course not as much as my Grandsir Garrison—he's a preacher— would expect of me, but I still have hard feelings about the Yanks. Now I know the good book talks about 'vengeance is mine saith the Lord.' Well, it ain't revenge I'm after, I'd just plumb like to get rid of all Yankees, period, and be done. Sherman's march to the sea has had a real effect on me, as far as the Yankees go."

"I can see the war's made a bitter man of you," said Angus. "How old are you, lad?"

"Seventeen, I will be eighteen in August."

"Seventeen, well by golly, you are a big one for seventeen. You must be six feet tall or better. Not surprised the army took you, being as how I've seen many babes in the woods fighting this war, but you must have left a woebegone family behind."

"That I did," sighed Will. "My papa was in the 29th Alabama Infantry, and I felt I wanted to do something, so I lit a shuck for Tennessee with a neighbor boy, signed on with the cavalry, and here I am. I knew it was the right thing for me to do, but my momma almost had a running conniption fit! Grandsir lectured me profusely on his trip to Nor Leans in 1812 and about the futility and waste of war. He pretty much said I was a danged fool to join up with a losing cause, but he let me make my own decision. Guess I was blinded by the romance and adventure of the thing, but now I wonder what I was so fired up about. I'm weary down to my brogans and I just want to go home! There have been times I kick my butt for not hearing my Grandsir Garrison's words, war is pure hell. Has what your grandpa said to you about war been true?" asked Angus.

"Yes, most of it—some of it much worse," Will allowed. "Grandsir said I'd see men do wicked things, and I reckon I done a few of them myself, I'm ashamed to say. I have come to realize war isn't a romance, no matter how many banners are flown and how many pretty plumes officers stick in their hats."

Angus guffawed. "Will, I believe you've got some philosopher in you. I am reminded of what a very smart man, Benjamin Franklin by name, once said, 'There never was a good war or a bad peace.' I have to tip my hat to both of you for such insightful observations. You're a right smart fellow, Will, lad!"

"Well, if I am so smart, why did I join up?" laughed Will. "But here I am and I can honestly say I did my best. Sgt. MacDonald, I want to say thanks again for helping me out."

"My pleasure, son, you'd have done the same for me," replied the sergeant. "And make it Angus. I think it's best if you rest up today and we can strike out for Greensboro tomorrow. Then we'll get ourselves out of fair North Carolina and as far away from the Yankee army as we can."

"If it's all the same to you, I'd rather get going today," said Will. "I feel like a new man after a good night's sleep and some vittles."

Angus shrugged, "Suit yourself, lad. Let's take it easy, hear? I wouldn't want that wound of yours to start seeping along the way."

"Say, Angus," said Will. "Was I just delirious, or did I hear you say we have to turn in our guns?"

"You heard me right," Angus replied. "Johnston got pretty much the same deal from Sherman as Lee got from Grant. The officers get to keep their side arms, private horses, and baggage. We common soldiers have to turn in our weapons and accoutrements. We can keep our haversacks, blankets, canteens, and other personal stuff. I reckon we can get some papers for our horses, as well."

Will shook his head ruefully. "I don't mind giving up the guns I was issued, but I've got several more that I damn well would hate to part with," he said. "What if we don't bother showing up in Greensboro? What if we just ride home and act like we don't know the war is over?"

"Lad, now you are delirious," said Angus. "Maybe you can play that dumb, but I'm not that good an actor. You know as well as I do that the Yankees' feelings toward the South have been getting uglier by the day ever since Lincoln's assassination. Without our parole papers, there would be nothing to stop a zealous bunch of Blue Bellies from blowing our heads off and leaving us in a ditch."

Will thought on this. "Guess you could be right, but not without a fight from me as long as I can shoot and I am able to defend myself," he said with determination.

He staggered over to Cat and began removing his cache. Besides the authentic Navy Colts, he had the Sharp's carbine which he carried in the Hope saddle scabbard, a Confederate-make Leech and Rigdon Colt percussion revolver picked up on the field of battle in Resaca, and the Griswold and Gunnison Colt copies he had originally been issued.

"Land's sake" Angus exclaimed. "You don't believe in traveling light like the rest of us, do you, lad? Your horse's poor back rose up about a foot when you took all that iron off of her."

Will laughed and said, "Well, my papa loves guns and I reckon the acorn don't fall far from the tree."

He removed the purloined Colts from his holster and replaced them with the Confederate-issue guns, and then he began to dig a hole underneath the Chinquapin tree with his knife. When he was done, he deposited the Northern Colts, the Sharp's, and the Leech and Rigdon six-shooter in the hole. He added some of his spare powder and ball. Then he filled in the hole, smoothed out the area, and placed some brush and fallen branches over all.

"Don't reckon I'll forget this old tree as long as I live," said Will, wiping his hands. "I aim to stop by here on my way home. I have another horse fitted with a saddle, if the Yankees will let me keep him. I will load this stuff on him. I branded him and this one with our Alabama brand the W bar C (W-C) I have the branding iron amongst my plunder."

As the two soldiers sat talking, they both had drinks from the whiskey bottle, suddenly Will fell backwards. Angus sprang to his side to examine him. Will had been hit in the shoulder by either an errant accidental discharge or someone had shot him on purpose. Regardless, he was hurt and the blood was covering his jacket. The bullet hit him high in his shoulder.

"Lad," said Angus, "that is a bad hit. The bullet must have been spent, as it is still in you. It needs to come out. I will help you over to the medical tent so a doctor can remove it. I suggest you drink as much of this rot gut whiskey as you can.

It is gonna hurt like hell, unless they have laudanum to give you. Will followed the instructions from Angus even though the whiskey made him want to vomit. Getting Will to the surgical tent was a slow process. Angus explained how Will was hurt. The surgeon was not busy and gave his drunken patient sufficient laudanum to pass out, but not before Will received a promise of no amputation and no Yankee prison.

The two then worked their way back to their horses. Angus led Will back to the campsite so he could figure a way to make a pack saddle out of the Army saddle. If he could keep the bay gelding he had liberated over in Tennessee from some reluctant Yankee troops, he could put all his guns on it unnoticeable to Yankee eyes.

Angus set about stowing his gear on his horse, all the while eyeing his headstrong new friend with some wariness. "I don't know lad," he said. "I think you're taking an awful chance. We're bound to meet up with Union patrols on the way home. I wouldn't want to be caught with any firearms with me in that eventuality."

"Everything we do in life is based on the choices we make," said Will automatically. He dimly recalled hearing the phrase before, but he couldn't recollect exactly where.

The companions struck camp and set off for the army surrender tents at a leisurely pace. Their respective regiments had moved on without them, which troubled them not at all, the war being over and done, for all practical purposes. Most all the Confederate troops would pass Greensboro. They camped overnight and made the outskirts of Greensboro the morning of April 28, a Friday. There, they were engulfed and carried along by a milling throng of Confederate soldiers, early arrivals like themselves, who shared their bewilderment of the parole procedure. They were an exhausted bunch, tired and trail-worn, dressed in a ragbag variety of uniforms, but they conducted themselves with great dignity.

Recognizing Sgt. Renfro hovering on the fringes of the crowd with his ever-present corncob pipe stuck in his mean little mouth, Will rode over to him with Angus close behind.

"Corporal William Cain reporting as ordered for our parole, Sergeant," said Will, dropping to the ground.

Sgt. Renfro looked as if he had seen a ghost. "Cain?" He said incredulously. "Boy, I had given you up for dead."

"No, sir," said Will. "I was shot all right, but Sgt. MacDonald here took care of me."

"Well, I won't try to disguise the fact that I'm pleased," said Sgt. Renfro. "Probably shouldn't say it, but you were always one of my favorites among the boys and I'm glad you'll be going home to your family intact."

"No thanks, the last few days, to some Yankee trying to kill me after I went through everything without a scratch." He told the sergeant about the two wounds.

"That is completely bad. We are not going to have an easy time after being surrendered. Mark my words, they will step on us every chance they get. Y'all be keerful goin' home. Sure good to see you, Cain."

"Thank you, sir," said Will. He wanted to say the sergeant had certainly hidden his feelings well all those years, but thought better of it. It seemed to him the sergeant's bellicose nature had mellowed considerably, owing perhaps to the relief of the surrender, he seemed almost kindly now, if that were possible. "Sgt. Renfro, Angus and me was wondering what we're supposed to do."

"You see those tents over yonder?" Said Sgt. Renfro, gesturing toward a pair of tents about a hundred yards away. "Get in the parole line with everybody else and turn your arms over to the ordnance officer in at the first tent, then move on to the next tent, where you'll get your parole slip."

"What about rations?" Angus spoke up. "The rumor I heard is we're to get several days worth."

"That's a fact and you're just in time," replied Sgt. Renfro. "The grub only arrived this morning by rail from Raleigh, courtesy of the Union government, bless their hearts. The Yanks are distributing it from those wagons yonder."

"Thank you, Sgt. Renfro," said Will. "Sir, I don't suppose I'll be seeing you again. It was a pleasure serving under you, and I'd be honored to shake your hand."

Sgt. Renfro maneuvered the corncob pipe between his gritted teeth and blinked his brimming eyes. He took Will's hand and squeezed it warmly. "It's not manly to cry boy, but I've been keeping so much inside myself all these years, I'm about to come a gusher," he said. "Now be off with you and enjoy a good life!"

Will and Angus joined the parole line, conversing amiably with each other and their fellow soldiers until they reached the first tent. Will surrendered his G&G Colts and accoutrements to the ordnance officer. When asked if he had a rifle or saber, Will replied he had had both upon a time, but had lost them in the fog of battle. The ordnance officer looked skeptical, but with a long, monotonous task ahead of him, he didn't press the point.

In due course, the companions moved to the parole tent, where two officers, representing the Union and Confederate armies, respectively, sat behind a rough hewn table. In a solemn ceremony lasting no more than three minutes, the Confederate officer wrote the date and Will's name and regiment on a printed form, then signed his own name and passed the document to the Union officer, who made his signature.

"Sir," said Will, addressing the Confederate officer, "can I have something to show that my two horses are mine? They both have Alabama brands the W bar C on their right shoulder. I had them when I joined up."

"Certainly, private," said the Union officer shuffling through a stack of papers. He removed a sheet, filled in the necessary information, and shoved it across the table toward Will, leaving blank the number of animals or color. "You fill that out as to markings and brands."

"That's it, then," said Will tentatively, "the wars over and I can go home?"

"It is and you can," said the Confederate officer wearily. "God bless you on your way home and I want to thank you for serving our cause, corporal."

Will exited the darkened tent and stood blinking in the sunshine. When his eyes had adjusted, he read the parole

> "GREENSBORO, NORTH CAROLINA, April 28th 1865
>
> In accordance with the terms of the Military Convention, entered

into on the twenty-sixth day of April, 1865, between General Joseph E. Johnston, Commanding the Confederate Army, and Major General W. T. Sherman, Commanding the United States Army in North Carolina, Cpl W. R. Cain of the 53rd Alabama, has given his solemn obligation not to take up arms against the Government of the United States until properly released from this obligation and is permitted to return to his home, not to be disturbed by the United States authorities so long as he observes this obligation and obey the laws in force where he may reside. He has been granted permission for the horses branded W-C to accompany him home."

Will could not make out the officers' signatures, rendered in haste, but they seemed of little significance. He found it ironic that the bloodiest war on human record, which had taken the steam on so many high-minded words and slogans, should come down to such a cold, bloodless document as this.

When Angus emerged from the parole tent, they mounted their horses and rode over to the rations wagon, laden with sacks of cornmeal and bacon wrapped in white butcher's paper. There was a Union first lieutenant in charge, assisted by a sergeant with an ill-favored face and a cocky Yankee attitude.

"Hand me up your sack, Johnny Reb," the lieutenant called to Will. "Sergeant, fill this up with some wholesome Yankee food for our vanquished friends here."

"Much obliged, Lieutenant," said Will pleasantly, ignoring the officer's taunt. "I've been eating' the best the Union Army had to offer these last several months. Every time we Rangers captured a supply wagon, we would eat high off the hog. I tell you what, that food was good! If this is better than that, it will be something to write home about, sir."

"You mean you can write, boy?" Said the sergeant and jabbed the lieutenant in the ribs with his elbow. Chuckling, the sergeant tossed a five-pound bag of cornmeal and a parcel of bacon in Will's haversack, and then did the same for Angus.

"That's all you get," he said. "Now, you boys go home and realize your faults for starting this mess, and next time you pick a fight do it with somebody you can whip."

"My group whipped you Blue Bellies near about every time we fought," said Will stonily, looking the sergeant straight in the eye. "If you Yanks hadn't had such a lopsided advantage over us Rebs numbers-wise, it would be us sending you home. If you ever bring your surly attitude down to Alabama, you can look me up around Elba. Will Cain is the name. I'll be more'n happy to kick loose that insolent Yankee attitude y'all have."

A deafening whoop went up from the Confederate soldiers within earshot. The sergeant gulped and laughed nervously.

"No hard feelings, kid," he said. "Now, get on with you. Next!"

"Come on, Angus," said Will. "Let's go where the air is clean."

He lightly spurred the mare and she stepped out quickly.

"What put a burr under your saddle, Will?" said Angus. "More trouble with the Yanks is the last thing we need right about now. I know you're a big lad but discretion is the better part of valor, or so they tell me."

"Sorry, Angus, I couldn't help but flare up," said Will. "I know Jesus said turn the other cheek, but it ain't always easy. I often think about what St. Paul said, that if it is at all possible, live at peace with your fellow man. I have a hard time being peaceable toward these Yankees after following them through Georgia and North Carolina and seeing their bloodthirsty actions. I don't know if I will ever tolerate rude behavior again however, being shot at surrender time has not elevated my opinion of Northern troops."

Angus gripped Will's good shoulder and gave it a fatherly squeeze. "Well, lad, let's us try to live peaceably at least until we can get home, all right? Don't think it is in the Bible, but I hear tell you catch more flies with honey than vinegar."

CHAPTER 5

The companions camped in Greensboro that night and embarked on the long journey home the next morning. Their first stop was Jamestown, where Will recovered his buried cache of weapons and his bay gelding that he had left tied to the tree. Untying the animal, he led it to water and found an area with grass so he could feed. He also picked up three old blankets that he could use to hide his cache.

"Angus I am going to keep this horse. Tonight I will use the small brand the 53rd farrier made for me and rub grease and dirt over the W-C so it will appear an old brand. I think I can make good use of the saddle, to help carry my other weapons. I will hide them under my blanket and the blanket roll on this saddle." Will insisted on openly packing the northern-make Navy Colts in the waistband of his trousers, the butts of which his roundabout and shirt tail would conceal when he sat on his horse. Angus pronounced it a foolhardy move, but Will would not listen to him, despite the coat's discomfort in the heat of the day.

The companions figured it was 700 miles or so from Greensboro, North Carolina to southern Alabama and hoped to log twenty-five to thirty miles a day. At that rate, they reckoned they would be home in a month, maybe a little less, barring any trouble with their mounts.

Along the way, they found good grass for the horses and stayed at isolated farms where, in many cases, the soldiers who had surrendered close to home had already returned. They were shown uncommon hospitality not only in these domiciles, but also in the homes where the sons or fathers would not be coming home. Angus was a rather garrulous sort and Will enjoyed listening to his war tales and his stories of hearth and home.

"What did you do before the war, Angus?" asked Will one afternoon early in May. That morning they had crossed the South Carolina border into Georgia. The tree-studded mounds of the Blue Ridge Mountains loomed hazily before them like the furry humps of a great sea of resting camels.

"Was a school teacher, probably not a real good one," replied Angus. "We still got the farm, though my wife had a hard row to hoe these last four years. I sure thank God for that woman. She is a keeper! She taught school for me the first year I was gone, but she couldn't keep up the farm and teach. Her brother came home from Chickamauga, pretty much a cripple. He got a minie ball in his hip 'twas fortunate one of those hasty sawbones didn't take his leg off. After he healed up, he has been a big help for my wife in keeping up the farm and minding our four kids. I assume you folks raise some horses?"

"Yes, I raised this one from a colt," said Will proudly. "My Grandpa Cain got her from the Chickasaw Indians a long time ago over in Virginia. He used to drive cattle from Elba to Virginia and sell 'em. One time, he saw these exceptionally fine horses and brought six of them home. This little mare is really fast in a quarter-mile race. None of the horses in my commissary unit could touch her! I call her Cat on account of she is that quick."

Angus grinned. "Right good name. You have much family, lad?"

There was nothing he would rather discuss than his family, with the exception of horses. "Well, there's my momma and a brother, Nathan, who is thirteen. Had a sister what died about eleven years ago, I believe. Our fourteen year old cousin Polly lives with us. My mother dotes on her, like she was her own. She's an octoroon—still considered a colored person by law. My papa's grandpa willed her to us after he died."

"She was your family's slave, then?" asked Angus.

"Oh, no," said Will. "My great-grandfather set her free in his will.

Anyway, papa and momma don't believe in slavery. They're always saying it goes against Jesus' teachings. Polly is like my blood sister. She is as smart as a whip, pretty as a hummingbird, does her ciphering real good and writes, and rides a horse good as any man. My momma's folks adjoin us with their farm. All together, Grandsir Garrison and we got 180 acres. My grandsir's got two black families workin' for him, but they've been free all along."

"Sounds real nice," said Angus. "Now as for this Polly lass—sounds like you've got your cap set for her, mayhap?"

"No, my sister is what she is. My papa says he believes she is the child of one his randy red haired cousins in Arkansas, making her my second cousin, we don't care if she is mulatto, we love her."

Will pictured Polly in his mind. As pretty and smart as she was, at heart she was a rough and tumble tomboy who liked to Indian wrestle and play King of the Mountain and had not the usual feminine aversion to getting dirty. She was a mite on the skinny side for his taste, and he had never thought of her in a romantic light.

He couldn't imagine marrying a woman unlike his mother, and Polly was his momma's copy, the very model of feminine refinement and beauty. He wondered how the years had treated both of them, and if Polly had changed.

"No, sir," said Will. "Polly is just a good friend. She will make some white man a wonderful wife, away from Alabama, maybe up in the Indian Nation."

"If you say so," said Angus. "But in my experience, friends make the best helpmates."

"Polly is my best friend. We used to do everything together, even wrassle until momma said Polly was too old for that type of stuff."

They rode on for a while in a companionable silence.

"Can't wait to get home to 'Bammy," said Will at length.

"Me neither, son," said Angus wistfully. "Me neither."

The companions pressed on. Fortunately, they met with no misadventure and except for the odd taunt and insult, the Yankees they met along the trail mostly left them alone. South of

Atlanta near a settlement called Aberdeen, however, their luck ran out. It was late morning as two Federal soldiers, both sergeants, approached them on horseback, passing a whiskey bottle between them. Will was cautious of them, for they were drunken and boisterous. They halted in front of the companions and eyed them with disgust.

"Where did you get that buckskin horse, Reb?" said the larger soldier. "You look like a thief to me if I ever saw one. We don't put up with horse thieves, do we Charlie? Specially Rebs. We hung a couple of Reb horse thieves only yesterday."

"I didn't steal this horse. She has my family brand on her. It matches the permission slip from the Federal paroling officer," said Will mildly, though his blue eyes were flashing. He wondered if the sergeant's hanging story was truth or bluster. "I have a paper signed by a Confederate officer stating that these horses are mine. We have come all the way from Greensboro, North Carolina, where we surrendered without any trouble and we don't want any trouble now. We just want to go home undisturbed, like our parole papers promised."

"Looks like we got us another snivelin' Reb, Mike," laughed the other soldier. "Wonder why they lasted so long in the war, snivelin' like they do. Remember all the snivelin' the two we hung yesterday did? They cried like babies as we put the ropes around their scrawny necks."

Angus guided his horse up next to Will. Knowing the boy's feelings about the Yankees, he was eager to defuse the situation. "We don't mean to cause harm," he said apologetically. "We both have our pardons and animal papers."

"Well, then, hand them over damn quick, you Rebel trash!" spewed one of the sergeants.

Will and Angus reached into their shirts for their papers. The sergeant took a deep pull from his bottle and grabbed roughly at the documents in Will's outstretched hand, nearly tearing them in half. With bleary eyes, he glanced at the documents and murmured "W. R. Cain, 53rd Alabama," before dropping them to the ground.

"Pick 'em up," groused the drunken soldier.

"Get them yourself, you drunken slob," Will shot back hotly.

"You smart mouth Reb pup. I'll put out your lights in a minute. Yore bleedin' already, I can make you bleed more," the soldier warned. "Pick up those papers like I said."

"Give me a drink of that whiskey, Charlie," said the other sergeant. He took a hefty swig and laughed evilly. "Say, let's just shoot this Reb son of a gun here and take his fancy horse, then hang the other one."

Unnoticed, Will had slowly unbuttoned his roundabout and had his right hand on the grip of the Navy Colt. He had decided if the soldiers went on with the threat he would kill them both, he was not going to be a peaceful man to hang.

"Let's do that, Mike," the big soldier agreed. "Except hangin' takes too long, let's just shoot both of 'em and take their nags for our trouble."

Will saw the man reach unsteadily for his pistol, Will jabbed the spurs into Cat. She responded by jumping into the other horse, instantly unsaddling the drunken man, who toppled to the ground with a heavy thud. Before the other soldier could retaliate, Will grabbed him by his kerchief and dragged him from his saddle, momentarily forgetting his wounded shoulder. The move brought intense pain and made his eyes water and his shoulder start to bleed freely.

Will leapt from Cat and struck each man a solid blow in the temple with the butt of his Colt. After retrieving his papers from where they had fallen, he took the unconscious men's pistols and secreted them in his haversack. Every move he made caused pain to course through his shoulder, when he got through with these two he would have Angus rewrap it.

"You go on down the road, Angus," said Will. "You have no part in this, and if anyone gets in trouble, it will just be me. I will catch you soon and have you try and staunch the blood in my shoulder."

Angus whistled appreciatively. "Lad, you are quick to strike and with force! I do declare you have definitely got a hair trigger! You say you were brought up in church. No offense, lad, but I think I'd best hightail it down the road. Can you get the men on their horses?"

"Angus, I was churched regularly, but perhaps, I slept through too many teachings or maybe it is my Scots' blood, and I see it leaking out of me. Can you try to fix it?"

"As far as getting them on their horses, there is more than one way to skin a cat," said Will. "Better get goin' Angus, just in case we have more Blue Coats for company. I'll meet you down the road a mile or so."

After Angus had ridden off, Will tied the hands of the two soldiers to the stirrups of their horses. Mounting up, he took the horses' reins and led them quickly into the trees with the unconscious men dragging behind. He untied the men and let them fall roughly to the ground, whereupon he smacked their heads again for good measure with his pistol butt and went through their pockets, finding thirty dollars in gold. He was about to smack the horses' rumps to send them running when he noticed they didn't have a U.S. brand. They were fine looking animals, a sorrel mare and a midnight black gelding. Why not keep them? He said to himself. He was going to heat up the branding iron anyway.

Will knew the big Yankee had learned his name from his papers. He could only hope to put some distance between himself and the soldiers before they came to. Leading the two horses, he rode off parallel to the road Angus was on. Presently, he spotted Angus just ahead and rode behind him three miles or so, then called out to him and rode over. He had a painful dismount. Angus tried to help him through the painful process.

"What are you doing with those horses?" asked Angus suspiciously.

"They ain't got no Yankee brand, and I reckon they been stolen from some Confederate soldiers or a family," Will replied. "Finders, keepers, I always say. I am going to brand them later tonight with yore help."

"Ah swan, Will, you are a reckless fool!" Angus protested. "What if those Yanks trail us?"

"They won't follow," said Will resolutely. "I put them out so hard they may not wake up for a couple of days.

We'll be long gone by then. Must be about noon—if we ride hard, we can do twenty miles by midnight. We'd best split up then."

"I wish we didn't have to travel so fast," said Angus. "My old horse is not as fleet as that animal of yours."

"Here, ride one of these and lead your horse behind," Will suggested.

"No sir, I shan't be caught dead riding a Yank horse, branded or not."

"Suit yourself. Just take this twenty dollars Yankee money. You ride ahead and I will catch up later."

Angus took the gold pieces Will offered. "Say, Will, how come you have Yankee dollars? All I got is worthless scrip."

Will consider telling Angus about the small fortune he had hidden in the skirts of his saddle but decided it wouldn't be prudent. With poor times ahead, the lure of easy money would be a sore temptation, he reckoned, even to a schoolteacher who seemed the very definition of trustworthiness.

"I guess you could say I profited a little from the war," Will said at length.

“Say no more!” Angus chortled. “I’ll chalk it up to the proverbial spoils of war and leave it at that. Well, lad, I’m making a bead for Opelika. Just keep traveling that way and with any luck, our paths will cross. If I don’t ever see you again, I’ll know you have gotten caught, shot, hanged or made it home to Elba unscathed. I hope it’s the latter. I will wait in Opelika as long as I can.”

“Wait up for me in Warm Springs if I am over two days,” said Will. “Thanks again, Angus, for doctoring me back yonder in Carolina. After today my shoulder is starting to hurt like hell. Sorry I got you mixed up in this fix. I too am in a hurry to get home.”

“That’s fine, lad,” said Angus. He dug his boots into the horse’s ribs and rode off at a trot. “It seems trouble is always to be just around the corner,” he called over his shoulder. “Take care of yourself, you hear? If you don’t show up in Warm Springs, I will assume the Yanks got you.”

Will touched the spurs to the mare and turned south. Cat settled into that ground-eating lope that she could keep up for hours, with the other horses tied head to tail, keeping pace. Will kept his eyes open all around, since he didn't want to be caught napping.

The full implications of his rash act finally hit him. He had come out on top this time, but next time his temper might land him at the end of a noose. He could defend his freebooting ways during the war as part and parcel of the whole chaotic experience, but the war was over now and what he had done was just plain lawlessness. What would his mother and Grandsir say if they knew what he did? They would cry and Grandsir would give him a stern tongue-lashing for sure. Moreover, what would papa say? Will prayed with all his might that his papa was still alive and that as a fellow soldier he would understand, but only if the war had changed papa the way it had affected him. He reasoned that he, Will Cain, would never be a pushover again not as long as he was armed and breathing.

About midnight, Will loped into a little settlement called Imlac and stopped at a tavern with a carriage parked out front. Ever watchful now since the morning's events, Will took a good look around the room before he went in and undid the flap on his holster. Two middle-aged men sat at the bar, deep in conversation. They looked like city dudes, salesmen maybe, wearing bowler hats and oxford shoes. On the other hand, they might be carpetbaggers from up north. Rather than provoking them, Will decided to play it safe and be friendly.

"Evenin', gentlemen," said Will as he bellied up to the bar. He was relieved when the men ignored him and carried on their talk.

"Howdy," said the saloonkeeper, an affable-looking man with a shiny bald head. "Are you on your way home, son? You have a lot of fresh blood on your shoulder."

"I know," Will said, "I need doctoring soon."

"We ain't got a doctor anymore. He went to war."

"Reckon I will last till Warm Springs. Sell me a bottle of Old Crow to help me along. Yes, I am heading home to Elba, Alabama. Hate to travel at night, but got to get home to my family and the farm. What's the next town of any size beyond

Imlac? There is a lot less blue coats at night."

"That would be Warm Springs," said the saloonkeeper. "It is about fifteen miles south. The wagon road is good. You are headed in the right direction for Warm Springs."

"Know if they have a blacksmith there? I want to get a set of shoes on my horse."

"Yeah, they got a pretty good one. Don't know how he is about shoeing horses, but I hear he does a tolerable job on plows and wagons."

"Got anything to eat in here?"

"I got some cornbread and sorghum surp on hand."

"That will hit the spot. What about something to drink?"

"I've got beer, whiskey, and well water."

"No beer, thank you, but I will take a slug of whiskey."

"You got it," said the saloonkeeper. He poured two fingers of Old Crow in a shot glass and cut a giant chunk of cornbread from a cast iron skillet on the stove. He put it on a plate and slathered it with syrup from a wide-mouthed jar.

"That's a right generous portion," commented Will. He wiped his hands on his britches and set to eating the cornbread and syrup like a starved man, gobbling it down in a few bites. He threw the whiskey back, felt it warm his innards, and belched quietly. "What do I owe you, mister?"

"Fifteen cents for the whiskey," said the saloonkeeper as he wiped the bar. "The cornbread is on the house for what you boys done for us. It's the least I can do. I still got a young-un out there somewhere in the infantry. Last me and the missus heard he was tryin' to stop Burnin' Billy Sherman."

This brought a sarcastic laugh and comment from Will. "Well, we didn't get that done, though we fought him from Atlanta east. General Johnston just surrendered us at Durham Station, North Carolina a couple weeks ago. I was cavalry and we got to keep our horses, so I traveled faster than your son will. Them that are in the infantry are walkin' kinda slow, since you don't go real fast when you're hungry and war weary. Hope for your sake and his that he comes home soon."

"I welcome that, son."

"Say, y'all see many Yankee soldiers around these parts?"

"No, guess we're too small a place to apply much attention to."

"Well, you can be thankful for that," said Will. "I'll take another shot of your goods and be going on to Warm Springs." He flipped a coin on the bar. "Here is a silver dollar for the drink and conversation."

The saloonkeeper pushed the coin back at Will. "Don't want your money, son. Like I said, I honor your sacrifice and the blood you are bleeding now. 'Sides, you remind me a little of my boy and maybe by treatin' you right, I'll see him again."

Will stuck the coin back in his pocket. "I'm much obliged to you, sir. Is there any water for my horses around?"

"Water troughs are across the street at the mercantile store."

"Thank you, sir. Good night."

"Good night, son."

Will took the horses across the street whereupon they each one selected a place at the trough. Cat nuzzled the water then took a couple long drafts. He spoke gently to the mare as she drank and stroked her flank.

"Is that enough, old girl? We got to be going," he said and swung into the saddle with a nauseating wave of pain. He used his right arm to mount, which was backward to his normal mount. "A few more miles and we can rest and feed you."

He never touched the spur to her, for she seemed to have a sense of haste and direction and struck her long lope. He made Warm Spring long before dawn, stopping outside of the settlement in a patch of pine trees. He almost fell out of the saddle from the pain. Loosening the cinch, he watched and waited. Only the night music of katydids and spring peepers met his ears. The coast seemed to be clear. He did not have a clear knowledge of where he was. He lay the single rein on Cat's withers and let Cat have her head and he would trust the Lord to direct her where to go as he had no idea where he was. Cat stopped in a flat spot with grass where he fell out of the saddle almost passing completely out from the pain and loss of blood. He had strength to spread his blanket on the ground and have a good drink of Old Crow, chasing it with water, then Will stared up at the fading stars, thinking about the saloonkeeper's kindness. "You never know when you might meet a friend," he said aloud, "or need six good ones at hand as he cradled his pistol to his chest."

He went to sleep with his pistol in his hand. His sleep was restless, with his shoulder hurting every move he made. When he awoke in the early morning, he could see a house about a quarter-mile away, where a lady was hanging out her wash. Saddling up, he rode toward the house hoping to be able to get a bite to eat. He was not feeling good at all. He had sweat on his head and his shoulder pained him terribly.

As he rode up it was apparent he had startled the woman. She had been singing Bonnie Blue Flag and had been intent on her washing. She had turned, looking wide-eyed and startled, quickly raising her hand to her mouth. Then she saw his gray jacket with blood on it and he could notice her relax slightly.

"Sorry ma'am didn't mean to scare you he mumbled, would y'all have any food I could buy for breakfast? My name is Corporal William Cain, from southwest Alabama, going home to my family and farm. Was just hoping you had something I could buy to eat, ma'am. I do not feel good at all. If you are not queasy, would you take a peek at my shoulder? It is leaking and the blood has a smell to it, and I don't think that is a good sign."

"Corporal Cain, my name is Betty Croshaw. My husband went off to war two years ago and has not returned yet. I don't have any food. The Yankees came by and cleaned me and the boy out. I would not sell you food if I had it. We are on the same side."

"Thank you, ma'am, for those thoughts."

As he spoke, he began to weave and fall out of the saddle. The woman rushed to help him, apologizing for just talking to him when he was so hurt. Struggling, she eased his hot body to the ground. He was running a high fever. She called her young son, Jason, and between the three of them, they managed to get him up to the front porch where he collapsed on the floor in a heap.

In a stupor, he had a moment of clarity. "He mumbled he needed to get up and care for his horses. She held him down gently and talked soothingly to him, saying all the horses were in the pasture with water; the buckskin was still under saddle but the bridle was off and she was eating. Going back into the house, she got several clean cloths to bandage his wound and cool water to wipe his face. Will just laid there, as her face and reality faded in and out as she ministered to him. Several hours later, he came to a numb awareness, and sat up.

"Ma'am, my name is Will Cain, from Alabama. Thank you for caring for me. I need to get up and care for my animals. Ma'am, I am very hungry. I remember you saying you had no food thanks to some damn Yankees. Do you think you could ride to town and get us something to eat? The mare is plumb gentle. Would you ride her to town and buy some food? I am starving."

"Mr. Cain, I can ride a mule, guess a horse would be easy. I have told you before that I had cared for the animals. Don't worry anymore. Again, my name is Betty, Mrs. Betty Croshaw. I will care for you as I can."

He reached into his pocket and handed her several dollars in silver. Take my mare and a tow sack buy enough to last several days. Get whatever you think we will eat. Get me a bottle of Old Crow and some candy for the boy. Speaking of the boy, the saddle that is on the bay mare, leave it on her and the boy can ride along with you. The bay will follow behind the mare easily. I will lay right here and sleep, after I get a dipper full of water, please."

Jason brought the water and Betty gave him some dried white willow bark powder to help break the fever that had started to rise.

Betty and Jason rode off to town without any problem. Jason was plumb tickled to ride the mare.

Will went to sleep quickly and did not awaken till Betty woke him to eat. She brought the town doctor to look at the wound. He was not pleased with the yellowish traces of pus seeping from the wound, with blood that was brown with a red tinge and a smell of rotten meat. He gave Will some laudanum and then probed the gunshot hole. He told Will he was going to open his shoulder up. In probing the wound, he located the bullet lodged against the shoulder blade and the only way to extract it was to cut it out.

"While I am not a strong advocate of alcohol, this time, I suggest you drink as much whiskey as you can with some laudanum so you will sleep while I work. It won't be easy on any of us, especially you." The doctor cleaned his shoulder with whiskey and carbolic acid, took out his scalpel and slowly made an incision after determining Will was unconscious. Betty then sent her son riding around as she tried to keep her stomach down and help the doctor as he needed.

"Doctor, it seems that you have been operating for hours, but I am certain it hasn't been that long."

"Ma'am it has taken a while, but you have managed to be a big help. It won't be long now. I just have to tie off some blood vessels and an artery, back out, and see if my stitching was good. Just hang in with me."

"I am not quitting, so don't worry. I can truly see how terrible war is."

"Life in general is hard. Birthing babies is hard on women folk, as you undoubtedly know. So we take the good with the bad, and go on with life."

Betty had bought a chicken when she was in town. She put it in the pen and she would dress it after Will regained more strength. She had planned on dressing it and making a big pot of chicken and dumplings along with some corn fritters but Will was to weak to eat.

After a few days of potato and turnip soup, Will was showing signs of recovery and hunger. She killed and dressed the fat hen, and made a large pot of chicken and strip dumplings. She had to encourage him to eat even though he said he was hungry. "Please eat, Will. The chicken broth will do you good," she said.

Will ate till he thought he might get sick. Betty and Jason ate a lot also. She gave Will some more willow bark and he went back to sleep.

On a distant morning, other than his shoulder hurting, he felt fine. "A few more days and I will be up and around."

"I don't think so," she said.

Jace came and thanked him for the candy and the horse ride. "You are welcome, my man. Let's go have a look at the buggy." It was a wobbly procession to the barn. He was weak as water, but knowing they would need more food than she had bought, he had to get the buggy going as soon as possible. "What's wrong with the spring buggy?"

"One front wheel is firmly stuck in place and will not turn."

"Mrs. Croshaw, can you find me a pole to pry the buggy up so we can block the front of the buggy up when I get it lifted? Here is a block of wood to put under it if you can." He struggled to get the pry pole under the wagon. His shoulder complained and began again to bleed heavily. He clamped his jaws together tightly, and got it placed

"I will give it my all," she said. "Now Jason, you stay out of Mr. Cain's way."

"Momma, did you hear Mr. Cain calls me a man, am I big enough to be a man?"

"I am sure if Mr. Cain said that, then you must be one in his eye."

Will leaned down hard on the pry pole and Jason quickly added his weight to help lift the buggy as Betty pushed the block under the axle. "The wheel is still touching the dirt Mr. Cain," she said.

"Here is another piece of wood, ma'am, put it on top of the big one."

"Okay, Mr. Cain, it will clear now."

"Betty, if you cooked all the food you bought when you went to town the other day, then tomorrow we will go back to town, and buy more."

"We really don't need to go so soon, Mr. Cain. There is plenty for a few more days and you will be better healed and the trip will be easier on you."

"Hey, Jace, I wouldn't be a bit surprised if there was not some hard candy for a four-year-old boy at the store. Your momma brought you some. I figure to get a bunch for us all."

"You really think so, Mr. Cain? And I am almost five, not four."

"Jason, Mr. Cain won't be going to town tomorrow or for several days after that. He is hurt more than he wants to admit."

"I know there is candy there, and I want you and your momma to call me Will, not Mr. Cain."

"Momma, is that okay?"

"It is okay," she said, "as long as Mr. Cain calls me Betty."

"That is fine with me, Will said, I can do that."

Several days later, he felt stronger but he hurt when he moved. It was all he, Betty and Jace could do to get him in the buggy.

The trip to Warm Springs was quick. Getting down very slowly from the buggy, he put two gold double eagles into Betty's hand. "These are yours to buy what food you want."

"Mr. Cain, oh, I mean Will, you can't mean this, you may need it later."

"There is more where that came from and besides that, the Yanks I took it from can't use it no more. They were prone to give it to me. You just buy whatever you want."

Entering the store, Betty was skeptical as to what to buy. She felt Will was serious in his gift. She told the clerk she wanted fifty pounds of flour and twenty-five pounds of corn meal. Then she turned to Will with a questioning look on her cream-colored face and pink cheeks.

"Go on, that ain't enough to last long. Get a big ham and a couple sides of bacon, Irish potatoes and sweet potatoes, sugar, salt, ten pounds of coffee, five pounds of pepper corn, and eggs—beings as how your chickens are all dead—baking soda and fifty pounds of dried beans, plus anything else you like or need. It's all paid for by the Yanks that were dying to see it go to a good cause. They were just dying to get rid of their money."

"Is that all, ma'am?" The clerk asked.

"Yes, sir," she replied.

"No, it ain't," spoke up Will. "We need two gallons of coal oil, a sack of assorted hard candy for the lad here, and a bottle of Old Crow, for me. And a couple of chambray shirts for the lad also, and two pair of overalls for him and a new sun bonnet or two for the lady, along with enough gingham to make three dresses, and two pair white stockings and some buttons, thread and a pack of needles. And

I noticed a can of lavender bath salts and a pair of shoes for her, so she don't need to walk barefooted any longer. And we need two half-gallon glass jars."

The clerk said, "That pair of double eagles won't buy all that."

Will, felt Betty clasp his hand.

"Y'all want to cut the order back?" The clerk asked.

"No, not on your life," said Will. "I told the lady to buy what she wanted. How much more than forty dollars do you want? I have many more dollars, and turn that note page around so that I can check your figures. I know my sums real well."

"I totaled it up and you are about fifteen dollars short."

"We can cover that easily, so let me see your figures," Will said.

"Will, that is more than enough, please put some back."

"No," he said firmly.

"Here is the paper for you to check," said the clerk with a look of disdain.

Will started totaling up the goods. "I think you made an error right here," he said, showing the clerk the figures in question. "It appears to me that you made a mistake in your totaling of the purchase. I make it to be fifty-two dollars even. You wish to recalculate?"

"No sir. I see my mistake and I am sorry."

"No problem with me," acknowledged Will. "Mister, you can load our buggy. Please mind the eggs."

Betty released his hand reluctantly and grasped it back as they stood at the buggy.

Will took notice how well she filled out the old dress from the chest.

After arriving at the farmhouse, Betty was in a hurry to get supper started. It had been a while since she and Jason had eaten a full meal and the young man responsible for their food had been hungry when he rode up. Potatoes were on to boil for mashed potatoes and she was going to make ham flavored milk gravy. Moreover, make some long awaited coffee. They had stopped at a black family's farm about two miles away and he purchased a gallon of milk and six hens. They put the hens in a sack. Her prayers were being answered, not like she expected, but answered. Stephen's absence still troubled her mind.

Will told the farmer they would be a regular milk customer.

After a tremendously filling supper, Will went to the creek to take a bath. Returning, he awkwardly and with pain, helped Betty fill the galvanized tub up on the porch and heated water for his shave.

"Don't shave that big mustache off," she said. "I like it." She put Jason in the tub first, out on the front porch. Will sat with his Old Crow and a cup of water. The first drink slammed the back of his throat with a kick. From then on, he sipped his whiskey and followed it with water. It was a comfortable taste and he tasted quite a bit before Betty came out with fresh coffee and a cup. She sat down in the chair next to him and the smell of lavender assailed his nose. They talked over many things, most of it centered on her being lonely and alone.

Will related to the lonely feeling even when he was among his messmates, there were many times he was so lonely he thought he would cry. "A person does need close companionship," he stated as a matter of knowing the fact.

They talked this over for a long spell a love based on friendship was extremely important.

Betty agreed, especially after a relationship between two people was close. Even though she and Stephen had no giddy feelings, there were friendly feelings. "There were times I missed Stephen so much, that I would come out here and holler at God for being so cruel to me. At night, I would hug my pillow and cry, it seemed like for hours, and still find no relief. It would start over the next morning, same old rut. I was going crazy for someone to share my thoughts. And even if Stephen and I were not in a real romantic love, we shared feelings. And the times at night when I gave myself to him, I wanted it to be an abandoned love, I pretended it was. But it was comforting to lie close to someone.

"Oh, Will, it's the little things, touches, hugs, kisses and the conversations about life and other things couples do in our lives, the giving to the other for the benefit of both, such as we do when we read to each other. I especially like to hear you read Byron, even though he was effeminate. His words are so tender and you repeating them make them personal to me.

"Will, I want something, if you would do it. I know it isn't completely right, but I have a need. I want you to hold me gently but firmly. Would you stand behind me and hug me?"

"Yes, I will." He realized, as he pressed her to him, she was firm, yet soft, and fit so nicely against him.

She turned towards him and put both of her arms around his neck, clasping him tighter. "Now kiss me if you want to."

"Do I want to? My heavens, that has been on my mind most of the day, and I have never kissed a woman before. From what I have seen between papa and momma, they enjoyed it. I have looked at your full pink lips all day. I wanted to try and kiss them but I didn't want to frighten you. I didn't know how to go about it."

"Will, I am not frightened at all." She tilted her head up and put her hand behind his head. She pulled his lips down to her moist and hungry mouth, searching for something he was not sure he had.

If this was what kissing was all about, no wonder his momma and papa liked to kiss each other so often. She held his lips to hers until he thought he would stop breathing. As soon as he regained his breath, she kissed him again and again.

"Will, I don't really know what made me get so carried away. I have never considered kissing anyone but my husband. It has been such a long time since I have been held by or talked to by a man. I couldn't help myself. I do hope you believe and understand what I am saying."

"As I said, I have never kissed a woman on the lips before," he mumbled. "It was pleasant, but it has aroused in me feelings I never knew existed. I don't know what to say, except I like being with you, touching you, talking to you and watching you walk around. I have an idea what you want but that is not for us, at this time.

Will, you may be all that stands between me and insanity. I have lain in bed for hours hugging my pillow and not being able to sleep. I would go outside and scream because of my loneliness and fear however then you come along to help us when there was no one else that could. I don't know how much longer I can hold on to my sanity."

Her tears ran down her cheeks like a river and her heart-wrenching sobs racked her body, with strong convulsions. She was clinching her arms around him so tightly, he was unsure if she could turn him loose. Even with the pain to his wound he stood close to her, enjoying having her so near.

Will was bewildered to say the least, somewhat adrift in his reactions to this lovely young woman.

Betty was having inner conflicts: her will, emotions and moral convictions jostling for a dominant position. Three of them could readily justify total surrender to the caresses and kisses, but knowing she was a married woman, she knew better. She was frustrated but very glad Will had the strength to resist their wants.

"If this is what love feels like, then I love you," smiled Will.

"I wish to explain about Stephen and I and how we got together," she said. "He was married and his wife was pregnant when the war started in Virginia, so he came here to escape war, never thinking a war was coming—. This was in 1858—never thinking it would encompass the entire south. He and my brother Tommy became close friends. We went on picnics together, to church together. Susan was not doing well with her pregnancy. When the time came for her delivery, they went to a doctor in Hamilton who had a staff. She became very weak and never left the hospital. Stephen found a wet nurse for Jason and, after a few months of his mourning and our being together so much, he asked me to marry him. I felt I could not refuse such a nice hurting man. Therefore, we married without all the feverish courtship. As close as Tommy and Martha were to him and Susan, they were not thrilled with the quickness of the romance. I became Jason's mother without any difficulty. Soon after the war began, Stephen received a letter from his mother about the federals invading Virginia. He soon enlisted and Tommy enlisted about six months later and I have not seen or heard from Stephen since.

The next morning, Will was in the barn looking at chores to do as soon as he was able. Hearing a horse come to the house, his heart leapt into his throat. Was this Stephen returning home? His thoughts were hopeful it was not, but knowing he really did not want him dead. He came toward the house to see Betty rush out to a man on a tired brown mule. The man only had one arm. She caught the mule and began to lead him to the barn. "Will, I want you to meet my brother, Tom Kelly. Tom, this is Will Cain who has been my and Jason's benefactor the last few days."

"Well, sis, I see something has put a look of hope back on your face."

"Yes," Betty said. "Mr. Cain came riding up several days ago wanting to buy breakfast, he had a bad wound in his shoulder. The town doctor came out and cut the bullet out of his shoulder and after he healed a bit he was hungry. I explained to him that we didn't have any food and he offered to go with us to Warm Springs as soon as he was able to ride the buggy and buy food if I would cook it. Of course, there was no way I could refuse such an offer. We left soon after he fixed the buggy and we went to the mercantile store and he bought food, enough so that now I can invite you and Martha over for a meal."

"Mr. Cain, may I ask how you managed to buy a passel of food? They won't take my Confederate script. What little scrip I have left, after my running off to expel the Yankee invaders, has certainly messed up my family, and I don't know how a one-armed man can make much of a living."

"Mr. Kelly, I happened to be where the Yankees who had money couldn't use it, after they quit breathing, so me and my friends took it. I was glad to share with Betty and Jace, especially after hearing about Chickamauga. I was there in that mess."

Betty turned and went to the house.

Tommy said, "I can see you have done something for Betty. I only hope you didn't do too much. I must ask you a question you didn't act like a stud horse did you?"

"Not on purpose. Yes, I was attracted to her, Tom, but only Betty can answer such a question. I don't talk about those things. If you were not her brother and had two arms instead of one, I would slap yore jaws hard. I can truthfully say I never forced anything on her but food and clothing. Before you leave you need to talk to her about our conversation and get some food for your family."

When Tom finally left, Will was sitting on the porch with his glass while Betty drank coffee. She mentioned that Tom had asked her about them. "I told him that you had not treated me anyway but what was a necessity and you only forced food, and clothing on me and Jason."

"Will, this may not be the time to bring this up, but my heart and mind are going in different directions. I let you into my being as a need of mine and now I feel you have stolen my heart. In fact, I would be in a dilemma now if Stephen came home. I do not think I could go with him if he asked me to. I know I love you more than anything, I could ever think of. I just want you."

"That is a serious way for us to be, Betty. I want to be around you, not for just the physical pleasure you bring me. I relish your company, your voice, and your touch, besides the way you think about deep things, which make me judge my own opinions. Betty, I have been here almost a month and I truly have enjoyed being with you. However, I feel I should be starting home to ease my momma's fears. I hope you understand. I have written her trying to explain my tardiness due to my wound, I am going home in the next few days, and parting from you will be extremely hard. My leaving will give Stephen more time to show up and you to think about us in a quiet way. If he doesn't come home, I want to marry you and move you to Alabama. We have a big farm where we could live and support ourselves. I know you would like it there and my momma is a sweet woman. You two will get along fine, I just know it. Betty, I would like for you to be my wife, right or wrong, God knows my heart."

"Will I would like that also, at the proper time, now however, is not our time, not until the situation with Stephen is final. From now on, we can be satisfied holding hands and talking, and keep our kissing to the minimum. I think that more kissing would lead to something that is wrong in God's eye."

A few days later, he brought home an Airedale terrier and he showed Betty how to train it, so that it would be a watchdog and a companion for Jason. Will explained that the dog would grow to about forty-five pounds. He also bought additional hens and a rooster for eggs and meat. Tommy Kelly had reconciled himself to Betty and Will's relationship and he agreed to break up the old garden spot for their food. Will also left the buggy horse for their transportation. He was trying to do everything he could do in his love for Betty and watch his money as it must meet all their needs including momma.

The moon and stars were bright as they were sitting on the porch with Jason curled up to his dog, Butch. Will spoke, after a protracted silence, that it was time, he must go home to his family.

"The time for my sad departure is here. I know it is sudden, but tomorrow I am leaving for Alabama. I am going to make a place for all of us. I plan on being gone a month and if Stephen has not come in contact with you, I will come move us to Alabama, providing y'all want to go. So send me a letter when it is decided."

Betty tearfully went to bed. Will knowing his weakness for her body lay down beside her with the quilts between them? He was not going to make a move against God's principles.

Early the next morning, after a good breakfast, he walked Betty to his horse. They stood by Cat hugging and talking, neither one wanted the separation to happen. He leaned down and said to her, "This is the last kiss until I come for you. I love you with all my being. I could only wish it had happened differently, but it didn't. Please be careful. Here is enough money to keep you and Jace till we get together. No matter where I go or what I do, you both are in my every thought. The buggy horse is staying here for you."

Jason, you and Butch take good care of yore momma."

With a lingering kiss, he mounted the saddle and leading the other horses, started west at a lope, keeping anyone from seeing his tears pouring down his face and the sobs in his chest. It was going to be difficult for them all. However, for him it would be agonizing.

Will held a steady lope to Warm Springs, where he stopped at the blacksmith and had all the shoes checked on the horses. He also bought a half a sack of oats and a bottle of Old Crow to pass the time away. Hamilton was the next town. Arriving there, he went to the livery stable. He was planning to spend the night in the barn.

The stable man directed him to the last stalls on the right. As he was leading his horses down the alleyway, he saw Angus's horse in one of the stalls. "Does that horse belong to a Mr. Angus MacDonald?"

"Yes, it does," replied the stableman.

"Do you know where MacDonald is?"

"Yes I do," the man said. "He is in jail. It is down there on the corner."

"What is he in jail for?"

"Drunk and fighting," was the terse reply.

Will strolled to the jail finding the sheriff sitting in a straight back chair cocked back against the wall.

"Say, Sheriff, I understand you may have a friend of mine in jail, a man named Angus MacDonald."

“Yes, we do. He has about thirty days to go to finish his sixty days.”

“What all did he do to get such a long time for fighting and resisting arrest?”

“The fact is, we thought he was going to stomp the other guy to death.”

“That don’t sound like the Angus I know.”

“Well, it was his parole papers that said who he was.”

“Is there any way I can get him out quick?”

“Yes, just pay the thirty dollars fine and he can go.”

Will walked back to the cell. He spoke quietly. “Hey, Sergeant MacDonald, rise and shine and greet the new day.”

Angus rolled over and opened one black and purple eye, stared for a moment, while he collected his thoughts. “Will Cain, what are you doing here? I fully expected you to be home in Elba or dead thank the good Lord you are here. I need to get out of here.”

“I know and I will get you out soon as I pay your fine of thirty dollars.” He returned to the sheriff’s desk, paid the fine, received a receipt, and was told to leave town by tomorrow.

The deputy opened the cell, giving Angus his parole papers, gun, and some Confederate paper that had been in his pocket.

"Come on, Angus, let's go on to Alabama. They want us out of town by tomorrow. Angus, your old horse is looking better with all the feed and no exercise." Will paid the stable fee, and gave Angus money for two bottles of Old Crow and a sack of fried chicken and corn dodgers, to ease their hunger later on. They left town at a good fast trot.

CHAPTER 6

"It is about forty miles to Opelika," commented Will when they rode out of town. Late in the afternoon, they arrived and turned into the livery stable.

"Y'all got room for our horses?" He asked the stable hand.

"Yes, we do. Right down the alleyway. The last stalls on the left tie them in the stalls, I will hay them later."

Angus asked Will if he had enough money for him to get a bath.

"Yes, I do, and I see a barber shop and bath house across the street. How come your clothes are so clean?"

"The sheriff couldn't take the stink, so he had them washed. When I get home, I am going to burn these gray rags and try to pretend I never went to war."

"Not me," said Will. "I am going to wear this gray coat till it rots off, then I am going to get a tailor to sew me a new one. I am so proud of us standing up for Southern rights. I am always wearing gray. Angus, where are you bunkin' tonight?"

"Reckon, they will let us stay with the horses?"

The stable man said for a quarter they could sleep in the stalls. Will leaned back, wondering what the future would hold and if the two yanks were on his trail. Cat sidled over and took up her customary watchful position over him. The last thing he saw as he dozed off was her taut, grayish-yellow belly, looming over him like an autumn sunset. His thoughts turned to Betty.

"Hey, wake up!" The liveryman called from outside the stall. "I didn't mean to shout, but when I came in that mare was standin' over you like a protectin' angel. She laid her ears back, so I scooted out for safety. She is a different animal for shore, and not only in looks."

"She is that," Will said agreeing. He stretched luxuriously and patted the animal's muscular rump.

A moment later, Angus stuck his head in. "Morning, Will, you ready to get started?"

"Almost," he said. "I want to buy some things for home." He bought several yards of calico and gingham cloth for momma and Polly to cut dresses from, a Barlow knife for Nathan, powder, caps and balls for the pistols, and a nice Briarwood pipe for his papa—it even had a silver scrimshaw band on the stem. He also bought coffee for the trip and bacon to fry.

"Angus," he said, "I want to eat now, though, 'cause I really don't want to stop till tonight unless I commence to leak. Guess we can get a bite across the street."

"I ain't got any money for meals," Angus admitted shamefully. "I done spent my last dollar on whiskey several days ago just before you got me out of jail."

"What did you do to get all that jail time? You may tip the jug but fist fighting is different."

"Well, I was minding my own business when this carpetbagger started runnin' his mouth about how we Rebels got taught a lesson. He kept flapping his lips until I couldn't take any more. So, I did what you would have done. I smacked his jaw as hard as I could. He went down, but being a scrapper, he got up. So I had no choice but to hit him again, and I hurt my hand. So while he was laying there I decided to do the Highland fling on his head and chest. I reckon these folks had never seen the fling danced so hard, guess I did a number on him. They thought I was going to kill him. The sheriff slugged me with his pistol and I went to sleep, waking up in jail with a sore head and a black eye. I think some other folks beat on me while I was out, because the Yankee lover never laid a blow on me."

"Come on, you old rascal," he said and put his arm around his friend's shoulders. "I'll buy you a meal." At the café, they ordered ham, eggs, fried potatoes and pie. Will was in a good mood he could almost taste his momma's pecan pie. It was better than this one.

They had a regal breakfast and had the horses packed and ready an hour later. Will paid for their sleep in the stall.

They headed southwesterly toward Union Springs, about forty miles away and hit town about seven o'clock in the evening. Angus looked around and found a place to eat, a clean little restaurant with red and white-checkered tablecloths. Eggs, biskits, a bacon and coffee were six bits for both of them. They made camp on the edge of town and put the nosebags on the horses.

"It looks like it's going to be a good night to sleep out in the open," said Will. "If we find good traveling tomorrow, we can be in Troy tomorrow night. From there, it will be a short sprint to Elba. If everything goes right, me and the horses will be home in two days, praise God." That evening, they made camp on the side of the road by a lazy creek, where they drank a little and talked a lot.

"I'll be turning off at Troy and run on down to Indigo Head to see my pap before I go home," said Angus. "My wife and kids should be there at my folks' place. She allowed they would go down there for a couple of months after she and her uncle got the crop in. I certainly hate to part company, Will. Even if you do get a wild hair now and again, it's been good traveling with you."

Will had lain down on his back and was gazing up at the stars twinkling in the inky sky. He thrust one arm behind his head for a pillow and took a deep pull from the bottle.

"Angus, have you ever thought about heaven?" He asked in a faraway voice. "I mean, as being a real place where a person goes after they are dead?"

Angus sat down beside Will and rocked back on his forearms. "Tell you the truth, Will," he said uncomfortably, "I'm not a particularly religious man."

Will continued to talk as if he hadn't heard Angus. "Not that I think everyone that dies is going to heaven. I think only those that have had a deep personal relationship with God get inside. Just being good, don't get you up there at least that is what I believe. I am depending on God's grace and mercy because of some of the things I have done in the name of war. Not that I have murdered anyone, or something like that, but I have had a lot of terrible thoughts and exhibited a lot of unkindness toward others, I think, that would keep a person out of heaven quick as murder."

"Could be, Will," said Angus noncommittally. "I never really thought about it."

Will rolled on his side, propped his cheek on his elbow and regarded his friend. When he spoke again, his voice took on an ardent note. "You know, Angus, the Bible says that all the temple stuff that Moses made was a mere shadow of what he saw when he was with God on the mountaintop. I think heaven is a real place, with everything that's good and pretty on earth up there only a thousand times more glorious. I cain't imagine a true paradise without horses and by golly, the Bible says heaven has got 'em! And my family and Betty will be there. I only pray you are.

"My wife drug me off to one of them brush arbor meetings. I silently repeated the words the circuit rider said, so I reckon you will see me in heaven, since God is so forgiving,"

Angus leaned forward and grabbed Will's wrist. "You ain't figuring on dying, are you? You got some kind of premonition? We've come a long way from the killing grounds, to be talking about dying now."

"It is not dying I am concerned about," said Will. "I'm just thinkin' about living out my life and having a family. I doubt if my pa ever worried about dying. He never wrote us much of the war, but every letter was about coming home and farming as if the war was just a hiccup in his life that would go away in time. Lord, I hope I find him home. So don't worry about what I said, Angus—it was just some woolgathering by a boy who has seen his life change, mayhap not for the best."

Angus smiled. "All right, lad, let's sleep on it and we'll talk about it tomorrow." He produced the whiskey bottle from his haversack and guzzled a good inch of the brew. "Ah, nothing like a snort to bring on pleasant dreams," he opined. "Want some, Will?"

“No, thanks, Angus,” said Will. “I just want to lay here and think about papa, momma, home, and Betty.” He watched the cottony clouds scudding across the face of the waning moon. “I am but a speck in this grand old universe,” he murmured as the sandman came, “and I’m sure glad of it.”

The mare nuzzled him awake at first light. The dawn was foggy and the air smelt of rain.

“Cat, you are a wonder and more reliable than a rooster,” said Will, yawning.

Hearing voices on the trail, he put his hand on the Colt Navy and waited. Presently he spied a couple of tattered wayfarers approaching. They barely lifted their haunted eyes in acknowledgement as they trudged past. Will noticed the tiredness in their step and the desperation in their hushed talk.

“Hey, fellas” he called out to them. “Don’t shoot! Do y’all want something to eat?”

Angus was awake now. “What is it, lad?”

"Just a couple of fellow Southern travelers I have invited to eat."

The voice of one of the men sounded back. "Yeah, we hungry," said the elder one. "Feel like my belly's growed to my backbone. Y'all ain't trying to trick us up and shoot us, are you?"

"Nothing like that," said Will. "We are war weary travelers like you, on our way to our home in Coffee County, Alabama. I'll strike up a fire so you can see us better, and I'll throw some bacon in the pan and put the coffee pot on to boil."

The two men came back warily and stood before Will and Angus. They looked like starving scarecrows in their gray rags.

"Y'all really got bacon and coffee?" said the young man hopefully. "We certainly would be obliged if you had some to spare."

"Got plenty," said Will jovially as he stoked the fire. "And I bought some corn dodgers yesterday. They are cold, but really good especially if we find a flat rock to heat up, and then lay them on it. Coffee has more chicory in it than coffee, but it's better than water."

The men hunkered down by the fire. "We haven't eaten in a day or three," said the elder man. "I have drunk a lot of water to make the hunger go away. My belly got to sloshing' around so much you could hear it a hundred yards away, ah bet."

The bacon fried quickly over the hot fire. Will took the point of his knife and speared two slices each for his guests from the skillet. Angus handed them each a warm corndodger.

"Eat up, friends," he said. "We only got one extra cup, so y'all will have to share for the coffee."

The men ate hungrily and the first helping was gone in the blink of an eye. Will fried more bacon and Angus kept the corn dodgers coming. They enjoyed serving their guests and forgot their own morning hunger.

After the third helping, the elder soldier apologized for not saying thank you sooner. "It was bad manners on my part, but my mother taught me not to talk with my mouth full," he joked. "Now if we don't get the drizzles from eating so fast, we will be right fine. Say, ah notice you fellers ain't had nothing."

"Shucks, Angus 'n I have been pleasured just by watching y'all eat," said Will as he cooked up another slab of bacon.

"Well, ah thank you again," said the elder soldier. "Ah swan, boys, ah never figured on bein' treated this good. It is a long trip to Louisiana a-foot. Seems like all we been doin' the whole war was walk and now my shoes are worned out and all the rocks in the world are right where ah put my feet!"

Will looked at the battered rawhide moccasins hanging limply from the old soldier's feet. It was evident he had made his own foot coverings. Good shoes had become the rarest of commodities during the war. Will being in the commissary unit, he had become accustomed to men begging for bits of untanned leather to use for fashioning a crude pair of shoes or Indian type moccasins, Will figured the old soldier had done just that, but he made no comment.

"You boys want a pull on this here bottle to cap off your meal?" asked Angus.

“I don’t mind if ah do,” said the older man and took a good swig before passing it on to his companion.

Will and Angus each took a dodger and some bacon, leaned back against their saddles, and dug in.

“Y’all want some more, just help yourselves,” said Will. “By the way, my name is Will Cain and this here is Angus MacDonald. We are both on our way home and hope to be there tomorrow, if the good Lord’s willing and the creek don’t rise.”

The elder soldier stuck out his hand. “My name is Isaac Spooner and this young man is my nephew, Thaddeus Lee. We are from over the Louisiana way in West Feliciana Parish. We sure appreciate this hospitality. The folks we’ve come across are as poor and hungry as we are. Ah certainly hope it improves between here and home. If it doesn’t, my wife and young-uns may be starved to death.”

“It’s been slim pickings in the villages we come across, too,” offered Angus. “Of course, Will had a few Yank coins to dole out and ease everybody’s pain. Friends,

I'm here to tell you, this is one charitable son of the old South!"

The fog was lifting and the sun's rays were filtering through the pine trees as Will got up and fed the horses and tacked them up.

"Hate to run out on you," he said directly, "but we are going to have to leave you boys now."

"Y'all do what you gotta do," said Spooner. "Now that you have fed us, we may lie down for a few hours. Lawd, my old feet are hurtin'! If'n I ever go to war again, I'm gonna do like you fellers and be in the cavalry."

Will led his mare over, reached into the tow sack, and pulled out a handful of corn dodgers. "Here, these will get y'all down the road a day or so." He handed Spooner a five-dollar Yank gold piece. "An' mebbe this will help put some new leather between your feet and those rocks."

"Ah, swan!" said Spooner, marveling at the shiny coin. "Son, this is mighty white of you, but ah hope it ain't stretchin' you out any."

"Don't you worry about it," Angus put in. "This boy can pull gold money out from behind your ears!"

"Well, y'all ever get down Louisiana way, come see me," said Spooner. "You'd be welcome as the rain, day or night, summer or winter."

The bay nickered. Will walked over by it and loosed the reins from the bush where the mare was tied and led her back to the campfire.

"Tell you what, fellows," he said, grinning, "I've got too many horses to keep up with and I'd be obliged if you'd take this one off my hands. Here, take her. Light as you fellers look, she won't complain about you riding double."

Struck speechless, Spooner took the reins. There were tears in his and his nephew's eyes as Will and Angus said their farewells and struck out southwesterly upon the trail.

"Will Cain, you beat all I have ever seen!" said Angus when they were out of earshot of the two men. "I declare, you are the most giving man I know of."

Will laughed. "Wasn't anything a Christian man shouldn't do? Besides, easy come, easy go, I always say. Someday, they will pass it on.

CHAPTER 7

The next morning, Will and Angus came to a crossroads. Knowing the time for parting was nigh, Will's eyes gleamed with emotion. Fearing he might start weeping, he fidgeted with Cat's bridle to distract himself from his feelings.

"Well, Angus, guess I had better light a shuck to Elba," he said. "It has been a pleasure and right enlightening to travel with you. If you ever get up my way, hunt me up."

"I'll do that," said Angus. "What are your immediate plans, lad?"

"Tell you truthfully, I don't know what I'm gonna do," mused Will. "I wanna lay down and rest for a month of Sundays like ole Rip Van Winkle, but whipping the farm back into shape will take priority, and there's cattle and hogs running wild in the canebrake to be brought in. My work's cut out for me, especially if papa ain't home yet, and I have Betty to think on."

"Think positive, lad," said Angus, extending his hand. "He's probably on the front porch, waiting for you."

Will took Angus's hand between both of his and shook it warmly. "Thanks, Angus, for your company and all your kindness," he said, his voice breaking. "I'll never forget you."

"Nor I, you," said Angus solemnly. He opened his palm and marveled to see a twenty-dollar Yankee gold piece. "You know, lad, I can only hope my sons grow up like you. Don't you need the money?"

"Naw, I'll get by," said Will. "Besides, don't forget my motto easy come, easy go. See you some day, Angus."

"So long, Will," said Angus. "And God bless you!"

Will spurred the mare and she loped off, with the geldings loping along beside her, keeping stride. Will had his mind set on the homecoming.

He shouted to Cat, "We're going home, girl, we're really going home." The landscape began to look real familiar. Cat picked up her pace—she could smell home.

Polly was coming out of the hen-house with a basket of eggs when she looked up and saw a rider with several horses coming at a strong lope. She had a keen eye and recognized the rider on the horse in an instant.

"Momma!" she cried as she ran at breakneck speed to the house, yelling, momma come quick! It's Will! Will's come home!"

"Are you sure it's Will?" said Ellen skeptically, as she eyeballed the horse and rider which looked nondescript to her tired eyes. "Are you sure, Polly, are you sure?"

"Yes ma'am. I'd know Will and that buckskin horse of his anywhere."

"Oh, Polly, it's an answered prayer! We haven't had a letter from him for the longest time and the last one said he was recovering from a bad wound. The war went so bad for us all. Thank you, Jesus, my boy has come home!"

Will thundered into the yard and set the mare up into a sliding stop. And the other horses milled around, flaring their nostrils and blowing.

"Momma I'm home, I'm home!" He drew his mother to his chest and whirled her 'round and 'round. He saw Polly standing by, sobbing for joy. Will grabbed her, gave her a big hug, and kissed her wet cheek.

"Polly, it is good to see you. I thought about you often," he said and backed up to take her in.

No longer skinny, she had blossomed into a fine specimen of young womanhood, and the curves of her budding figure stood out proudly against her homespun dress and pinafore. Her almond-shaped green eyes shone like gemstones in the honey-colored face, and her silky, crow-black hair hung past her shoulders. She seemed at once exotic, like some Arabian princess in a storybook, while retaining the tomboy look he remembered. She smiled demurely and he felt sensations coursing through his body, and the times he had with Betty caused him to know what the sensations were. In his heart, he repented about his sister, lordy she had turned out pretty. They would have to keep an eye on her, and keep the men and boys away.

"My, my, Polly you have growed a lot since I last saw you," he said at length. "Bet you have been a big help, too."Ellen tried to dry her eyes on her apron, but they kept leaking. "Yes, Polly has been a big help," she confirmed. "Don't know how I would have gotten by without her. She has growed up a bunch, 'tis true. Course, she is going on fifteen now and getting to be quite a young lady she turns a lot of heads. She could use some clothes that fit, for she's like to bust out of her old dresses."

He knowingly smiled as he walked to the mare, and took down the parcel with the yard goods in it, and handed it to Polly. "Take a look, sis, and see what I fetched for you and to make some new clothes out of."

"Momma, look here!" Squealed Polly, flouncing about the yard with the calico clutched to her breast. "There is enough material to make us lots of dresses." She hugged Will and leaped up to kiss his cheek. "Thank you, Will. Thank you, thank you, and thank you!"

"You're welcome, you scamp," said Will, smiling. Turning to Ellen, he asked, "Where is Nathaniel?"

"He is down in the canebrake, bringing out the milk cow."

Will grabbed Polly and swung her up on the mare. "Go find Nathaniel, Polly."

When she trotted off, Will fetched his haversack, took his mother's hard red hand in his and led her up to the swing on the front porch saying, sit down momma. I just want to look at you."

He gazed at his mother's face and basked in the infinite loving kindness that dwelled there. She was a little grayer perhaps and there was a hint of sadness behind her eyes, but she was just as pleasantly trim and pretty as ever in Will's eyes.

"A lot of things have happened since I last saw you," he said, his voice cracking. "I wasn't sure sometimes if I would get back or not."

"Oh, Will, I've waited for such a time as this since your papa left back in '61," said Ellen through her sobs. "Now I am one man short."

Will read the care on her face and knew the answer to his question before he asked it. "Papa's not coming home, is he, momma?"

"No, son," said Ellen gently. "We had a letter from your Powell cousins. They were with him from the first and said he was killed somewhere around Atlanta, June of '64. They said a sniper done it. Would have written you about it, but it didn't seem proper somehow to give you the news so impersonal like. And, I was afraid you might get the itch to desert if you felt like you was needed to home. The Powell boys say Bob got a Christian burial in Oakland Cemetery, there in Atlanta.

I was there at Atlanta, momma trying to find his unit, but there was nothing but confusion and killing we'll have to make it up there, one of these days, and pay our respects."

Will looked out at the fields, stretching away to the horizon, blinking away his tears.

"Damn that yellow-bellied Yankee what done it!" He exclaimed. "I'm sorry, didn't mean to swear momma like that, but I ain't got no use for the Yanks. The lot of 'em ain't worth one good Southern man like papa."

"I understand your bitterness, son," Ellen sighed. "It was a hard blow to all of us, but we persevered on the prayer that you would return, and the good Lord has seen fit to make it so. Nathaniel reminds me of you so much. He has been a big help and has grown into a man himself while you were away. He and Polly have kept me going when I didn't think I could. I know Polly is mulatto, but I couldn't have had a daughter that cares as much for me as she does and I love her so. Some folks around here think that's wrong, but I have read my Bible over and over and see no difference between white and black."

Will drew the Briarwood pipe from his haversack. "I got this for papa in Opelika," he said and passed it to Ellen. "He would've enjoyed smoking it late of an evening out here on the porch."

"That he would have," agreed Ellen, admiring it. "It is a pretty thing. Let's put it on the mantle. We can all enjoy gazing at it."

"How are Nanny and Grandsir?" asked Will, trying to sound cheerful.

"They are doing well. Both are getting a little slower, 'course they are close to seventy-five now. Your grandpa prays for you as regular as the sun coming up. They will be glad to have you home. I'll have Nathaniel hitch up the buggy and go bring them over tonight. I got some chicken and dumplings on the stove." She paused and added tantalizingly, "Along with some other fare like a pecan pie."

"Momma, may I tell you about something wonderful and complicated that has happened in my life? I pray you will be pleased. I wrote you I was helping a southern family who were out of money and food and the husband was most likely dead from the battle we were in at Chickamauga, Georgia. The widow woman had no money or any way to get any. She and the boy were completely out of food after some Yankees took their food and wanted to molest the woman. I bought them food and other things they really needed and chored up around the place. The woman is a few years older than me and clean, pretty and very industrious, just like you. We got along so good and it felt so right, I want to marry her, and I will. If the husband comes home, it is over, if he don't we will cross that bridge then. He has not contacted her in two years. Her name is Betty Kelly Croshaw. We are going to wait a bit longer to see if her husband comes home, but the war has been over a good while now and he should have come home or written if he was alive. Please don't think ill of us. We love each other, just like you and papa do. I can hardly stand being away from her. Don't tell Polly or Nathan yet, please wait a while."

"Will, you know Polly has dreams of marrying up with you. She has thought about it ever since you left. She will take it real hard when she finds out you want to marry someone else."

"Momma you raised me to think of Polly as a sister, and as much as I could be physically attracted to her, in my heart and mind she is my sister."

"Son, are you sure the woman did not trap you by offering you something that appeals to our sin nature, bein' as how you didn't have experience in these feelings?"

"Momma this was my first time to be kissed by a woman and it caused feelings I had never felt. I heard stories around campfires with my army friends, but never thought of doing anything like that. I reckon she could have trapped me but I wanted to be around her all the time. We sat for the longest times talking about most everything we could think of. We had many of the same ideas about family, life after the war, our futures—as far as we could see we had a future—understanding after the war there could not be much of a future for any of us. That is one reason I suggested she move here with us, we have plenty of land to live off of as a family."

"What will you and she do if her husband isn't dead?"

"I don't know about me. Betty said if she had to make a choice, she would stay with me. Betty has raised her step-son, Jason, since he was a baby. Stephen's wife died during childbirth and they were married some months later. Jace stuck to me like a tick while I was there and I grew to love the boy. He is smart, strong and very obedient along with being inquisitive."

"I need to talk to Grandsir and Nanny about Betty and myself."

"I am planning to have them over for supper tonight, momma said."

Ellen sent Nathan over to her parents' home to bring them over for supper and talk. When Grandsir came in, he immediately said how much Will had grown in spite of poor army food.

"I am fine, Grandsir, however, I need a heap of council." With that outburst, he launched into his present situation. Polly I would like for you to hear my story, sit down by momma please.

"Before I got home, I met a family in Georgia that were bad off, they hadn't heard from the husband in over two years, no letters no nothing. Staying to help, I fell in love with a married a woman with a young son. The lady's name is Betty and the boy is Jason."

Polly was visibly troubled by Will's story. Momma held her sobbing body close to her.

Grandsir said very solemnly. "Well, my boy, you seem to have stepped in a pile of poop or close to it, I hope we can clean it up. After a man is gone so long, it is not unusual to consider him dead, especially following the tremendous losses the South suffered. However you marrying this lady put's a different spin on my thinking."

"Ellen mentioned that she asked you about becoming trapped and that you think it is love, not some animal instinct we all share. Love is a word that gets the blame for plenty of things we do. If, as you say, it is a genuine thing between you and this lady, it may get a bit nasty if her long overdue mate turns up. Are you man enough to do what you have to do if it comes to it and mend dear Polly's hurting heart?"

"Yes, sir, I know I can. I know when you play with fire you get burned. I remember David and Bathsheba and all the conniving David did and the outcome of the baby dying. However, David repented and went on with life. I believe Betty and I can be just as strong."

"Counseling doesn't come easy or quick, so you will have to wait on my praying and conversations with the Lord Jesus. I will let you know as soon as I get a clear decision. It may not be what you want to hear, marrying her to salve your biblical conscience may be something that jumps up and bites you in the fanny."

After the Grandparents went home Will spoke to his momma "I only hope it is good counsel and that I can live with it," he said.

"It will be correct, whatever daddy says, rest assured about that. You will just have to wait. If this is really love the best start possible is what you want. Marriage is a lifetime of giving and receiving and sometimes a person feels it is more giving than receiving."

"We got any coffee, asked Will hopefully? Wanting her reaction but wanting also to move away from the conversation a wee bit."

"Yes, we do".

He strolled to the edge of the porch and hugged a post. "Say, momma where are pa's bagpipes? I may try to play us one of his songs tonight, just to remember him by."

When Nathan came out on the porch, Will said, "Nathan I have a present for you in a tow sack on my saddle I gar-on-tee won't disappoint you."

The boy leaped off the porch, retrieved the sack, and returned in a trice.

"What is it, Will?" he asked excitedly, giving Will the sack. "Will I like it?"

Will reached in, took out the purloined Colt Navy .36, and handed it to his brother. "Well, tell me Nate do you like it?"

Nathan ran his fingers up and down the pistol with reverence. "Wow! You bet I do. Where'd you get such a fine thing?"

"Spoils o' war as you might say," said Will cagily. "I've got some fresh powder, caps and lead. Later on, we will fire it up and see if you remember how to shoot. Be careful, for its loaded. An' never forget, the most useless thing in the world is an empty gun when you need it."

"He got me and momma some cloth," Polly chimed in. "Now momma can finish teaching me to sew. Then I can make lots of pretty things for us. Isn't that right momma?"

"Yes, child, yes," said Ellen in agreement. "I'll oil up the old treadle sewing machine and we'll get at it soon as things settle down to a boil."

"Polly, go fetch those old bagpipes from my cedar chest and bring them here please, said momma.

Will chose not to reveal he had close to two thousand dollars in Union money and how he had come about it. The money would surely be needed, for he was uneasy in his mind that gathering the cattle would be feasible, much less profitable. The prospect of taking on the Herculean chore at once scared and thrilled him.

"Where are the horses?" He asked generally. "I don't recall seeing them ridin' in."

Nathan tucked the Colt in his britches. "The horses are fine," he said. "We just keep them down in the canebrake so the Yankees couldn't steal them, or the white trash deserters that come and prey on folks. They are brash, likely to steal anything that wasn't nailed down. Got no respect for folks' property, just take 'cause they can. They ain't bothered us but they have been snoopin' to see what we got. Our sister is so pretty I keep that old shotgun loaded with buckshot just inside the door."

"That's wise of you," said Will. "Take the mare and the gelding out to the barn, if you please, and turn them and the others loose in the pen, after you feed them".

"We got plenty of horses now," said Nathan.

His eyes followed Nathan as he led Cat and the gelding to the pen. It was only about forty by forty feet and in disrepair, scarcely big enough to house the multitude of wild and semi-wild cows he fancied on capturing. Will knew in his mind that he had a big job ahead of himself. Rectifying the years of neglect would require a heap of work and he wondered if he would be equal to the task.

"I'm afraid you've come out of one war into another," said Ellen, as if she read his mind. "Won't be easy, getting the farm back into shape."

"I am more than able to do all things through Christ," said Will resolutely. He thought he and Betty were in Christ regarding holding hands and a quick kiss or two. It was hard to keep the Bible teachings in the front of all the action.

"I like it when you quote scripture, son."

"I have almost forgot how," he said.

"Here is what I see us doing," said Will, his eyes shining. "We haven't worked our stock since '62, when Nathan, Polly, and I had a feeble go at it. I met some Texans in the war and got me some good pointers on rounding up wild cattle, so things should go better this time. Me and Nathan will start driving the canebrake and bring in all the cattle and branding them up. I may have to take some of my money to hire a man or two to help, but so be it."

"Polly," Will, called out, "come here please, for a bit. I am so sorry I shattered that dream of yours. I love you too much to hurt you. You are my sister, my flesh and blood."

Polly gave Will a long hug. She was beginning to understand that their relationship was completely as a sister and brother, not as a future husband and wife.

“Will, the Powell boys got home a week or so ago,” said Ellen brightly. “They are young and strong, and I know they need the money. Polly can help you once in a while, too.”

“That’s fine,” replied Will, “but you’d best see if some of Nathan’s clothes will fit her. No doubt, she can wrangle with the best of ’em, but she can’t do it in a pinafore. Gonna need a good dog or two also, ’cause those animals are gonna be wild. Wish old dog Rattler hadn’t died, like Polly wrote me. He may have been past his prime as a cattle dog, but you couldn’t beat him as a watchdog. If he was still alive you wouldn’t have any strangers hanging around, I’ll warrant.”

Nathan had returned from the pen. “Cat sure looks like a million dollars of horseflesh,” he said to Will. He then added knowingly, “The geldings ain’t so bad, neither. Take it they are another war souvenir?”

“You might say that.” Will was grinning from ear to ear. “The long-legged bay mare is mostly thoroughbred”

“I think a colt out of her by Old Dan would be a dandy.”

When Nathan and Polly had gone, Will led his mother to the porch and slumped down wearily in the swing. Ellen sat down beside him and stroked his hair lovingly.

"I think I'll wait awhile before I pester the Powell boys," said Will. "Coming home from the war and all, it takes a while to get over it."

Seeing Will's eyes cloud over with hatred, Ellen gathered him to her breast. "I know it was terrible for you, son. Having to fight your own kind, it is almost like brothers against brothers."

"Those Yanks ain't my brothers," Will snarled, "I'm sorry please don't talk to me about the war. I am still convinced we did the right thing, but there were lots of terrible things happened. What the Yankees did in Georgia and North Carolina to people's homes was uncalled for. It has brought about some changes in my attitude, and not for the better, I fear. I know you and papa and grandsir taught me different, but I sometimes acted contrary to Bible teaching. I have asked forgiveness and I know I got it."

"Of course you did. God promised to forgive if we asked him to," cooed Ellen as she stroked his hair and wondered what transgressions her sainted son could possibly have committed.

"I'm so sorry papa had to die, for he had so many dreams about us and life," Will sighed. "I wish I had known him better. It makes me sad I didn't take the time as I could have learned so much before he went off to war. If heaven is like I think it is, I will have time to make it up while I enjoy fellowship with Jesus and papa."

Ellen smiled wanly. "Go-wan in the house and clean up son. I will get you a pair of your papa's pants and a shirt. I think you can wear them, for you're a lot bigger than you were, and after we get some meat on your bones, you'll be bigger still. You will be a lot bigger than your pa for sure, 'fore all is said and done.

Will rubbed his cheeks critically with the palm of his hand. "Momma, I'll go put the water on the stove to heat. Think I will shave, since I'm getting tired of this hair on my face, except for my mustache. I shaved regularly in the Army, and then for Betty, except she wanted me to keep my mustache."

Ellen smiled for Will's beard was little more than red peach fuzz but his mustache was big. She followed him into the house and while he put the buckets on the stove to heat, she watched his limber movements with pride. Her son had become a strapping young man and he stood ramrod straight, with a soldier's erect bearing. His piercing eyes were as blue as a robin's egg, as blue as his father's, if not more so. In fact, he had so many of his father's traits and features, it was like her beloved Bob had come back from the dead.

After Will had gone to the back porch to clean up, Ellen knelt at the kitchen table and prayed quietly "Oh, God in heaven, my Bob went home before he could see what he and I had produced. He would have been so proud of the man his son has become. I thank you, Lord, for bringing him home safe. I have felt so alone with all that is going on, Lord, and I have turned to you for solace. I am so grateful to have a man in the house again. Thank you, Lord, thank you. Dear Lord I thank you for helping us with the farm and healing Polly's broken heart."

A few minutes later, Will stepped in from the porch, freshly bathed and clean-shaven with his hair combed and parted, looking bright as a new penny. Ellen's heart skipped a beat. In the blue denim shirt Bob had bought on a trip to Mobile, he bid fair to be his father's twin.

"You're the mirror image of my Bob when we were courting," said Ellen proudly.

"Papa's shirt's a mite tight in the shoulders and chest," said Will, preening at his reflection in the kitchen window. "I do believe the sleeves are too short, but I can roll them up."

"You look fine, son," said Ellen serenely.

A little while later, Will was stowing his gear away in the room he shared with Nathan when he heard Nathan and Polly drive up in the wagon with his grandparents and rushed out to meet them.

"My, you've growed up a bunch the last two years! I didn't notice it so much the other night when we had supper over here. I do declare you're the spittin' image of your pa, except you're a danged sight bigger. Why, you're a regular high pockets! What do you think, David?"

"He's a Goliath, all right," said Grandsir.

Will looked into his grandfather's eyes, so lively and full of wisdom. Will had always admired Grandsir's great stature, and now they were roughly the same height.

"Grandsir, it is good to be in your presence again," he said solemnly. "I hope you have a good word for me from God. I have been praying about the situation."

"Good to see you too, son. I do have a word of God I will share with you later. I hope you receive it," said Grandsir.

The two men embraced and stood clapping each other on the back for several moments.

"Grandsir," said Will, "you look just like you did before I went off to war. I remember our talk and everything you said. It sure wasn't no party and it was rough on me. I have learned a lot. Some of it I won't ever use again, but what I learned about me will always be in my possession."

Grandsir nodded his head sagely. "I can see you have grown a lot boy in the last two and a half years and not just size-wise, your mind has grown along with your body. Didn't figure with all the news we got about the Rebs' dearth of supplies that you got that much to eat."

"Well sir, I was in the commissary department so I got to do some choosing before the other soldiers, being as how we took most of it from the Federal troops," explained Will. "Course, I felt sorta guilty eating what the fighting men needed, and there wasn't much food to go around. They had me herding Texas cattle around to feed the soldiers and every once in a while, the Yankees would try and take them. After we beat them off, we got to eat the food they had been freighting to Federal troops. It was fresh and usually pretty good. We shared with our troops, but we ate first, and we got to take anything else, such as clothes guns or horses, or whatever we wanted."

"Just like ants at a picnic," observed Grandsir, laughing appreciatively.

"I didn't have any idea Will was coming yesterday, but the good Lord knew, and he gave me a sign," said Ellen as the family gathered around the table. "That's why I and Polly fixed up this here Sunday feast."

Will's mouth watered at the bounty. Besides the chicken, there was cornbread, mashed Irish potatoes, summer squash, fried okra, a big plate of cathead biskits with gobs of butter on the side, and a tantalizing jar of mayhaw jelly. He spied a pecan pie cooling on the sideboard.

"Momma you could cook for God!" exclaimed Will, which caused everyone to laugh.

"Shush your blaspheming'!" Ellen scolded him, but she was grinning ear to ear. "But I can't take all the credit. Polly is a wonder in the kitchen and did her fair share and Nathan has proven to be a right good farmer. He growed the squash and okra in a garden patch behind the house, and we've shared and shared alike with the neighbors the whole war. God has blessed us, and I reckon we're better off than most."

She turned to Grandsir. "Daddy, would you please say grace?"

"Heavenly Father," said Grandsir in his preacherly tone, "we thank you for what your Son did on the cross for our salvation and restoration to fellowship with you. We thank you for the safe return of Will and ask blessings on those families that will be setting an empty place at many tables tonight. Those men walking home bless them. Bless this family you have given me and Nanny. Yes, Lord, and bless the food we eat and nourish it to our bodies. We know our future is in your hands. Amen."

"Amen," echoed the family in one voice. There followed a happy commotion as the dishes were passed around and everyone sang the praises of Ellen and Polly's cooking.

"Will, what are you going to do now that you're home?" asked Grandsir.

"Well, Grandsir, I am thinking I will start to gather as many cows from the canebrake as I can. Don't know if I will mess too much with the hogs, just yet anyway. Will most likely wait till fall when the mast is heavy on the ground. They will be bunched up better than and be fat as ticks. These cattle will take most of my time. How many you think we got, between you and papa?"

"Gracious sakes, boy, I wouldn't want to hazard a real guess, but it will scare all get out of seven hundred head. We already had about three hundred head when your pa went to war."

Will cogitated as he slathered his biskit with butter. "I don't know about that, Grandsir," he said. "I spent time with some boys from the Eighth Texas Cavalry and from what they tell me about cattle, if we had three hundred heads four years ago, we should have four to five times that now due to natural regeneration, as they called it. The way I figure that, we ought to have at least fifteen hundred head."

Grandsir whistled. "That's a lot of cattle, son! How do you propose to catch them?"

"Well sir, me, Nathan, and Polly will scare 'em out of the canebrake and drive 'em across the pasture and into the corral," was his reply. "If they're stubborn about being rounded up and corralled, we'll do like those Texas boys and ride 'em down, throw a rope on 'em, and drag 'em into the corral."

"Well, you ain't from Texas," Grandsir laughed. "Watching you trying to round up all those stray cows will be more fun than a circus! You will have to fix that pen, or corral as you call it. Sorry shape it's in now. It wouldn't keep one old bossy milk cow in if she wanted out. The job will take lots of planks and posts, which will cost money, and we're dreadful short of that commodity around here. You sure are taking on a mighty big challenge boy, and all the odds are against you."

Will stopped chewing for a moment. He guessed this was as good a time as any to divulge his wealth.

"I've got a bit of money that amounts to over three years of working income for farmers like us, in fact. Us boys in the 53rd had no qualms about taking it off the Yanks we captured and killed in the raids. It just seemed part and parcel of war. I've prayed about it, and I don't see that I have done anything wrong."

Ellen's face turned ashen. She knew her son had taken human life, but to hear him come right out and say it shook her to her core.

“You killed them, Will, and then took their money?” She said weakly.

“It was war daughter, not a church social,” said Grandsir. “Well, son, you can sure do some good around here with Yank money.”

“Yes, momma the dead don’t need money.”

“I aim to save most of it, Grandsir, as a cushion against the hard times to come,” said Will. “Rather than using milled lumber, I figure I can shore up the old pen with pine sapling posts and build a bigger one the same way with some hired help. Me, Nate, and Polly will round up as many cows as we can or bust a gut trying. I understand there is a market in Mobile that ships them on to Nor Leans for slaughter. We can drive ’em there.”

“That’s a right long Odyssey, to Mobile and back again,” said Grandsir doubtfully.

“But it can be done,” said Will a trifle insolently.

“Don’t set your cart before the horse, boy,” said Grandsir, getting a little hot under the collar. “Without a good dog or two, you’re just whistling Dixie, as it were.

I think Caleb Lowery should have one or two prime specimens."

"Caleb Lowery?" said Nathan incredulously. "He is an old drunk."

"Mind your place, young man!" Ellen thundered.

Grandsir tousled Nathan's hair. "Out of the mouths of babes," he said. "Sunday at church, we will ask around. Will, you can too, seeing as you'll be in church, also." Grandsir turned a hopeful eye on Will. "Won't you?"

"Yes sir, if it's one thing I've missed, it's goin' to preachin' regular."

Grandsir smiled. "It pleases me to hear you say that, son. War makes some men cruel and ornery. They get stained inside from so much bloodshed and forget how to walk with the Lord."

"Not me," muttered Will a little guiltily, feeling his Grandsir's eagle gaze cutting through to his soul, however I do admit to shooting a few that acted like they needed to be shot."

After dinner, Nathan and Polly drove the old folk's home. Will was impatient, to say the least, to take the set of bagpipes out of the closet. The bag was in need of oiling and the reed was in need of scraping cleaned a little, but that would have to wait. He took a deep breath and started playing a slow Robert Burns tune, “Mary Morrison,” a favorite of his papa's and one he was also partial to. Next he tried “The Rigs O’Barley” and was movin' into “Flow Gently, Sweet Afton” when Nathan and Polly walked in.

“Who mashed a cat?” Nathan quipped. “I could hear it squealing out by the barn.”

“Well, I am a bit out of practice,” said Will, chagrined.

“Don’t you listen to him, Will,” said Polly. “Nathan was just saying how pretty you play and that he wanted to learn to play the pipes himself some day.”

“How did it sound to you, Polly?” asked Will, eager for more praise.

“It sounded good to me—as far as I know what a bagpipe should sound like. I have heard only you and papa play them.”

Nathan snickered as he headed to his room. “That’s high praise, girl.”

“You hush, Nathan,” said Polly, grinning. “Good night, I’m going to bed, too. See y’all in the morning.”

"Good night, Polly!" Will said as she walked away. "Is momma in the house?"

"No, she isn't," said Polly, pausing outside her room. "I suspect she's out in the yard, thinking and crying. She does that a lot at night, since papa died and before you returned home."

Will went outside and found his mother sitting on the bench under the old oak tree. "What you doing out here by yourself?" he said as he sat down beside her and took her hand.

Ellen reflected for a moment before answering. That had always been her way. "Oh, just thinking how proud your papa would have been at this moment, seeing how fine his oldest boy has turned out, and about the good time we all had at supper. Will, you have set up a big job for you and the children, and a wife of sorts to care for."

"I know gathering the cattle will be a lot of work but I think it's the only thing to do and we can handle it. As far as Betty is concerned, when she gets here she is a worker who will fit right in."

Ellen laid her hand on Will's cheek. "Well, you go on thinking and I'll go on praying and ask God to open the doors we are to walk through and close them we ain't supposed to walk through. Any time you want to sit and talk to me, go right on ahead, for you will find me a patient listener."

Will looked up into the spreading canopy of the oak. Night was falling and the bugs had begun their soft monotonous songs. He heard Cat whinny in the corral and the lonesome lowing of cows from the canebrake. In front of his nose, a lightning bug rose and fell with the flashing of its bright yellow belly. With great care, he reached out, caught it, and watched it crawl along his palm. He raised his hand, blew the bug from it, and watched it rise into the dark sky. Thanking God he was home safe and sound!

"It's good to be home," he said, snuggling against his mother.

"Oh, son, I'm so happy you've come back whole," Ellen cooed as a beatific smile lighted her face. "Don't you ever go roaming again?"

"I promise, not without a lot of sound reasoning, momma. Now I have both Betty and you to satisfy. You will like Betty and Jason they are good people. Betty is so kind and gentle like you and Polly are, that is one of the reasons I love her so."

CHAPTER 8

The old clock on the hutch was striking five o'clock when Will got up. He and Ellen had decided the night before that the first order of business should be a trip to Elba to get much-needed supplies and he wanted to get an early start. He had suggested taking Polly along, as it was a forty-mile round trip and he would appreciate the company. Nathan would stay behind for Ellen's protection.

He went to the stove and found some embers still alive, added some pitch kindling, and started a fire. Then he went to the well, drew a bucket of water, and set it on the sideboard. He washed his face and hands in the basin and set about making the coffee.

"Good morning," said Ellen, emerging from her room. "Will, this is a job for me, making coffee in my house."

"I'll finish, would you wake up Nathan and Polly?"

"No need to wake me up," said Polly. "I waked up when I heard y'all walking across this squeaky floor. What do you want to eat for breakfast? I will fix it."

Will thought she looked mighty pretty in her nightdress, even though it hid her blossoming figure. Nathaniel ambled in behind her, yawning and scratching his hindquarters.

"Just cook up a bunch of eggs and bacon, dear," said Ellen. "I'm going to make up a bunch of scalded cornbread later, so you and Will can have food for your trip today."

"What trip?" asked Polly excitedly?

"You and Will are going into Elba," said Ellen. "We're running low on everything."

"Can I go, too?" asked Nathan. "Like papa always said, I've got a strong back and a weak mind, so I can help."

"I figured momma could use you here," said Will, "in case of any trouble."

"Oh, let him go," said Ellen. "I'll be all right, and life's too short."

"Thanks," said Nathan.

Ellen and Polly served the boys breakfast, and then they sat down themselves.

"Polly, you done become a fine cook while I was away," said Will. He had assumed his usual posture of eating with gusto.

"I am surprised you can taste it, the way you're wolfing it down," she giggled. "I've seen hogs with better manners."

Will's face turned as red as his hair as he straightened up and removed his elbows from the table.

"Never mind, Miss Prissy," he said, trying to sound authoritative. "If you ain't needed to help momma, please go feed the horse. We'll get on our way as quickly as Nathan and I get back from the calling up the horses."

The threshold of the canebrake, a vast sea of cane, brambles, and piney woods ranging for several thousand acres toward the Florida panhandle, was but half a mile away. Will had trained all the mares to come to a certain whistle for grain. He put his pinky and index finger in his mouth and sounded the shrill, three-note call. Directly, they could hear movement in the tall cane. Four horses trotted out, followed by two filly colts and Fred, the old mule.

Will slipped a short shank of rope around the elder mare, Chickasaw, who placed her muzzle on his shoulder and followed him to the barn like a pet dog. Chickasaw was dam to Cat and her full sister, Cut Butt, so named because she bore a jagged scar on her rump where she had been horned as a young filly by a wild cow. Cut Butt and the other mares, Socks and Star, followed dutifully, with the unnamed fillies and Fred, the mule and the horses he had brought home from the Yankees, bringing up the rear. Will turned them all into the pen and scrutinized them closely.

Both Socks and Star, the beautiful Texas red dun with a white, nearly perfect five-point patch on her forehead. Both showed heavy foal. Cut Butt Polly's favorite horse, that she was now calling Smoky, showed no such signs. Will assumed she had aborted her colt and her womb was open and she would come into her breeding cycle soon. Grandsir had mentioned at supper he had loaned Dan out four months ago to Joseph Dykes, a neighbor whose pugnacious boys had a bad reputation in the county. Will rued the fact that the stallion was loaned out and vowed to make it a point to bring the stallion home at his first opportunity because he wanted Cut Butt to be bred as soon as possible.

By this time, Polly had fed all the animals and Nathan had harnessed up Socks, the buggy mare.

"All ready, Will," he reported.

"Good," said Will. "Run up to the house and tell momma we're going. Then you and Polly head on into Elba and wait for me at the mercantile. I am going to ride that thoroughbred mare.

Nathan trotted up to the kitchen door and called, "momma, we're off to Elba."

Ellen came out into the yard. "Y'all make sure you are real careful in town," she cautioned them. "It hasn't been the nicest place lately, what with them Yankee soldiers and white trash deserters hanging around."

Will went inside and came out with his holster strapped on and wearing his gray roundabout. "I need to get this washed," he said critically, brushing the coat roughly with his hands.

Ellen put her hand on his arm beseechingly. "Son, why wear it? Them Yankees might take it as a taunt."

Will had long ago made a vow to himself never to talk about Jerry's death. He wore the jacket to honor him, as he had requested, and for his own reasons. "I don't mind taunting Yanks."

"I just feel the desire, and I promised Jerry Bacon I would wear it with pride in remembrance of him," he said. "I want everyone to know I'm proud of my heritage. Is there anything you need?"

"We could use a barrel of flour, ten pounds sugar, and some salt." Ellen eyed his coat dubiously. "Will, are you sure you don't want me to fetch your papa's Sunday coat?"

"No," said Will firmly as he mounted Cat. "See you this evening."

"Please be careful with the children!" Ellen called after him.

When Will arrived in Elba, Nathan was standing on the wooden sidewalk in front of the mercantile, surrounded by three Federal soldiers a sergeant and a corporal, both with meanness in their eyes, and a fresh-faced young private. Swinging in by the wagon parked out front, Will judged by the frightened expression on Polly's face that there was something wrong. He locked eyes with Polly and told her quietly to stay calm. Will hitched Cat to the rail, walked past Nathan without acknowledging him, and went into the sheriff's office next door.

Sheriff Jedediah Sloan was pinning wanted posters on the bulletin board when Will entered. He was a tall, lanky man, fifty-five or so, with thinning blond hair parted in the middle and a walrus mustache.

"Well, hello, Will Cain heard you were back," he said, sticking out his hand.

"Good to see you. Lots of fellers won't be coming home, like your pa, God rest his soul."

"Thanks, Sheriff Sloan," said Will, shaking his hand. "Thought you'd like to know, Nathan is out by the mercantile, up to his elbows in Union soldiers. I think they are giving him a bad time. I just want you to be aware of that fact. In addition, another thing you need to know, we Cain's ain't taking any guff from Yankees or white trash. All we want is to be left completely alone and treated fair. I have seen enough blood to last a lifetime, but if it is necessary to spill some for my friends and family I am more than ready."

"Now I am going out there and see what the hell is going on. You want to come along, fine. If not, just sit here and watch the smoke. I aim to be law abiding, but I'll be darned if I'll see any Cain walked over by Federal soldiers."

"Now, don't go off half-cocked Will," warned Sheriff Sloan, but Will was already through the door.

"What's the trouble, little brother?" said Will. "Are these Blue Bellies bothering you?"

“They made some smart remarks about Polly I didn’t much care for,” said Nathan with a note of fear in his voice. “In fact, their remarks were downright disrespectful and crude.”

The corporal planted himself squarely in front of Will. “We didn’t say anything bad about this dark girl,” he said and shot Polly a lewd glance. “We just thought maybe she would rather be with men that had some money, rather than some snot-nosed Rebel boy.”

Then the sergeant, a squinty-eyed brute with a sallow complexion, lumbered over and nudged the corporal aside. He looked contemptuously at Will and spat a viscous black pool of tobacco juice by Will’s foot.

“What’s it to you, Reb?” He snarled in a loud, sandpaper voice. “We whipped you and your Gray Coat friends already, and I reckon I can teach you some manners now personally. We didn’t harm a hair on nigger girl’s pretty head. We were just looking for some fun in this one-horse town. She ain’t your property no more, anyway, or hadn’t you heard Lincoln set the niggers free?”

“She never was my property,” said Will coolly. “She is my sister if it is any concern of yore trashy self.”

“Well, fancy that!” said the sergeant. “Well, we would have had her over to that saloon by now if this brat here hadn’t stuck his nose in our business.” He indicated Nathan with a contemptuous wave of his hand.

Will knew he was in a tight spot. The big brute was so close to him, he could smell his whiskey breath and rank body odor. He wanted to back up, but knew the big man would take that as a sign of weakness. He was very glad he had the Navy Dragoon in his holster and the holster flap loose. Will knew all hell was bound to break loose and ran over some stratagems in his mind. His best bet right now was to bide his time and wait for an opening.

“If you had taken her to the saloon, you would be dead by now,” said Will. “Let’s get that straight real quick. I would have emasculated you with a dull knife. The South lost because of supplies and manpower, not because of blowhards like y’all.”

"Why, ain't you a cocky rooster!" jeered the corporal. "Guess I need to pull out your tail feathers."

"Yankee, you better get a lot more help, if you want to pull my feathers."

Will watched the two men, waiting for one of them to make a move. Without taking his eyes off them, he said, "Polly, move the buggy down the street, then you and Nathan go home now!"

"Gal, don't move that buggy or you'll wish you hadn't," barked the sergeant. He wheeled on the young soldier, who looked about Will's age. "Westermeyer go over and grab the horse and don't be slow about it, you yellow-bellied runt. Do what I say and be quick about it."

"Yes sir, Sergeant Baker," said the young soldier, saluting awkwardly to escape further hostility. As he advanced toward the wagon, Will took three steps back. He felt a surge of relief, having the freedom to move now.

"Polly, go on and back that horse out, like I asked you to," he said calmly.

Polly had her hands on the reins but sat still, frozen with fear.

The corporal started rolling a cigarette. He was a strutting little bantam of a man, compact and muscular. This type of man Will knew well, arrogant cusses, forever trying to make up for their short stature with their words or their fists.

"Hey, Reb ain't any real use you gettin' all het up about that brown gal," he said tauntingly. "Her kind ain't worth getting you kilt over."

Will felt his blood start to boil, matching his Celtic heritage. "Your opinion of 'her kind' wouldn't amount to a hill of beans, you Blue Coat pile of horse poop," he said. "If there is any killing done, it will most likely be your sorry butt."

The one called Baker guffawed. "You gonna let him talk like that to you, Snyder?"

"Why you uppity little cur," said Snyder to Will. He could see Snyder's fingers nervously brushing the butt of his pistol. "You won't talk so big with your skull caved in." Just then, Sheriff Sloan came out of his office and walked over to the buggy, grabbed the bridle, and turned the horse around.

"Young lady, take the buggy down the street like Will told you," he said kindly. When she had done so, he turned to the soldiers. "You men got a problem with these folks?"

"Hell yes, we do," said Snyder. "We got the same problem with all you Rebs, you ain't got any respect for your conquerors. We are gonna teach this Rebel a real lesson about how to treat his elders and his betters."

"Come on, Cpl. Snyder," the young private entreated him. "Let's head out and not start any trouble. If Captain Cooksey were here, you wouldn't be acting this way."

Snyder spat in the dirt. "That's all you know, Westermeyer. I'll do whatever I want, whenever I want. I fought these Rebs for the last three years, and I am so tired of the whole kit and caboodle."

"I'm asking you men nicely to go on back to your camp." Sheriff Sloan appealed almost desperately to Snyder and Baker. "The boy doesn't mean any harm."

"We come and go as we please," said Baker. "Now, why don't you crawl back to your jailhouse and stay there before you cause me to turn on you, old man."

The sheriff slunk away and stood in the doorway of his office.

Snyder laughed with contempt. "Guess that sheriff doesn't want to mess with real men, does he boy? He has left you in our hands. Tell me, boy, why you acting so high and mighty over that high yeller. You don't want to get underneath her skirts yourself, do you?"

"She is our sister, I'll kill you for that!" yelled Nathan. He lunged for Snyder. Will put his arm out and roughly pushed him back. Sheriff Sloan backed slowly into the jail. A moment later, they could see the sheriff's face peering through the window.

"You watch your mouth, you sorry Yankee," hissed Will. "She is a human being and a woman and she deserves to be treated like one, especially by scum the like of y'all."

Snyder lunged at Will and in that instant the big Colt Dragoon barrel smashed across his face, breaking his nose and laying his cheek wide open. A fountain of blood gushed from the wound as he staggered backwards with a loud yelp. Out of the corner of his eye, Will could see Baker drawing his pistol, but the Colt barked once and the big man fell backwards onto the sidewalk with a dull thud, writhing in pain. Will saw Snyder rush at him again, his eyes wild, his face a ghastly mask of blood and gore. Before he could draw his pistol, Will struck him hard and quick across the temple with the long barrel of the Colt. Snyder swayed in his boots for a half second, then his eyes glazed over and he toppled forward like a tenpin down on his face.

A crowd was already gathering as Sheriff Sloan came bounding out the door his gun drawn.

"Looks bad Will, real bad," he said quietly. "The Yanks might give you the rope for this."

"I seen you peeping out the window" said Will, looking the sheriff in the eye. "It might not have come to this if you had stood behind that badge."

The sheriff couldn't abide Will's accusing gaze. He quickly turned away and yelled, "Somebody go get Doc McCreight, quick!"

"I'll go," said a towheaded boy about eight or nine, and dashed toward the doctor's office, holding onto his hat.

Polly came running up and hugged Will's neck. He put his arms around her and felt her body tremble against him.

"Will, are you okay?" she said, her eyes glistening. "I was so scared for you."

"No need to be scared, Polly, it's all over now. These men ain't going to bother you no more. Here hold my hand if it will make you feel better." She did. Will felt brotherly love course through him.

"I ain't ever been so scared in my life!" said Nathan excitedly. "You sure stood up to them roughnecks. I never dreamed you were so fast with your hands. Boy howdy, Will, I want to be like you!"

The doctor came trotting up, short of breath and carrying a little black bag. He was a portly man in his sixties, bespectacled and ruddy-faced. People had never seen him without a cigar in the middle of his mouth. It was such a severe habit that his lips showed an indentation of the cigar, on those few occasions when he removed it.

He leaned over Baker, the soldier Will had shot. The man had passed out from shock.

"He's too bad hurt to tote him back to my office," the doc said. He nodded at two bystanders. "You men, get him into the saloon and onto a table. I cain't work on him bendin' over, my belly's too big! Some of you other gawkers help this other 'gentleman' inside, too."

The saloonkeeper had already cleared off a table by the time the men got Baker and Snyder inside.

"Walter, bring me a bottle of whiskey," Doc McCreight hollered. He took a hefty slug and poured some on Baker's wound. "I think he will be alright. Bullet was a long ways from hittin' somethin' vital. Put that other man in that chair over there an' get a rag on his cheek."

Doc McCreight waddled over to Snyder. The little man was fully conscious now and sat regarding the doctor with contempt.

"Mister, I'm gonna have to sew up your face," said the doc. "I ain't gonna lie to you, it's gonna hurt like hell fire. I think you had better swaller a lot of this Old Mule Kick."

"Old man, you hurt me and I'll carve your liver for sure," said Snyder. "Where is that Reb that hit me? I'm gonna break ever' bone in his body."

Will shouldered his way through the crowd. "I am right here, Yankee. You lay a hand on the doc or me, and I'll crack your head plumb open this time like a walnut."

Doc McCreight chuckled. He reached into his black bag and got out his needle and thread. "I believe he would, too. Now you listen to me, mister. If you are gonna be nasty about it, you can go back to your camp and let your medic take care of you and your friend over there on the table. 'Course, he may bleed to death on the trip, but that's your worry, not mine."

He puffed on his cigar to stoke it and ran the needle across the glowing red tip. "Now, if you know what's good for you, you'll sit still. You flinch and I'm liable to put out your carn sarn eye!"

Snyder took a slug of whiskey and braced himself. He whimpered as the doc began to sew up the gash.

"First Yankees I have ever treated!" The doc mused. "I have done hepped whites, blacks, Indians, horses and mules, but no Blue Coats. Now I got two in the same day! Not a milestone I care to repeat."

Snyder rose shakily to his feet and sought out Pvt. Westermeyer in the crowd. "You ain't heard the last of this, Reb," he said, looking hard at Will. "We're going back to camp and tell our captain what happened."

Sheriff Sloan walked over to Will. "I'm near about certain there will be some kind of military inquiry an' you an' I both will have plenty of explainin' to do. If the Federals come askin' around, I'll vouch for your side of it and your character an' try to calm things down. You ain't plannin' on leavin' the county, are you?"

"No sir, I ain't goin' anywhere," Will replied. "Hope your explanation is stronger than your help. I do appreciate you turning the buggy around, for that gave me the breathing space to get ready for what followed. But you sure left me high and dry after that."

Sheriff Sloan sighed deeply. “Son, you were spoilin’ for a fight afore I ever showed up. I thought the Dykes boys were bad, but you sure ’nough come home loaded for bear. If I was you, I would stay away from town. After this fracas, you’re gonna be a marked man. I wouldn’t be surprised if a lynching party came after you.”

“Sheriff, I was just defending my sister Polly’s honor,” said Will. “Unless you’re deafer than a snake, you heard what them Yanks said, and I whutn’t about to let it slide. Everybody on that street saw them attack me. I was just defending myself, which is my right. Now, we are gonna go about our business and leave. If you need me, you know where our place is. Just like I said, though, we are not gonna let these Blue Bellies walk on us. I know what they did to good God fearin’ folks in Georgia and North Carolina, and it will be over my dead body if they do it to us in my own backyard.”

“Son, I ought to lock you up for your own good and I’ve got every right to do so, considering you done this deed in my town,” said Sheriff Sloan. “But I figure things are going to come to ahead soon enough. You just go on about your business."

Nathan and Polly's eyes shone with admiration as Will led them to the mercantile.

"I need a barrel of flour, ten pounds of sugar, twenty pounds salt, and twenty pounds coffee, five of baking soda," he told the clerk." And if this young lady takes a shine to anything, put it on my order."

"Mr. Cain, I'm pleased to have your business," said the clerk, who fancied himself cultured. "I knew your father well and your Grandpa Garrison is a pillar of the community. However, sir, it is a known fact the young lady is not white. It is our custom to serve her class of people only in the back of the store. The front is reserved for—"

"Don't go any further, mister," Will interrupted him. "She ain't black to us, some folks think she is —not that it makes any difference to me, for a person's skin color don't mean no more to me than a pile of poop, but I just proved she is a lady. If you don't believe me, go over to that saloon. They's two bloodied up Yanks that'll vouch for my point of view. In the future, whenever Polly Cain comes in here, she gets your best service, same as any other white person. Understood, sir?"

"Yes, Mr. Cain."

"Good, I also need a keg o' sixteen penny nails and two spools of rope about eighty feet long and about a half-inch around, maybe a little less."

"I've got a spool that should do. The salesman said it was about seven-sixteenths."

"That'll do," said Will. "Nathan, put this stuff in the buggy. Polly you keep a lookout. I'm going over to that saloon and see how the doc is doing. Figure out my bill and I will pay you when I get back. My brother will need help loading the flour. See that you do it."

Yes sir, I will, I will!" said the clerk.

Will walked back to the saloon. The loudmouth, Snyder, had passed out from the whiskey. He could see that Doc McCreight had done a nice job of stitching up his face. He crossed over to Baker. The doctor was finishing up dressing the shoulder wound, his cigar bobbing up and down as he sung a few bars of "Aura Lea."

"Doc McCreight, what about this man?" asked Will. "Is he gonna make it?"

"He is gonna be okay, son. His shoulder will never be the same though, for the bullet tore up some of the muscles. He just passed out again. I gave him some laudanum, and I gare-own-tee you, he ain't feeling any pain. You need to sit down for a minute and have a slug of Mule Kick yourself. A little toddy for the body, as my papa and yore's used to say."

Will took a good slug from the proffered bottle. The potion tasted like liquid fire, not like Old Crow, and burned all the way down. He reached into Baker's coat pocket, fished out a five-dollar gold piece, and handed it to the doc.

"Why, thank you sir, I didn't expect any payment," said the doctor, biting the coin out of habit. "This is legal tender, all right!"

"The Bible says the workman is worthy of his hire," said Will. He reached in Snyder's pocket, extracted another gold piece, and went over to the saloonkeeper. "Walter, this here is for the use of the tables and the whiskey."

"I'm much obliged to you, Will," said Walter. "Thanks for the show out there on the street. If it comes to a trial, I'll vouch for you."

"Thank you, Walter," said Will, with a tip of his hat.

He could feel every eye in the saloon on him as he took another pull of Old Mule Kick and headed for the swinging doors. Out of the corner of his eye, he saw a grizzled old farmer stand up salute and start clapping his hands as he waved his gray slouch hat. Another man arose and did the same. Pretty soon all the patrons in the saloon were on their feet, applauding Will's heroism.

"Attaboy, Johnny Reb!" someone called after him as he rushed through the doors, blushing hot in his cheeks.

Back at the mercantile, Nathan and Polly were sitting in the loaded buggy, anxious to go home after the morning's excitement. Will examined the rope and figured it would be sufficient do his limited experience with roping. He had received a few lessons from the Clem and the other boys in the Eighth Texas. He told the children to wait for him while he settled his account.

"What's the total I owe?" he asked the shopkeeper.

"Flour is $3.50, coffee is $1.50, sugar is fifty cents, salt is thirty-five cents, material for the lady is $1.00, and the nails are $5.00," said the clerk as he wrote down each figure in his ledger. "Total is $11.85."

Will did the arithmetic in his head. "Sounds about right," he said, reaching into his coat for his cash.

The shopkeeper cleared his throat loudly and said confidentially, "By the way, Mr. Cain, when your father—may he rest in peace—was last in here before he went off to the war, he charged $1.15. As his heir, I wonder if you would be so kind as to take it upon yourself to pay his outstanding debt. If you do so, that would bring your bill to $12.95."

"Why sure, I'll pay that," said Will, who didn't much care for the man's tone. "We Cain's don't want to be beholden to no sniveling store owner. Tell you what, here is thirteen hard Yankee dollars and we'll just call it square. Give me a receipt marked paid in full and remember what I said about the girl!"

The befuddled clerk quickly drew up a receipt and handed it to Will. "Oh, dear," he said, smacking his forehead, "I forgot about the rope! It will take me a moment to figure the cost."

"Mister, I'm a patient man," said Will, "but I really need to get home."

"Beg pardon, Mr. Cain," said the clerk, smiling nervously. "Let's just say it's on the house. Consider it a gift for your services to the cause and for your show of chivalry this morning."

"Well, I'm much obliged to you," said Will, thinking better of the clerk. I don't want to be beholden to you or anyone. Here is two dollars for the rope."

"Thank you, Mr. Cain, and good day to you!"

When Will came out, Nathan said, "Boy, I can't wait to tell momma about this."

"Me, too!" said Polly. "Will, you're braver than that Sir Lancelot I read about."

Will gazed at them. Their eyes were lustrous with adoration and respect.

"I'll do the talkin' children," said Will sternly. "Don't need y'all blowin' this thing all out of proportion. I'll ride ahead. See y'all to home."

Ellen was rocking on the porch with her apron full of speckled butter beans in her lap. She was contentedly shelling the pods and tossing the beans into a bowl on a little table beside her.

"Lookit what Aunt Winnie give us," she said as he walked up. "Your papa was always powerful fond of speckled beans."

"Me, too," said Will quietly. He sat down beside her, scooped up a handful of beans and started shelling them.

"What's wrong, Will?" Ellen asked. "You look troubled. Where are the children?"

"They're comin'. The mare wasn't interested in slow travel, and I need to talk to you."

He gave a careful account of what had happened in town, trying to play everything down so his mother wouldn't worry and carry on.

"That's a shame it happened, son," she clucked. "You got to watch that red-headed Scots' temper of yorn and get that

Rebel chip off your shoulder. Like it or not, the war is over and the Yanks won. And with the other happenings in your life, you don't need to court trouble. The Federals may have won the war, but the battle for Southern rights will go on for years."

"The war may be over, but there are still battles to be fought, mark my word," said Will hotly. He got up and paced up and down the porch like a bobcat in a cage. "I don't mean to get all fired up, but when I see a Blue Coat, I seem to lose all reason. I can't stomach injustice, and when that soldier made remarks about Polly I wanted to close his mouth, permanent like. I didn't think it was wrong to defend her, even if she is an octoroon. She is like a sister to me, and she is as white as a lot of folk around here, and of better character."

"That's true, son," said Ellen wistfully. "That is why I don't get ruffled when she calls me momma."

Will knew Ellen was thinking about his baby sister, Ruth. He remembered how she had cried and cried and wouldn't suckle at her mother's breast. She was just three months old when she died, looking to Will like a scary doll with sunken cheeks and hollow eyes. They buried the baby at the cemetery at Corner Creek Church and the family put fresh flowers on her grave nearly every Sunday.

Ellen went on. "So God gave me a tan-skinned girl who loves me, and all she wants to do is please me. I really am not looking forward to the day when she gets to want to be married, and 'twill be a special man that I let marry her." She paused and added plaintively, "Promise me you will watch out for her, Will, if something should happen to me."

"Nothing's going to happen to you, but yes, ma'am, I will take care of Polly always," said Will earnestly. "When's supper gonna be ready? Setting Yankees straight is hungry work."

"It will be a while yet," said Ellen mildly. "The quicker you quit wearing a hole in the porch and help me finish shelling these beans, the quicker we'll eat."

Will sat down again and took another handful of pods. The morning's events had once again put Texas in the forefront of his mind. Part of him wanted to shuck it all and ride westward on Cat never looking back, but the stronger Christian part knew he was needed at home.

"Say, momma, pa never did tell me," he said, "why did granpa Cain go to Texas?"

Ellen looked into the distance and gathered her thoughts. "Near as I remember, your Grandpa Cain, his brother, Isaac, and a few more just thought things would be better in a new place. Texas being about as big as a country and the promise of free land, they thought they'd try their luck there. They left, oh, let me see, I think it was about 1854. You might not remember, for you was just five or six then. Your papa would like to have gone too, but I wanted to stay close to my folks. He didn't try and jump over the traces, like I thought he would, but he did go out to Jasper County, Texas to visit shortly after the other Cain's left. Those Hope saddles y'all ride and Star came from that trip, as you well know. Wish he had gone and stayed, if so then he might still be alive today."

"Momma, they was a lot of Texans in the war, perhaps papa's numbered days were up."

"Why are you all of a sudden interested in Texas, son?"

"I was friendly with some of them boys in the Eighth Texas, is all," said Will carefully. "They were mighty fine boys, always talking about wide open spaces, wild Indians, cows and horses. The one I liked the best, name of Clem Patterson he wants me to come visit him east of San Antone. But I know I'm needed right here, and I wouldn't go without your blessing, anyway."

Ellen caught the faraway gleam in her son's eye. It was the look of a man struck by wanderlust. She had seen it in Bob's eyes when he had come back from Texas, and it had never completely gone away.

CHAPTER 9

Sunday morning, Corner Creek Church was as hot as a brick oven. The children fidgeted or drowsed on the sticky pews while the womenfolk, waving homemade palmetto fans, stirred up the best breeze they could muster. The men folk suffered the awful swelter, as men folk are often do. Pastor Garrison was in rare form, delivering a thoughtful sermon about returning to God. Afterwards, he added a personal note.

"Friends, I want to take this opportunity to welcome my grandson, William Cain, back into the fold," said the old preacher. "He has been away these many months, doing his part for the noble cause that was lost, and has come home to his family, whole in body and spirit, whereas so many hundreds of thousands of our brave lads did not. Let us rejoice in his homecoming. Everybody say hallelujah!"

"Hallelujah!" they shouted.

Sitting in the back with Polly and Uncle Tootsie and Aunt Winnie, Will blushed as he felt the hands of the other black parishioners clapping him on the back and shoulders. Pastor Garrison paused and lowered his head in thought. When he raised it again, he wore a deadly serious expression.

"By now, most, if not all, of you have heard about the unfortunate incident in Elba involving young Will and three Federal soldiers," said Pastor Garrison solemnly. "I don't have to tell you good people that a story going from tongue to tongue is likely to pick up a few cockleburs of exaggeration or downright fiction. I want to set the record straight, here and now. Will was standing up for the honor of Polly Cain, a young lady of mixed blood his ma and pa took in and raised as their own. He was provoked to violence by the vulgar words the Federals directed at Polly, whom none of you will deny is a bright and lovely girl, respectful and kind as the day is long."

Pastor Garrison paused. Noisily a few throats were cleared and some parishioners shifted uncomfortably in their seats.

He went on, "By the ignorant laws of this state, Polly Cain is considered a Negro person because she has a smidgen of black blood in her makeup. But if you were to cut her, she would bleed red just like the whitest white man, and nowhere in that stuff of life could you identify the part of her that is black. This morning, ere the service began, I overheard rumblings amongst certain members of this congregation criticizing young Will's actions. I heard you say he should have turned the other cheek, and that he was wrong to sully his family's name by resorting to violence on behalf of a common colored girl. It is no coincidence that these comments have come from the same throats as those who insist on segregating this house of worship, forcing God's children whose faces happen to be black to take the rear pews."

A murmur of protest rose from the crowd. His blue eyes blazing, Pastor Garrison struck the pulpit with the ball of his fist and thundered, "Brothers and sisters hear me! If this terrible war has taught us anything, it should be that we are one blood, one people, one America! Have the rest of a good Sabbath day and God bless you!"

The preacher strode down the aisle and went out into the sunshine to receive his parishioners. Some thanked him sincerely for his candor, others nodded to him coolly, and a few made a point not to acknowledge the pastor at all. Caleb Lowery, a farmer and sometime trapper known to do moonshine and partake of it to excess, was among those.

Ellen, Nathan, and Polly hugged his neck by turns. Will and the black members of the congregation emerged last of all.

"Pastor Garrison, thank you for your forthright words," said Aunt Winnie. "Us black people are much obliged to you for sticking your chin out on our account."

"Dat goes dubble fer me," said Uncle Tootsie, pumping the preacher's hand enthusiastically.

"You are quite welcome, both of you," said the preacher.

"I plumb enjoyed your sermon, Grandsir," said Will. "And that last part! Boy, howdy, when you get het up, you really are het up!"

Grandsir's booming laugh died suddenly as he spied Caleb Lowery leaning against a pine tree on the grounds.

Lowery drained a pint bottle and threw it into the woods as he shambled towards Pastor Garrison and stood before him, his arms folded defiantly across his chest.

"Garrison, ah just want ye to know this will be my last Sunday in yore church house," he said acidly, his little pig eyes filled with hate. "Ah don't aim to have nuthin' to do with no nigger-lovin' church. It's bad enough you allow 'em in yore church house in the first place. Now you wan' us whites to act like niggers is our equals. Well, they ain't our equals. They ain't no better'n monkeys. Lazy, stupid, black-assed—"

"Enough! Caleb we are related as cousins but I might want to make up for our past differences, by hand."

Nanny Garrison emerged from the church, where she had been putting away the offerings and hymnals. The little woman drew herself up to her full height and wagged her stubby finger in Lowry's face.

"You have been drinking, sir, which is a sacrilege on the Sabbath," she said in a fierce undertone, "and you lack the grace and good sense to know the Lord's house and grounds are no place for a serpent's tongue. If you want to see a monkey, sir, look in the mirror. Now be gone with you and good riddance!"

Astonished, Lowery stepped backwards, his pig eyes fixed on the Westbrook family. When he had moved several paces away, he halted suddenly and spat at the couple, narrowly missing Aunt Winnie, and turned and then he trotted down the hard-packed clay trail.

"Let him go, boy," said Grandsir, noticing Will was about to take after him.

"Is that the man you said might have some good dogs?" asked Will dolefully.

"One and the same," said Grandsir. "But don't worry, son. I put a bug in lots of other ears."

Directly after church, Will recruited half a dozen of Nathan's fishing buddies to help repair and strengthen the pen. Lured by the prospect of easy money, the boys worked like stevedores cutting, fitting, and installing new pine rails and replacing the rotted ones. When they had finished by early afternoon, the forty-by-forty-foot pen was three rails higher and looked plenty stout to Will. He knew he would need to build a larger pen later on and figured to hire his Powell cousins for the job, but the refurbished corral would have to suffice for now.

Afterwards, Will and Nathan hunkered down outside the pen to go over Will's plan for rounding up the cattle. Will smoothed out a space in the dirt with the heel of his hand and sketched a rough diagram with his grubby forefinger. He was in a hurry to get started, and there was a thrill in his voice as he described to Nathan what he saw in his mind's eye.

"We'll drive the cows out of the canebrake and rush 'em into the pasture, then rope 'em one at a time and yoke 'em to those two big full oxen of Grandsir's. They can waller them around and then drag them to the pens."

"What you know about roping cows?" asked Nathan skeptically.

"Not much," Will allowed. "But the way them Texans I was friendly with could throw a rope that was a thing of beauty. My buddy, Clem, showed me how and I about got the knack of it. For dang sure, we will need to practice a lot, but it's just like throwin' a rock, the rope will go where a feller looks."

"Sounds easier said than done, big brother."

Will laughed. "You may be right, little brother! For sure, we are goin' to lose a lot of hide off our hands and elbows before it's all over."

Will became busy outfitting the horses for the roundup. Nathan watched as he set about making a loop in the end of the store-bought ropes. It looked to Nathan like a complicated process and Will did it with some skill. Next Will tied the lariats, each about forty feet long, with a string to the saddle horn so they could be jerked free in a moment's notice.

"Right impressive work, Will," said Nathan.

Will had a skeptical look on his face. "Thank you, I tied them as best as I could remember. The Texans call this loop the hondo," he said. "What we do is, we lasso them cows and tie them on the big horn of our saddles and pull them into the corral, it is as simple as falling off a log."

"And twice as dangerous," Nathan laughed.

The brothers rode the three-eighths of a mile over to Grandsir Garrison's farm and led the two oxen back. Their names were Midnight, the nigh ox, and Frank, the off ox. Midnight was black all over, but for the tip of his tail, which was snow white, and Frank was a brindle. They each weighed about fourteen hundred pounds. They came back with the ox wagon and a load of corn, plus two extra ox yokes. With Will riding Cat and Nathan riding the gelding Will had brought home from the war, the brothers trotted off toward the canebrake. They hadn't gone far, perhaps a mile or so, when they spooked a herd of about fifteen or twenty cattle. The critters tore off in a rush with Will and Nathan hot on their heels. The cattle ran for what seemed about two miles, and then began to slow up. Will went around and headed ten or so back toward the farm. Nathan came around and with both of the boys in the rear they moved the cattle toward the pen.

They had left the gate open by accident, but it proved a godsend. The two oxen were standing right outside the gate and, when they saw the wild cattle coming, they turned and trotted into the pen with the wild cattle right behind them. Will dashed up and closed the gate, hoping against hope that the rebuilt fencing would hold the wild beasts. The cows frantically circled the pen, looking in vain for a way out. One of the bulls tried to jump over the fence but didn't make the top rail and fell back in a dazed heap.

"Land O'Goshen!" exclaimed Will. "If we can hold them in the pen, we may have a good chance to get them roped and tied down. Let's back off aways and let them settle down for a bit and see what happens. Nathan, lope up to the house let them know what we have done and have Polly put on some coffee, for we need to celebrate some way and coffee is harmless and thrifty!"

After Nathan left, Will rode the mare up to the edge of the pen. The skittish cattle ran to the far side, which gave him a chance to see what they had. They sure weren't big animals about the same size as the ones he trailed in the army. He counted eleven marketable head in the pen, including a bull weighing about eight hundred pounds and a younger one of maybe half that, and six cows that weighed about five to six hundred pounds each, all with cavs about four months old. Then there were three heifers close up to caving weighing about the same. Most of the cattle were manageable enough, but there were six very wild ones—five cows and a bull—that would need to be gentled straight away.

Nathan came back with his mother and Polly in tow. The women peered curiously through the rails at the catch.

"Y'all done a good job, Will," said Ellen. "I'm proud of you."

"Thank you," said Will. "Nathan, come over here, please sir. I am going to go inside and see if I can put a rope on one of them. You keep your horse right by the gate and when I go in, close the gate behind me."

Will rode in as easy as he could. The bulls kept their distance, but one of the mother cows pawed the ground and looked like she was spoiling to fight. He took his rope off the saddle horn, swung it around his head, and tossed it at the pregnant cow, missing by a mile. Recoiling the rope, he swung it again, heeding his own advice to throw the rope where he looked. This time it landed on the ornery cow, but the loop was so big, it went over her head and came to a rest on her hips.

He was about to pull the rope back when the cow stepped backwards. When the loop was right under her hind legs, he jerked the slack and the rope caught both hind feet. Then taking a wrap on the saddle horn, he spurred Cat ahead and in doing so brought the cow down. He kept the pressure on the bewildered beast, moving ahead and gathering more slack.

What do I do now he wondered? Out of the corner of his eye, he saw someone enter the pen, put a rope on the cow's head, and tie it to a post. It was Polly! He knew then what to do. He backed Cat up and stretched the hapless cow out like a wad of taffy.

"Polly, please come over here and hold this horse steady while I get another rope on that cow!" Will cried.

"OK!" Polly yelled as she ran over and took the reins.

Will called Midnight and the old ox came right to him, just like a dog. Taking a short piece of rope, he tied the cow to Midnight's neck after fashioning a good knot. Then he took the rope off the cow's head and had Polly move the horse up until his lariat went slack. The second Will released the cow's legs she scrambled to her feet and tried furiously to hook him with her horns. However, lashed to Midnight as she was, all she could do was run in a circle around the docile ox.

"Thanks, Polly, for your help," he said. "That was mighty good work. Let's leave

Midnight tied up and see what happens. Is that coffee made?"

"I believe so," said Polly.

"Run up to the house then and fetch it and some cups, and if there are cakes, biskits or fried pies, bring some. I am getting hungry."

Disappointed at being demoted to an errand runner after all the excitement, Polly pulled a frown and sauntered towards the house, kicking dirt clods as she went.

The cattle all retreated to the far end of the pen away from the fuss with Midnight and the stubborn cow. Will called out to Nathan, "Hey little brother, come back over here by the gate and don't let any cattle out. I'm gonna see if I can rope that cow that is springin' up big."

He moved inside with the rope in his hand. The cow wasn't touchy like the other one, but she sought refuge in the middle of the group. Will swung the rope and let it fly. As soon as he let it go, he knew he had missed the mark.

"Just like throwing rocks, you knucklehead," he scolded himself under his breath. “Remember, look where your hand and arm end up.”

His next six attempts went wide, too, to Nathan’s great amusement.

“I see you over there, baby brother, grinning like a possum eatin' crawdads,” said Will.

“You ain’t gonna quit, are you, cowboy?” Nathan teased.

Will laughed. “Well, the situation reminds me of what this feller I’d known in the army once said to me ‘It ain’t that I’m givin’ up, I just ain’t gonna try no more!’ But no, little brother, I ain’t quittin’—I’m gonna give it one more try. Then I’ll quit!”

“A nickel says you miss,” said Nathan.

“You’re on!”

Will reckoned he had been rushing it. He took a little more time and pretended he was about to chunk a rock at a tin can. When he turned the rope loose this time, he knew it would go right over the cow’s head, and sure enough, it did.

“Guess I owe you a nickel,” Nathan laughed.

"Yeah," said Will, "but now comes the tricky part. Good thing this cow's pretty docile."

He jerked the slack quickly, if awkwardly. The cow sulked up and stood there, still as a statue. Will whistled. Frank the ox ambled over to him and stood by patiently. Taking a short piece of rope, he tied the cow by the horns to Frank's neck. Will smacked the ox's rump and it dragged the cow through the gate, which Nathan held open and closed after the animals went through.

Meanwhile, the other cow was bawling for her calf and it was bawling back. Will positioned himself behind the calf and it moved in front of him.

"Open the gate again, Nathan, and back up," said Will. "After me and the calf come through, shut it quick."

Will kept pressure on the calf from the rear and with its calling from the outside, the calf made a beeline for her. Will went through the gate leaned down and swung it closed, and slid the latch shut.

"Glad that's over," he said. "Don't know if this is gonna work or not, little brother."

“Sure it will, just gonna take some time,” Nathan reassured him.

Polly was walking toward them carrying a tray of griddle cakes and cups. Ellen was a step or two behind with an enameled coffee pot.

“Gentlin’ these cows is gonna be mighty slow and tedious,” said Will, wiping his brow with his bandanna. “We ain’t got enough oxen to neck all these cows together. I think I had best go over to the Gibsons and see if I can rent his four head of oxen for a few days.”

“That’s a good idea, son. Now you and Nathan sit down and have a bite. You’ve worked like men you deserve to eat like men.”

Will and Nathan sat Indian-style on the ground with their backs to the fence while the womenfolk served them. They munched the cakes and sipped the piping hot coffee in quiet contentment.

“Mighty good eats, ladies,” said Will, his compliment turning into a prolonged belch. “I been thinkin’, if we get them six head sort of gentled down in a few days, we can herd them in that old cotton field over by Grandsir’s house. It’s all grown up with wiregrass and I know cattle don't do really well on it, but I think it would hold them for several weeks. We can plow up some peanuts and throw the vines and all over the fence to 'em for feed and drive them in for water every day. Well, I'm off to the Gibson farm. Be back ere nightfall."

Will found Strother Gibson cleaning out his barn, he was a burly man with a mop of long hair drooping in his sunburned face. His most striking feature was his eyes two inquisitive orbs, bright as sapphires, glowing beneath his beetling eyebrows. He had the trace of a burr in his voice and practiced a Scotsman's thrift, and he had a reputation for always coming out on top in a business deal.

"Howdy, Mr. Gibson, how are you this afternoon?" Will called to him, loping up on Cat. "I come to talk some business with you. Can you spare me a few minutes of your time?"

"Reckon I can, Will. But the question is how much time do you have?"

"Sir, what do you mean by that?"

"I just got back from up at Elba and I heared about yore set-to with a couple of

Yankees. Everybody reckons they will come and arrest you afore too long."

"Well, they ain't come yet and guess I'll keep on keeping on till they do. I just stood up for my family. You'd have done the same, Mr. Gibson."

"Family?" Gibson snorted. "You mean that octoroon gal y'all got from old man Cauley?"

"Yes sir, I surely do. Polly is family to us, and I don't care if that gives half this county an upset stomach, don't anybody run over this family as long as I am alive. My papa said us Scots stick by friends and family to the bitter end."

Gibson stuck his pitchfork in the ground and wiped his hands on his overalls. "Easy, boy, don't get riled at me! I must admire your spunk. What is the business deal you want to speak about?"

"Mr. Gibson, I was wonderin' if you would favor renting out your four yoke of oxen?"

"What you gonna do, haul something? I'd have to know how much and where to, wouldn't want to risk hurtin' my animals."

"I wouldn't let no harm come to your stock, sir. It's like this I got some piney woods cattle we want to gentle down a bit and sell them off. We need money, just like everybody else. I figure on bringing the cows in, tying them up to the oxen, and letting 'em wear themselves out. I only need your oxen for about three weeks or so, and they will never be any further away than our home place."

"You shore come back from the war full of piss and vinegar," Gibson chortled. "I know several that come back, and all they want to do is lay around and drink."

"Well sir, as far as some of them boys drinkin', unless a person has fought with a bear, no one can tell what a man has gone through," said Will thoughtfully. "The hell of war takes people in different directions. It just made me mad and hateful at Blue Coats, 'cause we got a right to be free and make our own decisions."

"Yore preachin' to the choir, boy," said Gibson. "What do you figure on payin' for use of my oxen?"

"I will offer three dollars a week for each ox, which will be twelve dollars a week, and I will furnish the feed."

"All right, you got a deal son, and I wish you well, though it seems like a lot of work for them scrub cattle. Need to caution you in case you forgot. My oxen are bulls, so watch out around any cows you got that's in heat. If you need them longer, send me word, ya hear? The two off oxen are Brownie and Spot—names tell you what color they are. The nigh oxen are Scamp, the black one, and Blanco, the white."

"Thank ye, Mr. Gibson," said Will. "Here is twelve dollars for the first week's rent. If you will help me get them started, I will head out now, sir."

"Certainly will, son. Henry, come here!"

A rawboned boy of about twelve ambled up from the lean-to around the corner of the barn.

"Go help Mr. Cain here catch them oxen up," Gibson ordered him.

"Yes sir, pa," said Henry. He said to Will, "come on, sir, they's in the pen yonder."

After the teams had been readied, Will mounted Cat, who was spoiling to go, and tipped his hat at Gibson.

"I always heard you drove a hard bargain, Mr. Gibson," said Will.

Gibson laughed. "Usually son, but I like the cut of your jib. An' I ain't figurin' to git on yore wrong side. The war made a helluva man outta you, Will Cain. They's some kinda deep down power inside you, it flows from you like a scent almost. You're gonna make your mark in this ole vale o' dross an' tears, boy, mark my words."

"Aw, pshaw!" said Will, feeling equally proud and embarrassed, and loped away.

The sun was hanging low when Will got the teams home and turned into the pen. With great satisfaction, he noted that the cows tied to Frank and Midnight had been worn down to a nub and made nary a fuss when Will approached them.

"I got Mr. Gibson's oxen I paid for one week," he said upon entering the kitchen. "A little longer, if we need them. What we got for supper? I could eat a plate of stink bugs right about now!"

"We got the last ham from last year, along with gravy and biskits," said Ellen. "You can wash it down with your choice of fresh buttermilk or coffee. Bless her heart, Polly churned the butter this afternoon and made the biskits."

Will drew a hearty sniff and breathed out extravagantly. “Smells mighty good, that Polly is a wonder, indoors and out! You know, we better get Grandsir’s hired hands to kill and smoke us a couple hogs, even though t’ain’t hog-killing time, for we are not going to have time to do it our own selves.”

“Yes, Will,” said Ellen obediently. She smiled in satisfaction at how well her son was filling Bob’s role. Watching him eat, it was as if her husband’s ghost had sat down at the table.

After he washed and sat down to eat, Will noted the silence. “Where are the children?” he asked and chuckled. “Seems funny, me callin’ them children, Polly is but a year shy of me and Nathan is only about two years younger.”

“That’s because you are a man now,” she said with conviction. “Nathan went to bed about sundown—he was plumb tuckered out—and Polly is taking a bath in her room. Running around that dusty pen, she got real dirty. She is a gal that likes to be clean. She’s right persnickety that way.”

“She may be that, but she was a big help to me and Nathan today,” said Will admiringly. "She saw me having trouble bringing one of them ole wild cows down and stepped right in. Smart girl and pretty as a morning too. What a pretty sister I have, and a second cousin I believe, thanks to one of your grandpa Cauley's wild boys with the slave women."

Ellen saw the dreamy look in Will's eye and looked quizzically at him.

"When you boys slow down a bit and give us some breathing room, Polly and I will start sewing clothes for both of us," she said. "We are gonna need some firewood within the next two or three weeks, too. If you boys could drag up a couple of snags, Polly and I could commence to cut it up with the crosscut saw. Daddy had it sharpened a couple months ago."

Polly came in from her bath looking fresh and clean as a daisy. She had put on a becoming housedress Ellen had made from a potato sack and embroidered with oddments of fabric.

"Mmm-mm, Polly," said Will. "You smell like a breath of spring!"

Polly smiled shyly. "I found some old bath salts in the chifforobe and put them in my bath. The bottle said they were lilac, hoped you wouldn't mind."

"I don't mind, child. Bob give me them salts more'n ten year ago as a anniversary present. Seemed like a dang fool extravagance, but your papa, he was that thoughtful. Never got 'round to trying 'em myself, glad somebody could put 'em to use."

"Thank you," said Polly. "How were my biskits, Will? Good as momma's?"

"Girl, I ain't crazy enough to cut my own throat by preferencin' one or t'other. You and make the best bread in the county, and let's leave it at that."

Grinning, Polly gripped her hands behind her back and swayed her hips a little. "Will, I'd be forever beholden to you if you would you help me empty the water."

"Sure," said Will, getting up. "Come on let's get that tub out of your room. Next time you want to bathe, do it on the back porch and we won't have to tote the water so far. We can hang a blanket up for your privacy."

“Oh, she ain’t modest,” Ellen laughed, “whutn’t that long ago, I caught her skinny-dippin’ in Whitewater Creek!”

Will and Polly’s eyes met. Will felt an odd stirring in his heart and smiled crookedly. Polly smiled, too, and instinctively took his hand.

CHAPTER 10

Early the next morning, Will went to the pen and was surprised to see the cows and oxen lying down together. As he walked up to Frank, the cow necked to him didn't move a muscle. The same results were noted with Midnight and his neck mate.

"I'll be dadgummed!" he shouted jubilantly. "This is gonna work out better than I thought." He left the pen in a trot to roust Nathan.

Polly and momma were in the kitchen fixing a stick-to-your-ribs breakfast of ham, grits, and biskits.

"Where's that sleepyhead Nathan?" asked Will.

"Still a-bed, I reckon," said Ellen. "That boy does like his sleep."

"Come, Polly," said Will excitedly. "I figure you're ever' bit as good a wrangler as ole Nate. We are gonna tie those other wild cows to Mr. Gibson's oxen."

He ran ahead and saddled Cat and was standing by the gate when Polly arrived. She had changed quickly into some of Nathan's old dungarees and a flannel shirt. Despite the manly attire, she still cut a fine figure of a woman. There was excitement in her eyes at the prospect of working with Will.

"I'll open the gate and we'll go in together," said Will. "Just make sure the cows don't bust through."

Mounting the mare, he moved up to the herd and, taking his time, dead-aimed the rope at the first cow's head. Bingo, a ringer! The old boss tossed her head irritably, trying to dislodge the rope as if it were a big fly, then she stood stock-still.

Will eased up on the cow and whistled for Blanco, the white ox. The ox just stood there, chewing stupidly. Will moved Cat closer to Blanco and flipped the sack over his head and neck, then took a dally around the horn and backed the mare up. When the cow felt the pull of the rope, she went stiff. The mare kept backing up, dragging the cow right up to the ox.

"Polly, come here and hold my horse," called Will.

He dismounted and tied the head of the cow to Blanco's neck. Polly led Cat up some, and when the slacked rope was taken off the cow, Will slapped the ox on the rump and the old brute moved up, dragging the cow. That worked so well, he quickly remounted, had Polly move back to the gate, and moved up and repeated the process on the last two wild cows and tied them to Scamp and Spot.

That left only the bull, which proved harder to catch, but he too was finally yoked up to the biggest ox, Brownie. A right good show followed. The bull hooked at the ox, but they were tied so close to each other, Brownie had nothing to fear. In fact, the dumb brute didn't even notice the commotion. He just walked blithely away as the bull's stubbornly planted forefeet wore a track of deep grooves in the dirt. Will opened the gate and let all the animals out of the pen into the grassed-over cotton field.

Will gathered Polly up underneath her arms and spun her around. "We make a right good team, you 'n' me!" he said. Setting her down again, he kissed her cheek.

"What was that for?" said Polly softly. She touched the back of her hand to her cheek and peered at Will through sultry, half-closed eyes.

"Cat fur to make kitten britches!" said Will jovially. "Come on, let's eat!"

The Cain's had just finished breakfast when they heard horses outside. Polly went to the window and looked back at the family with a worried look on her face.

"Trouble, Will," she said meekly.

"Well, I have been expecting it," sighed Will.

Sheriff Sloan strode up to the front porch, followed by a tall Federal captain with a dignified bearing and three other soldiers. Will and his family walked out to meet them.

"William R. Cain," said the sheriff, his voice shaking, "you are under arrest for assaulting two Federal soldiers on May 27, 1865."

Will regarded his accusers stoically. Behind him, he heard the disbelieving murmurs of his family. "Is this what you call vouching for a body, Sheriff?" said Will nastily.

"He vouched for you, son," said the tall captain, sweeping off his hat and tucking it smartly under his arm. "I am Capt. Alexander Cooksey, Cpl. Snyder and Sgt. Baker's superior. Mr. Cain, you are fortunate to have a friend in Sheriff Sloan. After Cpl. Snyder came back to camp Saturday evening with his colorful account of the events in Elba, my men smelled blood. It was all I could do to stop them from tracking you down and stringing you up on the spot, as the penalty for a civilian assaulting Federal troops is often death by hanging. I admit I had half a mind to forgo the standard military inquiry and let them proceed, but the sheriff convinced me otherwise. Had he not ridden out to camp

Saturday evening and told me your side of the story, you would be a dead man by now."

Will looked at the sheriff and nodded his somber thanks.

"On Sheriff Sloan's advice, I met with Judge Botencourt Sunday morning," the captain continued. "After reviewing the matter with His Honor, I was inclined to treat this as a civil matter and let his court decide your fate. He is a good man by all accounts and you will receive a fair and impartial hearing. This is a highly unusual move on my part that I have undertaken in the interest of repairing North-South relations, if only in a small way, and one for which I trust you are grateful."

"I am obliged to you for that, Captain," said Will sincerely.

"So please, Will, come along peaceably and we will put this to rest," said Sheriff Sloan. "I promise you and your ma, you will be okay if you'll just cooperate."

"Sheriff, I will go with you, but not as a criminal in shackles," said Will resolutely. "I will go as a free man. Polly, please go inside and fetch my gray coat. Nathan, saddle up the gelding. I'm leavin' Cat for you. She's tried and true and you will need her in case—"

"You're coming back, Will, ain't you?" said Nathan haltingly.

Will smiled. "Quick as I can little brother. But just in case the Blue Coats keep me for a while, don't forget to feed and water them cows ever' day. In a couple of days, I think you can untie all the cattle. See that they eat well and keep 'em gentle. Y'all might go over to Mr. Gibson and tell him what happened. If he wants his stock back, drive them home for him. Tell Grandsir what has happened, too."

Polly came up with Will's coat. She bit her lip to keep from crying. "I don't want you to go to jail on account of me, Will."

Will smiled at her and laid his hand on her cheek. "I cain't think of a better reason for going to jail than defending a pretty girl's honor," he said and mounted the gelding.

"Gawd," croaked one of the soldiers. "These Rebs ain't learnt a damned thing. Boy, don't you know you'll have striped young-uns if you go race-mixin' with this yella coon?"

Livid, Will nosed the gelding hard into the soldier, sending him sprawling to the ground.

"It was remarks like that what caused your uncouth friends to get hurt in Elba," he sneered. "If y'all want some of the same, come on, I'm all ears."

"Benson, keep your mouth shut!" Capt. Cooksey barked at the soldier, who got up from the dirt, cussing under his breath. The captain turned to Polly and said sincerely, "I apologize, Miss Cain, for this man's vulgarity and lack of respect."

"When can I see Will again?" asked Ellen, wringing her hands.

"The court date is Wednesday, May 31st," Sheriff Sloan, answered her. "That's jest two days hence. Ellen, you and the children had best stay on the farm until then."

"Two days in jail?" said Will incredulously. The disgrace of imprisonment was a bitter pill.

"It will pass quickly," said Capt. Cooksey compassionately.

"Quickly, hell!" said Will. "I wouldn't be in this sorry situation if those men, Baker and Snyder, hadn't behaved like gutter trash toward Polly. And your man there, Benson, he's no better."

Capt. Cooksey tugged thoughtfully at the end of his long mustache. He was a young, idealistic man who, remarkably, was not made cynical by the war.

"You've got to believe that all Northerners aren't evil," he said sincerely. "I wish the two sides could just let bygones be bygones."

"Not that simple, I'm afraid," said Will.

The captain sighed. "You might be right, son. I wish you weren't. But you're not doing yourselves any good, still flying the Stars and Bars and such. The struggle's over for your people and it's time to forget the past and look to the future. Rebuild the nation make it whole again! Take off that roundabout, the war is over. Why would you want to keep wearing a symbol of your defeat?"

Will looked him dead in the eye. The image of Jerry lying dead underneath the sweet gum tree flitted across his mind. "I wear it to honor my friends who aren't coming home," he said. "And I also wear it because it stands for the unvanquished South and it says I am free."

"Very well," said Capt. Cooksey. "We will escort you into Elba, but you will go without restraints. The Army regards this as a very serious matter, Mr. Cain, and for that reason, the hearing will be expedited. This is for your benefit, as well, as any delay might result in my men succeeding in carrying out your lynching. I feel it is my duty to warn you that counsel will represent the two soldiers you are accused of assaulting from the Montgomery office of the Judge Advocate General's Corps of the United States Army. He is very good, indeed, at his job and is even now preparing his case. You may elect to be defended by counsel of your choosing."

"You mean like a lawyer?" asked Will.

"Precisely," said Capt. Cooksey.

"I reckon the truth is the entire defense I'll need," said Will.

"You do strike me as a scrupulously honest man," the captain replied. "I will not be present at the hearing, Mr. Cain. Good luck to you."

Will said a tearful goodbye to his family and rode with the sheriff and the military escort into town. He was fuming inside but had made up his mind not to show it. When they got to the main street, he noticed a good many bystanders watching the cavalcade pass. Several men saluted him, and he was fairly sure one pretty girl winked at him.

Capt. Cooksey and his men went back to their camp, after which Sheriff Sloan locked Will in a small, tidy cell with a cot, a washstand, and a Bible. He had never been in a jail cell before and chafed at the confinement.

"Your horse is stabled at county expense, Will," said the sheriff, returning from the livery. "Say, that took guts wearin' that gray jacket into town after what happened. Folks on the street noticed and I reckon inside they was proud."

"I seen 'em," said Will. "Sheriff, does you reckon I am in bad trouble over this little fracas?"

"It don't look good, Will," said the sheriff. "The pistol whippin' was bad enough, but to shoot a man—"

"I was only sticking up for Polly!" Will interrupted. "She hadn't caused no harm, and those loudmouthed bastards had no right to sully her that a-way. It's just the same as they done down through Georgia raping, burning, and stealing. I swear, war brings out the worst in men, and these Yank men must have more worst to bring out than most."

"Hear, hear!" said the sheriff.

"What's court going to be like?" asked Will, who had never set foot in the courthouse that he could remember.

"Well, you'll go before Judge Botencourt and he'll hear out testimony on both sides and make his decision—won't be no jury," Sheriff Sloan replied. "Dependin' on his mood, he might decide what to do Wednesday, or he may decide to cogitate on it. He's a right fair man, like the captain said. So don't despair, son, he might see things your way. But I have to warn ye, Will, the judge is a mite peculiar and sometimes he passes out queer punishments."

"How do you mean?" asked Will.

"Well, they were the time a couple years back this feller was accused of raping an underage girl," said the sheriff. The young girl's pappy wanted the boy castrated, but the judge had a different idée, that he cut me in on. I went to the trouble and expense of building a scaffold, which still stands behind the courthouse, and he sentenced the young man to hang. I marched the lad to the scaffold like it was a shore fired hangin'. When the lad put his foot on the first step, the girl screamed out that she was not raped, that she wanted the young man to have sex with her. The judge came around front of the lad brought out the young lady who said she was afraid her papa would hide her good if he knew she had consented to the act. The judge married them in front of the scaffold and they been together now for about ten years and have four children. That is what I meant about his different ways of judgment."

Will laughed uneasily and wondered what bizarre sentence the judge might mete out to him.

"Don't worry, son," the sheriff reassured him. "You're in the right and plenty of folks will vouch for you. It'll all turn out in your favor."

"I sure hope so," sighed Will. "Sheriff, I ain't much of a drinkin' man, but could you get old man Sharples to sell me a bottle of whiskey? I sure could use a taste right about now."

"I kin do better than that, Will—I will get one free for you. After all, the county and state owe ye something for servin' in the army. I 'spect Walter will be happy to oblige. Be right back."

The sheriff left and returned directly with an unmarked, amber-colored pint bottle and sat beside Will on his cot.

"Walter sends you this elixir with his compliments," said Sheriff Sloan. "Said it'll put hair on your chest if you ain't got it and take it off if'n you do!"

Will took the bottle and tossed back a good slug. "Tastes about like piss, but I've had worse." The whiskey hit his belly like a hot coal and he took another pull. "Actually, it's not so bad at all—this stuff grows on ye!" he enthused and gave the bottle back to Sheriff Sloan.

They passed the bottle for a few minutes, feeling no pain, talking idly of the war and the Reconstruction.

"Sheriff, there was a lot of folks in the county that didn't join the Confederate

Army at the start and then came in later," asked Will at one point "how come?"

The sheriff thought a moment. "Well, there are a lot of folk—in fact, most folk in Coffee and surroundin' counties and most likely the hull state—never owned a slave. So, seceding over slavery weren't an issue. But after the Yankee Army started invading 'Bammy, folks sorta took exception to havin' interlopers about, so they joined up. We been that way ever since time started. My daddy went to Nor Leans in 1812 for that same reason. The English had troops in our country after we had whupped them in the Revolutionary War, and t'weren't right. We are free people and aim to stay that way. And as soon as we get the Blue Coats outta here, just like we got the Red Coats outta Louisiana, we can go back to life as we know it. I ain't much of a prayin' man, but I spend a heap o' time askin' the Lord to take these Yanks someplace else."

"I hear that hell has plenty of room," grimly suggested Will!

Will spent the rest of that day and the next feeling like a squirrel in a cage. He passed the time praying or playing checkers with Sheriff Sloan or the deputy. Wednesday morning, Will awoke before the cock's crow. His mind lingered on the pleasant dream he had had of he and Cat, with wings on her hooves and her mane afire, soaring across the Texas plains. For a moment, he didn't know where he was. Then he beheld the bars and his spirit melted. He fell to his knees and prayed, "Dear Lord, please shine your graces on me this day."

Sheriff Sloan provided Will with a razor and hot water so he would look his best. He wondered if all the bruises on Will's face and his scared hands from chasing the cattle in the brush would be against the boy's appearance. He had Will wash as much of the scabs off as he could. The boy he looked ragged. He combed his hair and scrubbed his teeth with a hog bristle brush and tooth powder made from pulverized charcoal, the latter items also courtesy of the sheriff. Will declined his offer of a suit coat to wear instead of his Confederate gray. He looked very presentable for court.

A little past eight-thirty, Sheriff Sloan led his whole family in. Ellen and Polly were all teared up, so much so his mother could scarcely speak. The sheriff let Will out of his cell and there were hugs all around.

Grandsir said in a stentorian voice, "Will, my boy, God knows what you did was correct and He will see you vindicated. Keep your faith. Never doubt, never waiver!"

"Thank ye, Grandsir," said Will. "I needed to hear your counsel."

The sheriff asked Will to stick out his hands. "I hate to do this in front of your family, Will," he said, attaching the handcuffs very loosely, "but it's what the Blue Coats want."

The deputy led Will out the door and down the street to the courthouse, with the Cain's following sorrowfully. A good many of the townsfolk had come to show their support. They all turned their heads as the deputy led him to the first row of seats on the left. The sheriff and the deputy sat down on Will's right, with his family settling in on the row directly behind. The three Union soldiers from the set-to were sittin' on the right behind a small table. Snyder and Baker, the two soldiers Will had brawled with, wore identically smug expressions. Snyder's face was heavily wrapped up in white bandages and Baker's arm was in a sling. The young private, Westermeyer, sat with quiet dignity with his hands folded in his lap. Another young man, perhaps thirty, with sandy hair and a boyishly handsome face, was also at the table. He was in his army dress blues and had a look of fierce intelligence, bordering on animal cunning. Will reckoned he was the advocate Lt. Cooksey had spoken of.

"All rise," intoned the bailiff. Judge Robert L. Botencourt came in noisily and parked his tremendous bulk behind the bench. He was a big man, as fat as he was tall, with a red, jowly face that shook like pudding when he moved or talked. He wore his hair long in the back to compensate for his bald crown, from which a few hairs sprouted like corkscrews, and he sported a set of thick and bushy sideburns. He stuck a pair of old pince-nez spectacles on the bridge of his wide nose and read over the complaint before him. A moment later, he pounded the gavel and said in a deep southern drawl

"This hearing is now in session. You regulars in the audience know I am a fair man, but one given to interpreting the law after my own fashion and running my courtroom as informally as humanly possible. In a word, I am a man of unusual methods. We have here an unusual case that an uncommonly level headed Yankee captain and I agreed merits unusual scrutiny. Is the complainants' counsel present?"

"Yes, Your Honor," said the sandy-haired man, rising.

"And what might your name be, Captain?" asked the judge.

The counselor was taken back with a surprise. "Er, Lt. Curtis Gamble of the Judge Advocate General Corps, sir, at your service."

"Gamble, eh?" harrumphed the judge. "That is interesting name for an attorney. Where is William Cain?"

"Here, Your Honor," said Will, half rising to his feet and sitting down again.

The judge regarded him owlishly over his spectacles. "William Cain, you are charged with assaulting two U.S. Army soldiers in this township, Elba, Alabama, on the 27th day of May, 1865. According to your sworn statement, you felt these men were disrespectful toward a young black woman, one Polly Cain, who lives with your mother. You took the matter into your hands and caused bodily harm to both men, including the infliction of a gunshot wound. How do you plead?"

"Guilty, Your Honor."

"What did you say? May I enter a plea of not guilty for the defendant who lacks council?"

"Your Honor, I mean I am guilty of what you said, but I'm not sorry for it and I'd do it again."

There was general applause from the audience, which the judge silenced with a sour look.

"You're not helping your cause any, Mr. Cain," he said. "I take it to mean you believe you were in the right, which would constitute a plea of not guilty. Is that correct?"

"Yes sir, Your Honor."

"Very well, I have sympathy for you, Mr. Cain, because I know the young lady in question has been in your family for much of her life and is loved no less than if she were your sister by blood. However, that is no excuse for your actions. We cannot take the law in our own hands because we feel morally wronged. Federal law under Reconstruction says the punishment for shooting Federal troops is hanging, you are fortunate you were not hung. However, who knows? Before all is said and done, hanging may turn out to be my only option as well."

Will turned around and looked doubtfully at his family as the courtroom buzzed with the audience's reaction. The judge banged his gavel once and went on.

"Now, I don't mind telling the court that I aim to go fishing this afternoon. Therefore, I will expect the parties on both sides of this complaint to be quick in their respective testimonies. Let us hear from the complainants' counsel."

The young attorney rose, crossed his hands behind his back, and spoke in a smooth tone of voice. "Your Honor, in appreciation of your appointment this afternoon, I will dispense with my opening remarks and let my clients speak for themselves in order to expedite this procedure."

"Okay," said the judge, using the acceptable Choctaw word.

After being sworn in by the bailiff, Snyder and Baker took the stand in turn and told the same story of "minding their own business" and being "accosted by one William Cain, a local resident known for his hot temper. As to their alleged mistreatment of Polly Cain, a "mixed-raced young woman not related by blood to William Cain," both soldiers testified they had only tried to "exchange pleasantries" with her before being "attacked without provocation and with malicious intent" by the defendant. The young private, looking as frightened as a rabbit in a snare corroborated their testimony to discredit Will and absolve the soldiers of any wrongdoing. Will couldn't blame the lieutenant for that, but at the same time, he wished his own command of speech were less rustic.

Judge Botencourt called Will to the stand. He took the oath solemnly and sat down on the judge's left.

"Let's hear your side of this, son," said the judge.

"Well, sir, I reckon I don't know as many pretty words as these Yanks, but I do have a good handle on the truth, and what they say happened is a pure fiction. These two men Snyder and Baker whutn't saying nothin' pleasant to Polly that I heard, they profaned Polly's character right there on the street."

"Please share with the court the nature of these remarks," said the judge.

"I cain't repeat them, Your Honor. They were that vile nothin' but pure gutter talk that not any woman, octoroon or not, should have to listen to. Even if you gave me, something to write on I would not write it, I didn't talk that way in the war and I don't think them words."

Judge Botencourt took out his pocket watch from somewhere within the cavernous folds of his robe and checked the time. "The court will take your word for it, son. Now get on with it! I believe I hear the bass jumping down at Gray's Pond."

There was general tittering among the spectators as Will continued.

"Yes, Your Honor. Well, I told Sheriff Sloan about what was happenin' and for reasons he would have to tell you himself, he chose not to raise a finger."

"Is this so, Sheriff Sloan?" asked Judge Botencourt.

"Yes, Your Honor," answered the sheriff in a shamed voice.

"Continue, Mr. Cain," said the judge.

"Well, sir, seeing as how he weren't going to be any help, I told the sheriff point blank that no one was going to mess with the Cain family and went out to defend Nathan and Polly. Long story short, some hot words were said on both sides, and the sheriff did finally come out and helped Polly get to safety. Snyder threw the first punch then the other one, Baker, drew his pistol on me. I admit to pistol-whipping both of 'em and shooting Baker, but I did it to protect my sister's honor.

"Son, it is rather extraordinary that you would risk your own life to defend the honor of a young black woman, isn't it?" the judge asked.

Will thought about it a moment. "With all due respect sir, it weren't extraordinary, it was just the right thing to do. I like to think that people is people, no matter what color the Good Lord chose to paint 'em. Polly is an innocent young girl and my sister. It matters not if the court understands that or not, and the way these men was treating her just whutn't right. Besides didn't the Blue Coats come to free the Negro and see that they get treated fairly? If what happened out on that street was fair, then I'm hot-damn Burnin' Billy Sherman!"

The spectators erupted in a loud cheer and Judge Botencourt banged his gavel for order.

"Quiet, quiet!" he boomed. "You all are giving me a headache. Lt. Gamble, do you wish to question Mr. Cain?"

Will glanced at the attorney he didn't like the inscrutable look on his face.

"Not at this time, Your Honor," he replied.

"Very well," said the judge. "You may step down, son. Now, is there anyone present who wishes to speak on the defendant's behalf?"

"I do, Your Honor," said Sheriff Sloan.

"Take the stand, then, and get on with it," said the judge as he leaned back in his chair and took a pinch of snuff.

"I cain't account for why I didn't want to tussle with them Blue Bellies—err, Federal troops," said the sheriff, wringing his hands nervously. "I don't hold with them ridin' rough shod over us Southerners any more'n the next man, but it's a hard thing sometimes, expecting men like that, who seemingly ain't got no respect for anything, to respect a tin star. I reckon this is somethin' I'll be needin' to study on. Could be I'm gettin' too old for this job."

"Stick to the matter at hand, if you would, please," said the judge. He puckered his mouth like a fish and dangled his pocket watch in the sheriff's face. "And make it quick!"

"Yes, Your Honor. I heared and seen it all happen jest like Will said it did. The Federal men, they're jest not telling the truth."

"Very good, you may stand down," said the judge. "Anyone else have any direct testimony?"

Walter Sharples and three other townspeople took the stand and briefly collaborated Will's testimony. Many more volunteered to speak, but the judge denied them.

"That's enough testimony," said the judge. He noticed Nathaniel, shyly raising his hand. "What is it, young man? Got to take a pee?"

"No, sir," said Nathan. "I'd just like to say something, if you please."

The judge blew noisily through his blubbery lips. "All right, young man," he said. "But it had better be good."

After Nathan was sworn in, he took the stand. "I just want to say that I'm proud of Will for takin' up for Polly," he began, his eyes already beginning to glisten. "My papa was my hero, and he always will be, but he was killed in the war. Will's the man of the house now, and we couldn't ask for a better one. I reckon Will didn't win any medals in the war, but he ain't ever forgotten his raising. He stood up for dear Polly. It was the right thing to do, and it don't make any difference that the men was Yank soldiers. They were rude, nasty, and insolent. They got what was comin' to 'em. An' I'm proud my big brother gave it to 'em. That's all I got to say, sir. I love Polly so much if I was of age I would want to have her as a wife, I see her heart not any color."

A silence fell over the courtroom as Nathan stood down. Will nodded to him as he returned to his seat, whereupon the Cain family enveloped him in hugs.

"Not bad, not bad at all," said the judge, nodding his head. His meaty jowls swayed like sides of ham in a smokehouse.

Pvt. Westermeyer had been viewing the proceedings with mounting nervousness, twitching and fidgeting all the while. Suddenly he stood up and blurted out, "Your Honor, I take back my earlier testimony. Everything happened just like Mr. Cain said it did. I apologize to the court for saying otherwise. Guess I was just scared and confused."

Judge Botencourt raised his eyebrows and looked challengingly at Lt. Gamble.

"Your Honor," said the advocate, his face betraying the slightest hint of uncertainty. "In view of today's abbreviated session, I would like to request that the court postpone rendering its verdict and grant counsel time to arrange for additional testimony at a later date."

"Well, I don't know about that," said the judge harshly. "I was just about had my mind made up. How much more time are we talking about, counsel?"

"Only a day, sir," said Lt. Gamble.

"Very well," said the judge. He banged his gavel and announced, "This court will reconvene Friday morning at nine a.m.!"

There was nothing they could do but wait, Will urged his family to return home. His mood black, Will ate the dinner the deputy fetched him mechanically, without tasting a morsel. The big clock on the wall outside his cell read two o'clock when Walter Sharples came in. He exchanged pleasantries with the sheriff and the deputy and walked over to the cell.

"Howdy, Walter," Will called out. "I want to thank you for your testimony this morning."

"Glad to do it, son," said Walter. "I've got some good news for you. Thanks to your grandpa, word's all over town about your needing a couple of good dogs for your cattle roundup. Well, they was a feller from over near Opp in Covington

County passing through just now on business and he overhead some fellows talking about it my saloon. Turns out he raises cows himself over there and told me he had a passel of Hall's Heelers."

"What're them?" asked Will.

"Australian cattle dogs," Walter replied. "Smart dogs and just as full of vim and vigor as the day is long, the feller said, and good crackin' herd dogs." He said he would sell you a pair for $15.00. I took the liberty of paying the man $7.50 on deposit and he's gonna deliver the dogs here to the jail next week when he swings back through town." He called out to the sheriff, "That all right with you, Jed? It'd be too out of his way to take the dogs out to the Cain place."

"Now, Walter, you know I'm not runnin' a kennel here," laughed the sheriff. "But yeah, that'll be all right."

Will stuck his hand through the bars for Walter to shake. "You're a real friend," said Will.

The saloonkeeper grinned. "Don't mention it. You made my day by bustin' up them Yanks, and I knew you were good for the money. Your papa would have a beer at my saloon every now and then, you know. I was right fond of him. He was a good man and told many a crackerjack story. Least I can do is give his boy a hand."

"Here, Walter, let me pay you back right now," said Will. He took off his left brogan and fished out a wad of Yankee currency from the toe. "I always carry a few bills for emergencies," he allowed and passed the money to Walter.

"Much obliged," said Walter. "That ain't all, Will. This same feller said he knows a cattleman over in Mobile by the name of Sam McAtee that would probably be interested in your cows. He's staying indefinitely at the McLain Boarding House on First Street. Feller suggested you send him a telegram for a quote." He handed Will a slip of paper through the bars. "I wrote the particulars down for you."

"I cain't thank you enough for all you've done, Walter," said Will.

"My pleasure son," said Walter, "and the best of luck to you on Friday, I'll be there to lend my support."

When the saloonkeeper had gone, Sheriff Sloan came over to the cell.

“That’s mighty good news, Will,” he said. “If you like, I can send that telegram for you today.”

“I’d appreciate it,” said Will as he fished inside his shoe for more money. He handed a few bills and the slip of paper with McAtee’s information on it to the sheriff. “This should cover the cost of the telegram and what I owe to the feller from Opp that’s fetching the cattle dogs. If you don’t mind, just pay him for me when he comes and let me know when to pick ’em up.”

“I’ll send my deputy out to your place,” said Sheriff Sloan. “What do you want the telegram to say, Will?”

“Just say I’ve got some prime cows he might be interested in and ask him how much he’ll pay per head.”

“Gotcha,” said Sheriff Sloan, counting the crumpled bills. “Say, Will, how come you to have so much Yankee greenbacks? Ever’ body’s talkin’ about how free you seem to be with money when the rest of us is either broke or near it. Did you rob a Yankee bank or somethin’?”

Will reddened. It hadn’t occurred to him that people would notice he was seemingly so well heeled. He wasn't ashamed of how he had acquired his money, but it was no one's business but his family's and his own.

"Something like that," he replied and changed the subject. "Say, Sheriff, do you think you could get me some writing paper and a pencil? I've a mind to make good use of my confinement."

Sheriff Sloan went to his desk and fetched the stub of a lead pencil and a piece of coarse brown paper, both of which he passed through the bars to Will. "Who you writin' to, Will?" he asked.

"My Grandpa Cain over in Texas," replied Will. "If I come out of this mess without gettin' my neck stretched, mayhap I'll ride out there."

"Well, I'll leave it to you then," said the sheriff. "Meanwhile, I'll send that telegram for you."

Ellen had instilled in Will an appreciation of words and he rather enjoyed the almost mystical process of seeing his thoughts appear on paper. He sat down on his cot and, using the Bible for a desk, began writing in the graceful

Copperplate hand his mother had taught him.

Dear Grandpa Cain,

I trust this letter finds you and yours bearing up tolerably well in the after math of the War. It is my sad duty to tell you that a Yankee coward killed my papa outside Atlanta. I regret my mother has not written you previously but she has been distraught over it all. As you can tell by this letter, I was spared the same fate. I write to you now, however, from jail where I await my sentence for assaulting two Federal soldiers. The judge is a peculiar man but I like my chances.

I wish to ask you, sir, if I may prevail upon your hospitality, sometime in the near future as I have a desire stoked by my comradeship with some fellows from the Eighth Texas Cavalry, to see your Fair State. After rounding up our wild cattle in the cane breaks we will most likely take them to market in Mobile, after 'tis is all done, I may come for a visit."

If this is agreeable to you, please reply post haste.

From your loving Grand Son
William R. Cain, Jr.

When the sheriff returned a half-hour later, Will had just finished the letter. He was oblivious to the misspellings and punctuation errors and looked with pride on his own handiwork.

“You wouldn’t have an envelope, would you, Sheriff?” asked Will.

“Hard to come by,” said Sheriff Sloan as he fished around in his drawer, “but here’s one made out of wallpaper that’s already been used once. Just scratch out the old address and write the new one on t’other side.”

Will did so, addressing the letter simply to William T. Cain, Jasper County, Texas.

“Think that’ll get it there?” he asked Sheriff Sloan as he passed the letter through the bars.

“Reckon so, Will,” allowed the sheriff. “There cain’t be that many Cain's in Jasper, Texas. I’ll post it fer you. Say, Will, you’re not puttin’ the cart before the horse, are ye? I admit the judge seemed to sway your way today, but with that character, it could still go either way."

His grandsir's words echoed in Will's mind. Keep your faith. Never doubt, never waiver.

"I will get to Texas," said Will dreamily, "one way or the other."

Time passed for Will with a wintertime molasses-like slowness. He clung hard to his grandsir's words about keeping the faith, but all the while, he worried about what would happen to him and his family if he were sentenced to be hung or sent to rot in a Yankee jail. His mind toyed with the many other grim scenarios the eccentric judge might concoct for him.

Friday morning finally arrived. The little courtroom was again packed. Will's family was already there when the deputy led him, again handcuffed, to his seat. Sheriff Sloan had advised Will he would not attend due to other business and Will understood. Will noticed there were two other Federal soldiers sitting behind Lt. Gamble and his clients. They looked vaguely familiar, but he couldn't place them. As Will was sitting down, he felt a tap on his shoulder. He turned around and gazed into the amiable face of the man sitting next to Nathan.

"Remember me, lad?" said the man, smiling broadly. He had a wide, pink, smooth-shaven face and an air of amiability about him.

"Angus!" Will shouted. "I almost didn't recognize you without your beard. What the hell are you doing here?"

"Will!" Ellen rebuked him. "Don't forget where you are!"

"Sorry," said Will. "Angus, this is my family."

"We've met, lad," said Angus. "I have told them about our adventures together. Some of them, anyway! Heard about your plight over in Enterprise colorful news travels fast you know and thought I'd lend you my support, such as it is. I'm sorry to hear your papa didn't make it home."

"I appreciate it, Angus," said Will. "It went well Monday, thanks to Nathan and others speaking up for me. Your two cents certainly will help, if it comes to that."

"Will, why didn't you tell us you'd been shot?" said Polly tenderly.

"Whutn't no big thing," Will muttered.

"No big thing, he says," said Angus. He winked at Will and addressed Polly gravely. "Young miss, this lad was at death's door and would have fallen face-first across the threshold, if it hadn't been for the medical knowledge of yours truly."

Will grinned and said, "He's pulling your leg, Polly."

Angus leaned forward and whispered confidentially to Will, "Not a bad idea at that, laddie-buck. I've beheld beautiful women from New Orleans to Charleston, but I'd give this one the top prize. Those green eyes are enough to make any man forget his marriage vows."

"Well, you'd best remember yours, you old rogue," said Will good-naturedly and turned to face front as the bailiff ordered all to rise.

Judge Botencourt settled his round stout frame behind the bench and looked out at the spectators with a wide grin on his face. "It will please the court to know my fishing trip went exceptionally well, three bass and four catfish," he announced. "They were delicious! Now, lest the court think I was idling away the taxpayers' monies, I would remind it I always do my best thinking in commune with nature, and with cane pole in hand, I studied deeply on this matter. If Mr. Cain prevails—and I say with no prejudice that he should, unless Lt. Gamble has something good up his sleeve—he will suffer no retribution and will leave this courthouse a free and hopefully wiser man. However, if he should not prevail, I have cooked up a fitting punishment, and I promise you, ladies and gentlemen, it fits the crime."

The judge paused a moment to bask in the excited whisperings he knew his announcement would prompt, then went on.

"Lt. Gamble, the court granted you additional time to bolster your case. I trust you have used that time well."

"I have, Your Honor," said the attorney. "At this time, I would like to call Sgt. Charles Odom to the stand."

Will watched as one of soldiers sitting behind his accusers was sworn in and seated in the witness chair. Something about the man's movements sparked his memory and his heart sank. He turned around and mouthed one word to Angus, "Aberdeen."

Lt. Gamble addressed the witness. "Sgt. Odom, please tell the court what happened on or about the morning of June 10, 1865."

"Well, sir, me and Sgt. Laird there" he began, gesturing toward his companion in the audience, "were on routine patrol around Aberdeen, south of Atlanta. Our orders were to be on the lookout for Confederate deserters what didn't have their parole papers. Well, sir, we came upon these two cavalrymen what looked like might be riding stolen horses and asked to see their papers."

"And did they oblige?" asked Lt. Gamble.

"Yes, sir," replied Sgt. Odom. "Cain handed his papers to me, but I was a bit tipsy, sir, and I butterfingered them, I'm afraid."

"You dropped them," said Lt. Gamble, "because you were drunk."

Sgt. Odom looked embarrassed. "Not drunk, but getting there. It shames me to admit it, but owing to the war being over, Sgt. Laird and me—not to mention many more like us—had been getting a little carried away with our revels."

"Perfectly understandable," said Lt. Gamble. "Go on."

"Well, sir, I told Cain to pick the papers up, but he refused. The next thing I knew, the smart-talking young Rebel boy spurred his horse into mine and I was throwed to the ground," said Sgt. Odom. "I saw the boy's pistol barrel coming at my head and I went out like a light. Reckon he did the same thing to Sgt. Laird, for we both woke up in the bushes when night was coming on. We'd been dragged a good distance. Our horses and guns was gone and our pockets had been picked clean of thirty dollars."

"What did you do then?" asked Lt. Gamble.

"Well, sir, it took us the better part of a day to walk back to our camp and I immediately filed a report with my commanding officer," said Sgt. Odom. "Course, I knew the Rebel boy and his friend were long gone and I never thought anything would come of it, the big brass having bigger fish to fry, I reckoned. Well, sir, the long and the short of it is, on

Monday my commanding officer got word that Sgt. Laird and me was to make haste for Elba, Alabama for a hearing for a man whose name I will never forget."

"And why is that, Sgt. Odom?" asked Lt. Gamble with a sly smile.

"Because it was the same name as the man whose parole papers I had looked at that morning in Aberdeen," said Sgt. Odom excitedly, "and the same name I had filed the complaint about."

"Please share that name with the court, Sgt. Odom," Lt. Gamble said.

"W. R. Cain, III, of the 53rd Alabama Calvary."

"That will be all, Sgt. Odom," said Lt. Gamble. "Your Honor, if it please the court, allow me to elaborate on Sgt. Odom's testimony. In preparing my case, it came to my attention there were not one but two complaints against W. R. Cain, III, late of the 53rd Alabama regiment. Highly unusual, I immediately summoned Sgts. Odom and Laird to these proceedings from Georgia, but the distance involved precluded them from reaching Elba in time for Wednesday's session. They traveled by train to Montgomery and, as there is no rail line locally, came the rest of the way via stagecoach, and arrived late last night. I had hoped their testimony would not be essential to my clients' case, but with Your Honor appearing to lean in Mr. Cain's favor in Wednesday's session, I began to think otherwise and requested the extension."

"Understood, counselor," said the judge. "But the court doesn't see that Sgt. Odom's testimony is relevant to the charges brought against Mr. Cain for the offense that occurred on the streets of Elba. What happened in Aberdeen is regrettable, but a matter for another time and another court."

"With all due respect, Your Honor," said Lt. Gamble, "what happened in Aberdeen is indeed relevant to my clients' complaint. The assaults allegedly committed by Mr. Cain upon Federal troops in both Aberdeen and Elba are remarkably similar. In both instances, Mr. Cain, a civilian who had signed his parole paper in Greensboro, North Carolina, willfully committed two separate acts of aggression against soldiers of the U. S. Army, thereby establishing a pattern of violence. Furthermore, Your Honor, Mr. Cain violated the terms of the surrender agreement by having weapons on his person whom he should have turned in to the ordnance officer at Greensboro and which, on both occasions, he used to strike Federal personnel—an offense I remind this court is ordinarily punishable by death."

"Perhaps he did so and acquired the guns from some other source," the judge suggested.

"Only the defendant can say," said Lt. Gamble. "Let's ask him, shall we? I call William R. Cain to the stand."

His heart beating in his throat, Will rose shakily to his feet and took the stand. He placed his right hand on the Bible and recited the oath. As he sat down, he saw his grandsir nod almost imperceptibly to him.

"What about that, Mr. Cain?" said Lt. Gamble? "Did you turn your weapons in to the ordnance officer at Greensboro?"

"Some of them," said Will.

"Some of them," echoed Lt. Gamble. "Please clarify your statement, Mr. Cain."

Will sighed. "I'm sworn to tell the truth, so here 'tis. I only turned in the two Confederate-made pistols I was issued when I joined up. They weren't too swift, not as good as the Colts they make up north, and I have to admit. I buried the other arms I had collected during the war near Jamestown and came back for them after I surrendered."

"And were you wearing a gun when you encountered Sgts. Odom and Laird near Aberdeen?" asked Lt. Gamble.

"Yes, I was," said Will.

"And did you strike the men with the gun?"

"Yes, I did."

"And did you take their horses, their guns, and their money, and leave them for dead?"

Will, saw his mother's grim expression of hurt and disappointment.

"Yes, I did."

"Why did you do this, Mr. Cain?"

"They were drunk and rowdy and they accused me of stealing my horse, which made me mad as all get-out. And they were braggin' about the Rebels they had hung for horse-thievin' the day before."

"Did you believe their boast, Mr. Cain?"

"Naw, not exactly, I figured they were just trying to make themselves out big, like Yankees tend to do."

"So you felt it was your duty to take them down a peg or two."

"Well, in a manner of speakin', yes. See, the war changed me, like it done a lot of people. After all the Yankee cowardice and meanness I saw firsthand, I made up my mind not ever to take any guff off of them nor let them go ridin' roughshod over me or mine as long as I lived."

"Do you see yourself as a vigilante, Mr. Cain?"

"How's that?" asked Will.

"Do you think because the war has changed you, because it has made you an expert on man's baser instincts, that perhaps you are better qualified than, say, Sheriff Sloan to dispense justice as you see fit?"

Will thought for a moment. Whatever the consequences, he knew there was only one way he could answer the question. "Sometimes...sometimes, yes, I think I am."

“No more questions,” said Lt. Gamble.

“You may step down, Mr. Cain,” said Judge Botencourt.

Angus had been watching the proceedings like a man with ants in his pants. Finally he could contain himself no longer.

“Your Honor!” he jumped up and shouted. “I’d like an opportunity to speak on this young man’s behalf, if I may.”

Judge Botencourt shot Angus a reproachful glance. “I am nearsighted, not deaf. Who might you be, sir?”

“Angus MacDonald, Your Honor, of Enterprise. I traveled homeward with Mr. Cain from Carolina.”

The judge laced his pudgy fingers atop his freckled dome and, closing his eyes, leaned back in his chair. “Very well, but I warn you, Mr. MacDonald, I may fall asleep.”

Angus was sworn in and took the stand. He told the court how Will had come under his care after being wounded and of the uncommon generosity and compassion he had observed in the boy during their travels. He divulged that he was the other soldier with Will at the

Aberdeen incident and added a few more details, such as the fact the Federal sergeants had threatened to shoot him and Will and take their horses, which had caused Will to act as he did.

"I'll admit young Will has a fiery temper—redheads are like that, they say," said Angus. "But this is a good Christian boy who spoke to me of God and his family with the fervor of a preacher. Made an old heathen like me a little uncomfortable, but I never doubted his righteousness and his generosity, for I saw it in action time and again. I benefited from it myself, and there were two near-about starved Rebs we met that got to ride home instead of walking, thanks to Will's gift of a horse."

"Would this be one of the horses Mr. Cain took from Sgts. Odom and Laird?" asked Lt. Gamble, rising from his chair and approaching the witness stand.

"The same," said Angus. "Now you might say the horse weren't his to give, but the point is, we're talking about a boy who lives and breathes horseflesh. For him to part with a horse he could just as well have sold or kept for his own says a lot about his character."

"It does indeed, Mr. MacDonald," said Lt. Gamble. "But the fact remains, this individual you paint as a good Christian boy flouted the terms of his surrender and has admitted to this court he sees himself as not only above the law but also a better interpreter of it than those sworn to enforce it. Just because this presumably innocent boy who went to war came back from it somehow changed. I would submit to the court that the war has indeed changed Will Cain, and not for the good. Furthermore, that a man of his warped perspective and volatile temperament is a threat to society. While it is regrettable the war has put a sizeable chip on his shoulder, we cannot allow him or men like him to walk around daring others to knock it off, just because their war experience was less than pleasant."

Angus looked into Will's eyes. It was clear the boy was beginning to doubt his chances of exoneration.

"Lt. Gamble, you talk a lot about war," said Angus. "Were you in the war yourself?"

"No, sir, I was not. But I have heard—"

"You've heard a story, that's what you were going to say," Angus interrupted him. "Well, all us veterans could tell you stories. Thing is, we'd rather not. No, we'd rather not tell you about the maggot-eaten bodies of young men—babies, really—we saw rotting in the sun with their chests ripped open by projectiles and their eyeballs picked out by birds. We'd rather not tell you about the ungodly screams of men having their arms and legs sawn off without anesthesia, nor about those limbs piled in a ghastly heap that stank to high heaven ere they could be buried, Southern women gang raped by Federal soldiers. It don't matter what side we were on, Union or Reb, we all saw the same unspeakable things and suffered the same hardships that one-way or the other changed all of us, some maybe more than others. So before you go discounting how war might change a fellow, Lt. Gamble, I suggest you put yourself in the boots of the men that was there."

A slight ripple of annoyance played across Lt. Gamble's placid face.

"Most eloquent, Mr. MacDonald," he said. He turned to address Will. "Mr. Cain, do you still have in your possession the other horse you stole from Sgts. Odom and Laird?"

"I do," replied Will. "And the Colt pistols besides. I'll make good on the thirty dollars I took, too, if that's what you're drivin' at."

"Indeed it is," said Lt. Gamble. "Regardless of the outcome of this hearing, these items shall be returned to the sergeants forthwith.

"We don't want 'em back," Sgt. Laird spoke up. "Let the kid have 'em. Anyway, the horses weren't ours. Some of our men had stole 'em from a Rebel farmer they had beat up, just a few days afore the war ended. When we encountered Cain and his friend, we were drunker than Cooter Smith and acted like a couple of blackguards. I prob'ly would have done the same thing in his shoes."

Lt Gamble protested, "You're out of line, Sgt. Laird."

"Like he said, we don't want any of it back," said Sgt. Odom. "Laird and I were both good soldiers, but we got carried away there at the end and disgraced our uniforms. After what I've heard today, I figure the kid was a good soldier, too, only a little headstrong, and a good man besides. I don't want to see him in any more hot water. Lt. Gamble, you do what you have to do about this other set-to, but I ask you kindly not to pursue the Aberdeen business any further."

Lt. Gamble looked like he had just bitten into an unripe persimmon.

"If Your Honor is awake," he said testily, "perhaps he would at this time be prepared to render his judgment?"

Still reclining, Judge Botencourt opened one baleful eye and fixed it on the advocate.

"Whippersnapper, I never dozed for a moment," he said and yawned expansively. "I heard every word. Mr. MacDonald, I quite enjoyed your moving testimony. Your remarks, Lt. Gamble, were not so informative."

The judge rocked his girth forward and looked at Will and said, "Will you please rise, son."

Will stood up, ramrod straight. His mind went back to the stories his papa had told about a man that had lived five hundred years ago in Scotland by the name of William Wallace. He had a trial and was tried and found guilty for fighting for freedom and the rights of the oppressed. On the day of his execution, he stood straight as an arrow and told all he was only guilty of fighting for freedom. He was not afraid to die, for he had made peace with his God. Bob Cain said William Wallace died once like all brave men, whereas cowards die a hundred times. Will looked back at the judge with eyes of steel. He was ready to face his judgment.

"Mr. Cain, it seems to me in both instances discussed in this courtroom you were provoked to violence by your antagonists," the judge began, "were I not in my robes, I would go so far as to say your foes got what was coming to them. In my official capacity, however, I condemn your actions on the streets of Elba. While the court does not totally agree with Lt. Gamble's assessment of you as a vigilante and a threat to society, there is no mistaking your violent tendencies. Mr. Cain, the State of Alabama will not allow you to take the law into your own hands.

This time, it was Federal troops. Next time, it might be your neighbors. The court cannot take a chance on your wayward emotions should someone say or do something that violates your personal code of honor.

"I told the court earlier this morning I had worked out a fitting punishment, and I have. It is obvious you love your family deeply, Mr. Cain, and they you. In the difficult months and years ahead, they will need your brawn and resourcefulness to survive." He paused, reveling in the audience's anticipation. "But they will have to get along without you, I'm afraid."

A collective gasp arose from the audience. Will turned around and looked into the stricken faces of his family. Polly and Ellen were sobbing. Grandsir and Nanny hugged each other solemnly. Nathan's lower lip quivered and his eyes were on fire."You're not going to hang my brother!" he cried. "He don't deserve it!"

The judge banged his gavel. "Quiet! No one said anything about hanging. How unoriginal. What I have planned for your brother is worse than that and far cleverer, I daresay."

Will's heart was pounding so hard in his chest he thought it was going to come out of his mouth. He saw a terrible vision of himself in some Northern prison. He could hear the steel doors clang shut, like the gates of hell, and he could see the guards in the hated blue coats, laughing and jeering at him.

"William R. Cain," said the judge, "you have one hundred and twenty days from this date, June 30, 1865, to complete whatever business you may have in the State of Alabama so by September 30 1865 you will be gone, after which time you be considered in exile for a period of five years. It is the court's hope that, during that time, the pain of separation from your family's bosom will serve to teach you the art of self-control. If you are in Alabama during your exile, you will be confined to the state penitentiary for fifteen years. In addition, you are to pay punitive damages to Sgt. Baker and Cpl. Snyder in the amount of $50 each, said amounts to be paid in the sheriff's office within thirty days. Not that I care, Lt. Gamble, but is this decision to the satisfaction of the U.S. Army?"

"It is, Your Honor," said the advocate, smirking.

The judge banged his gavel. "So be it! This case is closed and this court is adjourned!"

Ellen, Nathan, and Polly rushed to Will's side. His knees were so weak, he thought he would fall, but as they held him so tightly, that was impossible. Grandsir and Nanny stood by, awaiting their turn to hug him.

"Well, son, it could have been worse," said Angus, pumping Will's hand.

"That's for sure," was his reply. "I'm much obliged for them silver-tongued words you said up there, Angus."

"My pleasure Will, I'd best be heading home now." He turned to Polly. "Young lady, you remind me of a poem

'She walks in beauty, like the night
Of cloudless climes and starry skies
And all that's best of dark and bright
Meet in her aspect and her eyes
Thus mellow'd to that tender light
Which heaven to gaudy day denies.' "

Angus bowed and kissed Polly's hand. "There's more but I've forgotten it! You folks take care, and if you need me just holler!" With a last wink at Will, he strode jauntily from the courtroom.

Ellen and Polly took Will's hands and walked beside him to the waiting buggy. Will helped the two of them onto the seat and Polly took the reins. Nathan took his place on the buckboard and the grandparents settled into their own carriage.

"Oh, Will, God bless you for caring for me," Polly whimpered. "I don't want you to go away. I want you to stay here."

"Don't cry, Polly," said Will softly. "I ain't gone yet. A hunnert-twenty day may not be a long time, but by cracky, I aim to make the best of 'em! Y'all go off to home now. I need to get my horse and see Sheriff Sloan. Now don't fret, I'll be home directly."

Will fetched the gelding from the livery stable and went inside the jail.

"Deputy told me what happened," said Sheriff Sloan. "I warned you that judge was peculiar, but at least you're not gonna be hung or go to prison."

"All things considered," said Will, "I'm right pleased with the outcome."

"That's the right attitude. Anyway, I've got good news for you. A reply just came from Sam McAtee."

He handed Will a Southern Telegraph Company telegram and he read aloud

"Will pay $10.00 head cattle upon review – STOP – no cut back?"

"Sounds like a fair price, but what does no cut back mean?" asked the sheriff.

"It means he'll pay the same price for any weight and sex," was Will's reply.

"Well, you got your work cut out for you, and I don't envy you the task."

"Ain't that the truth? Sheriff Sloan, thank you for all your kindnesses. If I have time before I leave Alabama, I will stop by and buy you a drink."

"Well, thank you, Will, for puttin' in a good word for me on the witness stand. Moreover, I apologize again for tuckin' my tail 'tween my legs when you coulda used my help."

"Aw, forget it I kin kinda see it your way, Sheriff. You got one of them danged if you do, danged if you don't jobs if ever there was one, and I don't fault you for turnin' the other cheek. Good Book says that's the best policy, but I'll be darned if'n it works for me!"

The sheriff laughed. "You're quite a young man, Will. If'n you kin keep your eyes open and your temper under a boil, you'll make somethin' of yerself. I'm afeard we are jest seeing the beginning of the mess we're gonna have with the Yankee Army in control. You're gonna come a-crost lots of men like Snyder an' Baker—you'd best learn how to turn that other cheek, at least some of the time. Still thinking about trying Texas?"

Will pondered a moment on that. Now that the die was cast, he had no doubt Texas was his destination. He felt the allure of the sprawling young state, still largely untamed as he heard tell it, tugging at his spirit. He just plain liked the sound of the word Texas, perhaps a rowdy place like Texas where a big boy with a big temper wouldn't have to turn the other cheek.

"Yeah, I've got family scattered from hell to breakfast, but I kindly figure on heading out West," he said at length.

The sheriff nodded. "I hear there is lots of opportunity out there. What was it that

Greeley fellow up north said? Go west, young man. That was right smart advice especially coming from a Yankee."

Will laughed. "I never figured on leaving here for any spell, what with and the family and farm to care for, but now I figure on giving Texas a look-see, especially if I hear from my Grandpa Cain. I just hope them five years pass quickly so I can come home. Nathan's a good boy, but I see how he is sniffin' the breeze, seein' which way it'll take him; he ain't gonna want to stay down on the farm all his life. Polly is a young lady now and will be looking for a husband ere long. I'm afeard momma is gonna be left pert near alone."

"I don't believe that Polly gal will leave your ma any time soon," said Sheriff Sloan. "They are a marvel to see, jest as close an' lovin' as any flesh 'n blood mother an' daughter. Say, Will, what you said up there on the stand 'bout people bein' people no matter how the Lord colors them, that sorta got to me. Seems to me that sort of thinking' is the thing that is we need all over this big ole country. Wherever you end up, Will, I know you'll do your family's name proud."

"I appreciate that, sir," said Will. "The good Lord willing, I'll head out West, where there ain't so many Blue Coats to keep a feller down. Don't care for 'em a-tall!"

The sheriff let loose a mirthful whoop and slapped his knee.

"Son, I sorta gathered that!"

CHAPTER 11

On the ride home, the enormity of his punishment hit him like a ton of bricks. Now he had to deal with Polly's feelings about he and Betty getting married.

The judge was a strange old buzzard, and he had been fair, Will reckoned, but exile from one's home state was harsh. How would his family get by without him? If something happened to Nathan, there would be no man of the house and all because Will couldn't turn a blind eye on injustice. Well, he was not going to change his character one jot from that direction, but he figured he'd better become a lot more careful in the way he acted on it. Seeing folks get treated right was something Grandsir and papa had tried to teach him since he was knee-high, and he'd not be a changin' that tradition this late in the game.

Will's mind raced with thoughts of the Herculean tasks ahead of him. Was he equal to them? Only time would tell. Once he got to Texas, he could work up a stake and send for momma, Nathan, Polly, and Betty. The thought of her name quickened his pulse and the picture of her pert figure in his mind's eye stirred his loins, reminding him of the pleasure Betty's body brought him. He would now have to include Betty in all the Cain plans.

When he stepped into the kitchen, the womenfolk flew at him like chickens in a tornado, just as he reckoned they would.

"Oh, Lord, my own flesh and blood, exiled from the bosom of his family!" Ellen wailed. "Will, where will you go? What will become of us?"

Polly threw herself at him and collapsed in his arms, weeping hysterically. “Oh, Will, I am so sorry you got in trouble over a girl like me.”

Will put his arms around her and for the first time, he realized he was holding a real woman, only with Betty he could be himself, where as Polly was young and yet pure, and his sister.

“Polly, you ain’t just a girl,” he consoled her. “You are family, the daughter momma never got to raise and the one she did. You’re one of us! So hush up that talk. The Bible says we are born with a purpose and we have a future. For the Cain's, that future will always include you. You are the sister I always loved.”

“What do you think will happen to us, Will, with you gone?” asked Nathan. Little rivers of tears streamed down his face and, every now and again, he would flick out his tongue to stem the salty flow.

“Buck up, little brother!” said Will hugging him and patting his back hard. “When I’m gone, you will be the man of the house, and I’m countin’ on your broad shoulders to bear the load. Right now, we’ve got a passel of work to do and we don’t have time to set around and worry. Worrying never done anything except get a person centered upon misfortune. We have to be positive about our future we cain't go stickin' our heads in the ground."

Ellen had calmed down some. "Please, son, I must know. Where do you plan to go?"

"After I get everything done around here, I think I will head to Texas. I've already written to Grandpa Cain."

"Praise God," Ellen exulted. Could it be that Providence led all those Cain's to Texas? "Yes, Providence led him there, praise the Lord, and now His Providence will light your path as well."

"Well, I don't know about Providence," said Will, somewhat amused. "It's more of an earthly urge that's pushin' me toward Texas. Sure, I want to see Grandpa and Grandma Cain, but I'm hankering to see Clem, that Texas cavalryman I told you about. He wants me to come visit him east of San Antone and I aim to take him up on it. If that don't work out, there is the whole west of America to see, Oregon, Colorado, New Mexico, and California. It's a big country out there and I will be working and sending money home regularly."

“But all the work here, Will,” said Nathan. “Three months ain’t a lot of time, and we still ain’t got any dogs.”

“We will soon enough,” said Will.

Will shared with them the deal Walter Sharples had made on his behalf with the cattle farmer in Opp. Then he produced the telegram from Sam McAtee and the family passed it around. Suddenly everyone felt better about the situation. Ellen started bustling around the kitchen, humming merrily, and Polly went to join her.

“What would you like for supper, Will?” she asked.

“Just whatever y’all got on hand will be fine. We need to eat early then get to bed. I have a letter that must get into the mail as it is a letter of importance to us all. A soon as we eat, I am going to Grandsirs, then on to town. Oh, and, how ’bout rustlin’ up enough corn dodgers for the next few days. Like as not, Nathan, Polly, an’ me are gonna be too busy to eat sittin’ down.”

Ellen put her hands on her hips and struck a defiant pose. “Will Cain, I am still the head of this house and nobody is gonna be so busy they cain't sit down to eat! You'll get proper vittles every day. Bodies cain't work on an empty stomach."

When they were all seated and well into the meal, Will stood to his feet, "Nathan and Polly, momma already knows what I am going to say. I was waiting to tell you about this but, until Grandsir spoke to me at the jail the other day, I couldn't even tell momma. Here goes some of the best news I have had since the war ended. Before I go to Texas, I must go back to Georgia and bring Betty and Jace here to live for a while. I know this is sudden on y'all but I had to wait on Grandsir's righteous God-given Council, which he gave me that at the jailhouse. He agreed that my marrying Betty was right under the present circumstances. I need to go write Betty so they can get prepared. I hope this is alright with you all. She is a wonderful woman with a big loving heart. I know she will fit into the family. So I am going to town in the morning. I would go now but the mail goes out only in the midmorning."

Will filled his cup with Old Crow and went out to the bench under the big Oak tree. Polly shyly came and sat by him. She put her hand on his arm. “I am glad for you, Will. I pray the best for you and Betty. I kinda felt some day you and I would marry. I reckon a colored girl can’t cross that line no matter how much she wants to.”

“Polly, your color hasn’t got anything to do with it, I see you as my sister and that is what is wrong. If you were Uncle Tootsie’s daughter or kin I would have considered it a privilege to have you as my wife. I have loved you as a sister and always will, so don’t go around feeling overlooked, unloved or unwanted, that is the devil putting those thoughts in your head, also momma says we are cousins.”

Nathan and momma came out at the tail end of the conversation. “Polly, sweetheart,” said Ellen, “it isn’t my business, but I believe what he said was true. Bob and I raised you as a sister to both boys, which is what we wanted. I am sorry if the ending is not what any of us thought. You will always be my daughter and the boys’ sister and we were sure your daddy was one of Mr. Cauleys’ sons and your slave mother. Polly nodded half heartily in agreement.

They all were up early the next morning and as soon as breakfast was over, Will grinned and said, "All right, Nathan, go see after the animals, please, sir, and do the milking while you are in the barn. I'm gonna make a run to town, and then we will ride down to the canebrake. I'll be back a long time before dinner, and it'd better be good!"

Polly tossed a dishrag at him as he headed out the door.

"It will be!" she and Ellen said in unison.

After his uneventful ride in to town Will returned home and entered a fresh area of the canebrake, thick with scrub pines and a few oaks, and harkened to the lowing of the cattle in the near distance. Cat listened intently, her ears twitching back and forth, alert and responsive to every noise. Presently he spied a motley herd of about twenty cows, some standing, some lying down, and all contributing to the ungodly chorus. He was upwind of the herd and shielded from their view by a screen of pines and brambles. The mournful song—ungh-hh! ungh-hh!—of one enormous bull was louder and more urgent than the rest. He was mostly black with grayish white on his shoulders and belly, his horns were short and curved inward, and the tips were ivory colored, as if they had been polished. These cows looked healthy to him, not reduced to skin and bones. He reminded himself to ask Grandsir about their lineage. He also spied among the wild herd the family's old red milk cow that had strayed and never returned home.

Will watched for a long spell, trying to get a lay of the timber. It sure looked like they came to this spot often. The herd started walking off, unaware that humans had seen them. As he rode home, he made a mental map of the area, for he would surely come back.

After supper, the family gathered on the pine bench in the front yard. It was a warm and humid night. A whippoorwill called somewhere in the coal-black night and received a sadly identical answer from afar. Every now and again, yellow veins of heat lightning played across the sky. Polly pointed out the Big Dipper and the other constellations Ellen had taught her. Nathan lit a dried cow patty so it would smolder and keep the mosquitoes at bay. Will turned the kerosene lantern down low and sat down next to Ellen on the bench.

"How did we get so much land?" asked Nathan drowsily. Even more so than Will, he felt an attachment to the land and took great satisfaction in seeing a crop come in.

Ellen took a moment to gather her thoughts. "Way back when Grandpa Cain decided to go to Texas, he wanted your pa to have that sixty-acre piece over yonder by the canebrake. He sold it to your daddy for sixty dollars, tellin' us he doubted we would ever inherit anything from him, so we could consider the value of the land above sixty dollars as an inheritance. We did well by that piece, growed lots of corn, cotton, sweet potatoes, and beans. He left a bunch in grass for the cows. Your pa wouldn't plant the same crop in the same place three years in a row—moved them around, said they did better, and I cain't agree more with that way of farming."

As she spoke, Will got up ambled about the yard, gazing up at the stars and letting his mind wander over everything that had happened in the last few days. He had a sudden case of cold feet. He wasn't so all fired sure he wanted to go to Texas, or anyplace else for that matter. He had come home to stay home and start making a living. Now fate had decreed he must leave his home state. Well, he would go, all right. Before he did though, he would give Grandsir and any other doubting Thomas's something to remember him by.

"Penny for your thoughts, son," said Ellen, coming up to him outside the barn.

"You scared half the life out of me!" said Will.

Ellen chuckled faintly. "Son, I learned a great deal about you at the courthouse. When you admitted to striking and robbing those Yank soldiers in Georgia, my heart broke. But when your friend, Angus, spoke up about your good deeds, it mended right up again. I reckon you've more than atoned for your actions and the Lord forgives ye."

"That's what I believe, too," said Will softly.

"I learned a lot about war, too," said Ellen. "What Angus said affected ever'body in that courtroom, I expect. It's hard to think of boys and men suffering the way they did. Makes me glad Bob's end was quick and he had a proper Christian burial. I understand now, son, why you don't want to talk about the war. And I understand why you say it's changed you."

Will didn't try to stop his tears. He fell into his mother's arms and sobbed like a baby.

"It's all right, son," she said tenderly. "You're back with your family now." For too short a while, thought Ellen bitterly, for too short a while.

The next morning, things started in earnest for the family. Will, Nathan, and Polly were in the saddle early and they made the canebrake by first light. Less than a mile inside, they emerged from the cane into some flat land covered with short grass and weeds the perfect stomping ground for cattle, they went left about half a mile then cut back toward where they heard the bellow of a bull. Riding Smoky, Polly saw the herd first. She was on Will's left, riding about a hundred yards away. She waved her arms frantically to catch his eye. Will looked over. She motioned to Will to go ahead while she stayed still. He moved up about fifty yards and slowly eased ahead. The mare's ears were twitching to beat the band. Polly was riding up now and motioning Will to keep going. He could hear the cattle going out ahead, and then Polly hollered "run dangit run!"

Will spurred Cat and she leaped into action. He was right on the cattle and they were going in the right direction, so he kept the pressure on. He took up his black snake bullwhip and gave it two sharp cracks in rapid succession. The lash made a report just like a firecracker, sending the cows flying in a panicked jumble. Will and Nathan drove them hell for leather, and after a fifteen-minute race, they came to the fence. Will cracked the whip again and moved over so he was below the double gate. Once more he popped the whip and the lead cows made a turn to the left, and there was Polly, heading them off. They turned back to the right, and when they did, Will cracked the whip twice and they ran into the pasture.

Will wondered how they were going to hold the restless catch, some twenty-odd head strong, in the pasture. Without being told, Polly loped ahead and sent the oxen out to mingle with the herd. Their bellowing presence had an immediate calming effect.

"Polly, that was a good thought," said Will. "It may have saved our day. Let's move them up toward the pen. I am goin' back to close the gate just in case they run."

Once the catch had been driven into the pen, Will rode up and admired their collection, twenty-three head including one blocky red bull, a specimen of impressive size with a straight back and big hindquarters. It was encouraging that several of the cows had his pa's brand on them, as they might gentle quicker than the wilder ones.

"Nice haul, big brother," panted Nathan. "I'm going up to the house and see if momma made that batch of lemonade she promised."

"Polly, you are a real help!" Will exclaimed when he was gone. "I could not find a better hand if I put an ad in the newspaper. You saw them cows right off and I almost never did!"

"I'm only doing my part," answered Polly. "After all, I'm one of the family like you keep saying, so I reckon them cows are as much mine as yours. I am powerful glad to be working with you. I just don't know what I will do when you have to go."

"Polly, you needn't fret about that. Everything will work out."

"Will, I don't think it will ever work out for me," said Polly sadly, "and now you want to marry another woman."

"Why do you say that, Polly? I don't like to hear you talk that a-way."

Polly's pretty brow furrowed in thought. "Many reasons, but mostly because I am considered black under the law, and there will always be people who will judge me and give me a hard time for that reason alone. I'm powerful fond of Uncle Tootsie and Aunt Winnie I think they are among the finest people in the community, white or black. I just don't feel black, and I am not drawn to black folks. It shames me to say it, Will, but if you didn't sit with me in the black section at church, I'd be too uncomfortable to go, even though Grandsir is the pastor."

Will considered this and could understand why she would feel that way.

"Momma, papa, you, and Nathan are the only family I've ever really known," she went on. "I barely remember my real mother. She died when I was small and another black woman took care of me, until I came here to live. What a sweet providence that was! Momma took me to her bosom as her own and taught me to read and to count, to sew, to clean house and to cook, to pray, and to love. She has been my rock. She is my real mother and I love her so."

"Polly, that's what we are supposed to do," said Will, fighting back tears. "Love one another, for we are all God's children. I know the way a lot of white folk think about black folk, that they ain't human and so on, but I know this they are just as human as white folk. I reckon God put a lot of thought into making people of different colors, same as he did for the birds and the flowers and such, and He hoped folks would appreciate his going to the trouble. It hasn't worked out that way, though. Seems to me too many of this old world's troubles have growed out of one group gettin' riled up over another group's coloration. Me, I'm a godly man and I only see one race, and that's human. Polly, it doesn't matter to me or the family whether you're one eighth-black or pure black, we love you as our own."

With Polly beaming at him, Will tossed a handful of corn fodder over the fence. The new cattle scampered to the other end of the pen, but after a few minutes, they approached the fodder tentatively and fed.

Will turned to Polly and said, "I think if we can feed these cattle a little fodder here in the pen and leave the gate open to the pasture, they will stick around, after they get used to eatin' here. What do you think, Polly?"

"Will, no one has ever asked me what I think of something important like that!" She exclaimed, her green eyes sparkling with pleasure. "I think it's worth a try, but where are we going to get enough feed to tempt them to stay?"

"I don't rightly know," Will had to admit. "Think I'll go over to Grandsir's and talk to him about it."

"Good idea," allowed Polly. She examined her grungy clothes with a frown. "While you're gone, I'm going to take a bath."

"Oh!" said Will, smirking. "On the back porch, I hope. It's a real bother havin' to tote that tub and water to and from your room. Bathin' out in the open shouldn't vex you none, you not bein' modest an' all."

"Close your mouth, Will Cain!" Polly scolded him. "I am a lady, and I aim to put up a proper screen."

Will arrived at his grandpa's house in short order to find the old man chopping wood.

"Howdy Grandsir!" he called. "Here, give me that axe and take a load off on that stump over yonder while I show you how it's done!"

"Be my guest," Grandsir panted and plopped down on the stump.

Will made the chips fly and worked up a real lather. After a while he leaned on the ax handle and said, "Grandsir, do you know where I might find some corn fodder for sale?"

Grandsir raised an eyebrow. "What you want that for?"

Will explained his plan to gentle the cattle enough to keep them in the pasture for a while before taking them to market. "I can hold a bunch more if I can do that," he said. "Polly and I think we can keep them from runnin' off by appealing to their bellies."

"You and Polly eh?" said Grandsir, grinning. "Well, I got some fodder I pulled last winter. You're welcome to that, seeing as how I've got a good many cows of my own in that wilderness, and you're bound to catch a few and have their upkeep on your tab. I recollect one Sunday at church Terrell Morris said he had some feed. Go ask him, and if you need the wagon to haul, you can use mine. You're sure settin' yourself up for a lot of' work, son, and I'm afraid it'll get the best of you."

"Grandsir, I ain't afraid of hard work," exclaimed Will and returned to his chore with a vengeance.

Grandsir watched him for several minutes with amusement. "That is a mighty good thing, because you got a heap ahead of you. You can stop chopping wood any time, son. There is enough to last me and Nanny from now till doomsday!"

"You're right, sir, I just got carried away with myself," Will panted. "I just don't like anybody telling' me what I can't do."

"Not telling you that, boy, just advising you to keep your head screwed on straight. Going well, is it?"

"I'll say it is, Polly, Nathan, and me brought in over twenty heads this morning. Say, Grandsir, I saw a bull the other day down in the canebrake that was pert near all black with gray on his shoulders and a black stripe down his back."

Grandsir nodded knowingly. "That's them old Spanish cattle from down in Florida. Old timers and Indians say they're the descendants of the original cattle the Spanish explorers left behind in the 1600s. Used to be, that's all we had around here. Then us folks from back east brought our English cattle out here—that is, the Guernsey's, Devon's, and the like—and interbreeding changed the color to red and white. Guess it makes a better cow for beef and milk. I am glad to see some of those old cattle around, for I hate to see things change completely. Losing the war is bad enough! We will see some changes, some good and some bad. Reckon the world will call that progress."

After seeing his grandmother and sampling one of her biskits and muscadine jelly, he was on his way to see Terrell Morris. He found the farmer coming in from his sugar cane field, followed by his two black farmhands.

"Howdy, Mr. Morris," Will sang out. "Don't know if you remember me. I am Will Cain, Pastor Garrison's grandson."

"Sure, I recollect you," said Morris. "You shore 'nough look like your pap, 'ceptin yore a sight bigger, but you got his face. Sorry yore pa won't be comin' home. He was a real fine man. The South's got lot to recover from, seems like we have lost the flower of our youth. 'Course, you went off real young and I'm glad to see you got back in one piece. What can I do for you?"

"Grandsir says y'all got some corn fodder, and I need some for a bunch of cattle we have caught."

"Yeah, I got a heap of it," said Morris. He was a beefy man, short and stocky as a fireplug, and just as red as one from years in the sun. Lot, I and Artimus got it in about three weeks ago. My few cattle can't eat it all, and I'd hate to see it go to waste. Reckon the Lord knowed you would want it, an' He knows I could use the cash. I reckon we got five to six wagon loads."

"What kinda price y'all got set on it?" asked Will.

Morris rubbed his meaty jaw. "I'll take two dollars a wagon load, if'n you do the haulin'. If we haul it, price goes up to three."

"I'll give you two dollars and fifty cents for it hauled, an' that's good Yankee greenbacks."

"Awright, Lot and Artimus will be at your place in the morning by six o'clock."

"Thank you, Mr. Morris. Here is the money in advance for three loads. An' I will settle up with Lot for each load after that, all right?"

"Shore thing Will, pleasure doin' business with you."

Returning home, Will smelled the savory goodness of coffee and fried ham before he got to the house. There was another fragrance on the air as well—

lilacs—and he knew Polly must be taking her bath. Sure enough, there was a blanket stretched across the back porch, just as he had suggested. From behind the barrier, he heard a soprano voice lifted high above the sounds of splashing water. He recognized the tune as "The Bonnie Blue Flag," but the words were unknown to him. He stood and listened as Polly rendered a full-throated but comically amateurish performance.

"My homespun dress is plain, I know
My hat's palmetto, too.
But then it shows what Southern girls
For Southern rights will do.
We send the bravest of our land
To battle with the foe
And we will lend a helping hand
We love the South, you know.
Hurrah! Hurrah!
For the sunny South so dear
Three cheers for the homespun dress
The Southern ladies wear."

"That's right pretty singin', Polly," Will sniggered as he stepped up on the porch. He stood before the blanket, which was affixed by clothespins to a length of cord stretched catty-cornered between a post and a window frame. This arrangement produced a small triangular space in which Polly could bathe in some privacy, but it left an open side that was shielded by only a handful of bushes, which Polly figured were adequate cover.

"You stay on the other side of that quilt, Will Cain!" protested Polly. "I'm as naked as a jaybird!"

"Okay. I promise not to peek. What was that ditty you was singin'? Don't believe I know it."

"It's called 'The Homespun Dress'! Shame on you, Will, for eavesdropping on my singing!"

"Can't rightly calls it eaves droppin' I wooden be surprised if Grandsir heard you over to his place. Can't rightly call it singin', neither, sounded more like a mess o' tomcats fightin' in a sack. Why, next time Nathan milks the cow, he's like to draw buttermilk!"

"Now that is a not a nice thing to say, Will Cain!" Polly fumed. "I don't claim to be an opera singer! There was a corn shucking at the church a couple years ago and I heard a group of white ladies singing it and I memorized the words. I was thinking about you, Will, when I came to the line 'We send the bravest of the land,' but now I think you are the meanest of the land!"

As she squawked, Will crept silently to the open side of the porch, where the quilt offered no shield and stood among the bushes. Polly sat in the tub, her back to him, fuming away in the direction of the blanket. A towel and her clothes were draped over the railing. She had pinned her long hair up, exposing the nape of her pretty neck, and the smooth, caramel-colored skin of her bare shoulders and upper back gleamed wetly in the afternoon sun. The high back of the tub hid the rest of her body from view.

As pretty as she was Will couldn't resist giving into an impish impulse. He put a bit of cold water in the bucket, tossed it over the top of the blanket and shouted as it came down on her.

"Boo!"

Polly nearly jumped out of her skin. A fountain of tub water sloshed a good two feet in the air. She craned her neck around and seeing Will, her green eyes narrowed to furious slits.

“Will Cain, you are evil!” she wailed, sinking as low as possible in the tub. “You get out of here before I call momma on you!”

Will had nearly keeled over, he was laughing so hard. Finally, he contained himself and stuck the bucket out.

“And just why are you handing me that bucket?” Polly inquired huffily. “I’m not ready to bail the water out yet!”

“I hear a bucket is awfully handy for helpin’ carry a tune, and Polly, you need all the help you can get!”

Will was too late in dodging the water she hurled at him. It struck him square in the face, but he kept laughing.

“Now, don’t take on so,” he said. “I was just funnin’ with.”

Just then, Ellen stamped out on the porch and peered around a corner of the blanket.

“What’s all this commotion about, Polly?” she asked. Then over the blanket she saw Will trying to sidle away. “William Robert Cain, what are you doing, lurking about?”

“You are her brother, get away from here now I am truly ashamed of you!”

“He was spyin' on me!” said Polly pitifully. “And he made fun of my singing.”

“I was not spyin,’ I was just having some fun,” Will protested. ‘Sides I didn’t see nothin’, and if that was singin’, I’m sorry I didn’t get my ears shot off in the war!”

“Hush your mouth!” said Ellen, laughing in spite of herself. “Polly finish up your bath and the next time hang up two blankets ’stead of the one! Will, get in the house, before I box yore ears. Supper’s nigh ready.”

When his ma had gone, Will called once more to Polly. “See you inside?” said Will.

CHAPTER 12

The next morning, the Cain's had just finished breakfast when Lot and Artimus arrived.

Will, yawned as he told the men where to put the feed. He had had trouble getting to sleep the night before, worrying about the best solution for branding the cattle. Will had a thought come to him, he would build a chute, wide at the top for feeding the cows through, but narrow at the bottom for slowing them up long enough as they scrambled through, so they could be branded, one at a time. He knew he had tarried too long in building a new corral and decided one sixty by sixty feet would fit the bill. He shared his plan for expansion with Nathan and Polly, who pronounced it a crackerjack idea. Ellen approved of his hiring his Powell cousins for the job, as she knew they could use the money.

An hour later, Will and Nathan dismounted at the Powell place. Bob Cain's mother was a Powell and he had always allowed they were a peculiar clan, keeping to themselves and rarely attending church or social functions. Although the Powell's lived but seven miles away, the Cain's saw them only rarely, but still there was a strong bond between the families in times of need.

Will's Uncle James Powell was sharpening a plow down by the barn. Powell was a bony, angular man with shoulders so broad and straight, he looked like he had a broomstick tucked underneath his shirt. He aimed his friendly, perpetually astonished-looking face at them and squinting his nearsighted pearl-colored eyes.

"Howdy, Uncle James," said Will. "How are you this mornin'?"

"Howdy do, Will," he said when he had confirmed the identity of his guest. "Heard you were back and done whupped up on two Blue Coats. More power to you! Step down and ease yore mind. Who is your companion?"

"Why, this is my young brother Nathan."

"So 'tis, so 'tis," said Uncle James. "What can I do for you two?"

"Well, we need some help for which I can pay Yank greenbacks. If you can spare Lucas and Little James, I'd be much obliged to you."

Uncle James strode over to a corner of the barn and brought out a cow horn with a wooden mouthpiece. He trumpeted three clear sharp blasts then waited a minute or so and did it again. When he was through, he was out of breath.

"They will be here shortly," he panted, leading Will and Nathan to the porch. "Pull up a chair and sit a spell."

Uncle James produced a brown and white jug of corn squeezin's from underneath his chair. "Made this batch o' medicine last week," he said. "Turned out rather well if'n ah do say so." He crooked his arm and hoisted the jug onto his shoulder and took a sizeable pull, his Adams apple bobbing up and down like a fish bobber, he then passed it over to Will, who followed suit. Nathan looked longingly at the jug and licked his lips.

"Don't tell Grandsir I led you astray," grinned Will, passing him the jug.

"I won't," Nathan promised. He struggled to hoist the heavy jug up to the proper drinking posture and took a long gulp. Lowering the jug, his grin turned into a wild coughing attack and his eyes bugged out like a bullfrog.

"Takes practice, son," chuckled Uncle James.

Just then, the two Powell brothers came up riding double on a roan mule. They drew back a little when they saw folks on the porch with their dad.

"Somethin' wrong, pa?" Lucas asked suspiciously.

"Not a thing," said Uncle James "Boys y'all member your cousin Will Cain and his brother Nathan. Will has somethin' he wants to talk to you about. Lucas is this dark headed one and this other one is Little James." Boys get off your mule and have a sample of my jug.

"Hi dee lads, said Lucas. Will, we were with your pap, right up until he got kilt. We have seen to it he got a proper Christian burial and we made a wooden headboard out of cedar that will last till you get a stone. Bob never stopped talking about you boys, Polly and Ellender, right proud of his family and thought he was doing his best to keep the South free."

Both men were lean and wiry and had a hangdog aspect about them. They sat down in two raddled rocking chairs and eyed Will with open idolatry.

"Well, I ain't seen you fellers since I was a sprout," said Will. "You've growed into fine-lookin' men." Privately, he thought the privation of wartime rested heavy on their stooped shoulders and in their hollow eyes. We all appreciate you getting him buried proper and writing momma. I know one lady that has been waiting over two years to hear about her husband. He was at Chickamauga the last she knew."

“We walked home with a fella named Douglas who was there at that mess. He said there was so many dead, that the bodies were all rotted before they could get them in the ground. They made the Yank prisoners bury them, just a big hole filled with remains.”

“We heard about a Will Cain that messed up them two Yankees the other day over in Elba.” stated Lucas breathlessly. “Was that you? We kinda figured it was some of Bob’s kin.”

Will nodded.

“I swear, Will, I would like to have seen that action!” said Lucas. “Wearing that gray coat shore gets attention.

“Yeah, it was right there in Atlanta tryin’ to stop ole Burnin’ Billy Sherman, that devil, a sniper hit your pap, said Little James. He was a tough, tough soldier. Sherman shore laid waste to that fair city."

Will gulped and blinked away tears. “I appreciate that, Little James,” he said. “Guess y’all heard Judge Botencourt gave me a hunnert-twenty day to get my business done and leave Alabama for five years. That is what I came over for. I need to hire some help and momma said I ought to keep the money in the family. We will need a new corral and a branding chute and help with the castratin' and brandin'. I can pay you fellers $1.25 cents a day, with hard Yankee coin, plus feed, if you want to work for me. Y'all think it over."

Lucas and Little James looked at each other and seemed to confer in some private, unspoken language. "Whuddaya think, pa?" asked Lucas, ken you get by without us a few days, we could shore use the money."

"Don't look at me," said Uncle James. "Bothen of you done fot in the war and managed to come home whole. Reckon you can make up yore own mind 'bout a Lil' bizness deal. Does sound like they can help us and y'all can help them."

The brothers again exchanged glances and turning to Will, nodded emphatically.

"We'll be there tonight," said Little James.

"Good deal," said Will, rising from his chair. Nathan got up too, a little wobbly and goggle-eyed from the moonshine.

"Glad to see y'all again," said Will. "Uncle James, please come over and visit us sometime. The door is always open for you and I'd be obliged to you if you don't tell momma nor Grandsir I took up drinking."

"That goes double for me!" said Nathan.

It was just after eight in the evening when Lucas and Little James arrived on the mule, each carrying their army haversacks. After they had turned the mule loose in the pen, Will met them on the porch and put them in his and Nathan's room. The Cain brothers would take up residence in the barn during their cousins' stay.

"I would be obliged if you had somethin' to eat," said Lucas, rubbing his belly. "My backbone has been talkin' to my stomach since dinner time."

"Come out in the kitchen and Polly will feed you," said Will. "We got fried ham with red-eye gravy and lots of cornbread, milk, or coffee. Momma has gone to bed, but Polly will take care of you."

The cousins stopped short when they saw Polly set the table. Will caught the look of wonderment in their eyes and smiled appreciatively as he made the introductions.

“Boys, this is Polly Cain, and Polly, this is Lucas and Little James. Lucas is the bigger one. In case y’all’re wonderin’, Polly is family. Her whole name is Polly Ellender Cain—named after momma.”

“How do, ma’am,” the boys said as one. We heard good things about you from your papa Bob. We were with him in the whole war he spoke of you in special ways.”

“Yeah, momma mentioned that. Glad to meet y’all.”

The talk was light and easy. After Will told them how Polly came into the family, the cousins accepted her as one of their own and bantered freely with her. Polly refrained from being too familiar with them, however, for they were white men and she understood she should keep her place. After the main meal was over, she fetched coffee and pound cake for dessert.

“I swan, Will, y’all gonna feed us like this all the time?” exclaimed Lucas. He let out a long, drawn-out belch. “We ain’t et this good in a coon’s age, Little James is thinkin’ he has died and gone to heaven.

Ain't that a fact little brother?" He added, kicking the boy under the table.

"Shore 'nough is a fact," stammered Little James, who couldn't take his eyes off Polly. "Ma'am, if'n you don't mind me sayin' so, you is about the purtiest woman ah ever seed."

Polly smiled demurely. "Thank you, James. Well, good night, see y'all in the morning."

"Good night, ma'am," the cousins chorused as they scrambled to their feet and bowed clumsily.

"Boy howdy, Will, old Bob was keerect about her being a peach."

Will said, "I get up about five and start the coffee, the wash pan and water is on the porch an' the outhouse is back toward the barn. There is a coal oil lantern by the wash pan. Good night, see you in the morning."

The next morning, Will rallied his cousins and sketched out in the dirt for them how he wanted the corral and branding chute built, outfitted them with axes and saws, and indicated the trees to be used for posts. Lucas and Little James were hard, conscientious workers and the labor progressed smoothly as they settled into a routine over the next few days. With Will, Nathan, and Polly pitching in between roundups, the branding chute went together quickly and the stout structure worked like a charm.

One morning a few days later, Will announced to all he was going to go to Georgia and bring Betty back. He left enough instructions and pencil drawings so that Lucas and James could keep on schedule with the corral and help Polly and Nathan trap cattle. He saddled Cat and led Chickasaw behind.

Being in a hurry, he pressed the two horses as much as he dared. They both had a long-lasting easy lope. By riding long hours, he was at Betty's door late the second day. Knocking on the door, it was opened by Jason. When Betty saw who it was, she squealed as if she was wild Indian, and she jumped into Will's outstretched arms, and kissed him with fervor. "I am so glad to see and touch you. Does this mean we are moving?"

"That depends on what news you have heard about your husband", smiled Will.

"Will, I have some news about Stephen," said Betty.

Will's heart sunk and his breath left him, and a feeling of panic came on him.

"Yes, what is the news?"

"Tommy was over in Hamilton last week and went to a meeting of Confederate soldiers, the meeting concerned a proposed pension by the Federal congress, for Confederate soldiers who had served honorably. It won't be much, perhaps eleven dollars a month, but the good news was he met a soldier that was at Chickamauga with Stephen, from Hood's brigade. He said Stephen was fatally wounded and died. He was in the same tent with Stephen. They had just taken Stephen out to make room for other wounded, and then the Yankees overran the hospital. Therefore, we can legally be married. I am sorry to know he died but at least now I know what the truth is and we can plan our future".

"Well, I had a problem in Alabama, said Will, some Yankee soldiers set upon Polly, I shot one, tho' I did not kill him and hit the other one with my pistol. Now the court says I must leave Alabama for five years. I am going to Texas to my grandfather Cain's home and for now you and Jason would have to stay on in Alabama with momma and the family. As soon as I am settled I will call for you, 'cus I do not want to be separated from you. I told momma about us and why I could not marry Polly. She finally understood my reason. Polly was harder to convenience as she wanted me for a husband for a long time. Grandsir will marry us and we will have a nice party. You will love momma and my family. Polly will work through her disappointment with patience and love and she will be fine, 'specilly when she sees how happy we are."

"Oh Will, I know there is lots of things happen' and some changes a comin' but I am so lookin' forward to bein' your wife, meetin' momma, Polly, and Nathan and being part of your family," said Betty.

Will gave Betty a big hug and kissed her soundly. He thought his heart would burst with joy.

"We'll buy you a pretty weddin' dress when we get to Enterprise. You'll be the prettiest bride ever.

"In the morning, we can take the cow and cav over to Tommy, and all the feed and chickens, then make a quick trip to Elba, and our future."

Tom and Martha were more than happy to get the cow and cav, but if Betty wanted them to, they would sell the cow and send the money to her.

"Not at this time," Betty said, "just keep the cow and the old mule y'all can use the milk, maybe raise a pig." They would keep the younger, faster mule so Will could go home and get ready to move on to Texas. They told the story about the problem with the Yank soldiers and Will's expulsion from Alabama. Will greased the light wagon up good and with help from Martha and Tommy, got it loaded and Betty gave them stuff she got from her mother. There was even room for the dog that had become Jason's constant companion.

They left early in the morning and Jason rode on Chickasaw thinking he was a big boy. The Airedale dog followed along beside him as they had become inseparable.

The late afternoon of the third day, they rolled into the farm, surprising everyone but momma, who said the Lord told her that they would be home before dark. The family sat around talking and getting to know each other. Jason was wide-eyed with excitement about all the people that were now his family,

Looking at Polly, Betty said, "Will did not do you justice, Polly when he said you were pretty—beautiful would be much more descriptive."

The next day about noon, the deputy rode out with word that the cattle dogs had arrived in Opp. Will, Nathan, Betty and Jason all made the trip into Elba, with Polly remaining behind to help Ellen cook for Lucas and Little James, whose appetites had proven insatiable. Upon the dogs delivery, Sheriff Sloan had paid the cattle farmer the balance owed him and confined the dogs to a cell and had given them food and water. They were handsome animals, compact, strong, with short, straight, bluish-gray coats, and tan points.

Will settled on the $100 he owed the Federal soldiers and sent Sam McAtee a telegram indicating he would be driving his cattle to Mobile in the next few weeks. The dogs were tied in a buckboard bed without a problem and they seemed to enjoy the ride home. Jason had his arms around both dogs all the way home. "Jason, Will said, you don't want to make your Airedale Jock, jealous over these two dogs. "I won't do that, Will, now I got three dogs."

Arriving at home the dogs received more victuals and Polly's hugs. Polly named the bitch Sally and Nathan came up with Nailer for the male.

At the end of eighteen days, the corral was finished and they had branded ninety-six head, of which they had castrated fifty-one bull calves. At this time, Will figured he had one hundred twenty-six cattle rounded up and could market at least sixty head. Not bad, he figured, for a few weeks work, and he was getting to know the canebrake much better. He was considering trying to get some more pasture, as he could see that the fodder was going to be an expense he didn't want. Betty, never having been a rider, entered into the riding like a bulldog in a dogfight, no fear and lots of try. Polly and Betty took to each other like a duck takes to water and they acted like sisters, with a lot of laughing and joking.

Will sat down on the porch swing with his cousins after he had gone to the barn and got his whiskey bottle out of his tow sack. He went in the house, got three tin cups, and poured a generous amount into each one.

"I want to thank both of you for the amount of work y'all have accomplished for me," he said. "I couldn't have asked for more. I said I would pay y'all $1.25 a day plus feed and a place to sleep." He added with a big grin, "Course, I didn't think two slim fellers could eat so darn much. Y'all near about worked poor momma to a frazzle cooking I figure your wages out to twenty-two dollars and fifty cents each for workin' eighteen days. Do y'all agree to that?"

"Yeah, that is about right," said Little James, "but me and Lucas feel beholden to you for more than feedin' and sleepin' us. Y'all went way outta yore way to make us feel to home, and we're much obliged for that."

Will took another drink from his cup. “I was more than pleased to do it. Been a real pleasure gettin’ to know family again and being able to help, ’cause I know there ain’t a lot of hard money around these parts right now.”

The Powell brothers finished their whiskey and refused a refill, not being heavy drinkers, and set out for home on their old mule. Will walked down to the barn to see about the cattle. Cat sensed his presence and walked over to him. She whickered contentedly as he rubbed her neck and scratched her head. Will climbed in the pen and walked over to Star. The mare looked ready to foal. She was swelling up good and her bag was filling out, it will not be more than a couple weeks he mused, Smoky was coming along nicely, as well. He shore needed to get the stallion home.

When he returned to the porch, dusk was gathering. He sat down on the porch swing and poured himself another shot. The kitchen door opened and Polly came out with Betty and they both sat beside him with Jace at their feet, where they were oblivious to the moon until it glowed over the top of the trees, shiny as a silver dollar on a field of black velvet. Will was aware that Betty was holding her body close to him. Her nearness produced a sensation much to be desired. Right now he had to think on other things such as going to Texas, getting with Grand Sir, planning a wedding and leaving for Texas alone. He had lost his feeling of freedom, sitting by Betty with all the pleasure she brings was all that was on his mind. She was his whole life and his commitment was to her. He didn't feel he had freedom any more to do what he would want, but only to do what was best for them. As his hero, William Wallace did, he had to follow his own convictions and do what he felt God wanted him to do. Will, said deep in his heart, "Devil, you will not steal my joy, you were defeated on the cross. I have the victory over you, when God is for me man cannot harm me."

When he remembered the war, he remembered how the Yankees only wanted to kill you and if they didn't, the food surely would. He never thought about the future. There were things he felt he wanted to have, but he was not thinkin' he would ever get them but he knew also, the Bible says, God will not withhold good things from those that walk uprightly.

Will recalled what Angus had said to him on the road home, friends make the best helpmates. He hadn't paid him much attention at the time, but now the words had rich meaning for him. Will looked at Betty, in the moon light, she looked to him like a storybook fairy princess too beauteous and rare for words, who might dart away on gossamer wings at any moment. They were friends, close friends. He felt so fortunate that he had stopped by her place and stayed to help, not out of a sexual thing but the desire to help someone less fortunate.

For the next several days they worked the timber and cane brakes.

It was several miles towards a little branch that ran the water until late summer the cattle never strayed far from water. Will eased up into the scrub timber and scattering of big pines. He looked down and there was Nailer, peering ahead and sniffing the air. "Easy boy," whispered Will. Halting the mare, he stood up on the saddle and looked intently into the brush.

He was mindful of just how much the exercise had in common with reconnoitering for the Yankees.

Presently, he heard the thoroughly masculine lowing of a bull, a deep down, throaty sound that warned other males to stay away or else come investigate and be prepared to fight. Then he saw him, a mighty gray bull in his full prime. He traveled on the fringes of about thirty cows, not like a stallion in solitary command of a harem of mares, but out where he could fight off another male and service every cow that seasoned. He had a big, thick neck that molded into a huge hump right behind his head, and his dewlap hung down low, showing his Spanish Iberian breeding. The other three bulls in and around the group were of no interest to the majestic gray. Will imagined they had halfheartedly tried the behemoth before but, being younger and less bold, had not proven his match. The gray was busy proclaiming himself loudly to any bull in the canebrake that wanted a challenge. He knelt at the altar of a sweet shrub and tore the ground with his ivory stiletto-tipped horns, first the right then the left, but he heard no answer to his claim of dominance.

Will watched in awe, never had he seen or heard of a bull like this. They were in position to chase them westerly toward Nathan and Polly. He needed to whistle, but with the bull making his throaty call, he was sure that Polly or Nathan would not hear him.

As he pondered the situation, Nailer started a slow sneak on the herd, his head low, his unblinking eyes intent, he was within a couple of jumps of three yearlings. The wind shifted and began to blow from behind, straight to the herd. Several old cows sniffed the air and started moving away from Will in the direction of Nathan and Polly. Will whistled, praying the sound carried, doing it again and again, a little louder each time. He received an answer to his left from Polly and with a loud Rebel yell he spurred the mare into a jump and cried, "Sic 'em, Nailer.

The flight was on! Right, wrong, or indifferent he, the dog, and cows were going west. He heard Nathan shout further ahead and then Polly's shrill yell from his left. Trying to dodge all the limbs was impossible. The only thing for it was to just hug the mare's neck and let her go. He caught a magnolia limb across his forehead that made him see stars. The blow nearly unseated him, but his grip on the big horn was strong. Small branches whipped his face constantly, stinging like yellow jackets. Nailer was biting any cow he could. The cattle started to veer off to the right. Will shouted to no one so much as himself as to what the cattle were doing and with the cows and cavs leading the way, the fence swam into view. He saw Nathan on the east side of the opening with the other dog, Sally. When the cows saw Nathan, they instinctively went to the left, and then turned right into the field. The great bull, turned back toward the brush, but Nailer and Will feinted at him and forced him back into the surge. Enraged, the gray charged the fence and squatted for a jump, but Nailer bit the bull's hocks and turned him aside.

Will called out to Nathan and Polly, "Stay in front of 'em and keep 'em here while I go after the wagon of fodder."

"Will, you are bleeding all over the place!" cried Polly. "We got to get you cleaned up!"

"First things first," said Will and took off like a shot.

Once all the fodder was scattered, the chaotic scene settled down. The oxen and milk cows crowded up to the fodder and began eating. This brought out the wild yearlings and the less timid cows. Soon, even the proud gray was enjoying the feast, but the three younger bulls still gave him a wide berth.

"Polly, you and Betty be the counters," panted Will. "Please count the cattle we just brought in." "I won't!" Betty protested with a stamp of her foot. "At least until I clean you up. You are a mess!"

"She ain't lying', Will," said Nathan. "You look like you come in second place in a pickaxe fight."

"Shut up, Nathan!" said Polly. "You go count those cattle, please, while Betty cleans up Will."

"Yes, ma'am!" grinned Nathan, giving Polly a mock salute.

"Let's get you up to the porch, Will," said Betty with deep concern.

"Shucks, you'd think I had been scalped by the Indians, the way you're carrying on," he protested.

"Hush!"

After sitting Will down, Betty went into the house and returned with a bowl of water, a rag, and a bottle of iodine. Ellen followed with a tray of coffee and hoecakes.

"Land sake's alive, Will, you sure got cut up," said Ellen. "Betty, here let me help."

"No need of that momma, I took doctoring. My grandfather was a doctor in Ireland. Is it proper to address you as momma?"

"Yes, child, if you wish or you can say Ellen. I would prefer momma, it sounds closer."

The whipping branches had punished Will's face something awful, raising long red welts and cuts that bled profusely. With infinite care, Betty cleaned the blood from his face, then gently touched the glass iodine applicator to the cuts all under the watchful eye of Ellen, who didn't care if Betty's grandpa was a doctor, Will was her boy.

"Ouch!" Will winced.

"Can't the baby take his medicine?" teased Nathan.

"How many did you count, Nathan?" Will asked him.

"Including the four big bulls, I counted eleven small bulls soon to be steers, twenty-six cows with calves, six weanlings, and seven cows without cavs. Fifty-four all total."

Will whistled. "That's a fair size sweep! Don't know if we can keep any more around, for feed is going to be a question. Think I had better run over to the Powell's place and get Little James and Lucas to come over tomorrow, and we will brand and castrate everything that needs it. We will keep the young she-stock around for a while an' get them sorta gentle. It appears like we can head to Mobile with at least eighty-one of our animals the rest is Grandsir's. We should catch up another sixty to seventy head before I head out that y'all can market later."

He turned to Betty. "Are you 'bout done, doctor?"

"Yes, Will, dear," said Betty solemnly.

"Good, I'd best be off to the Powell's. Nathan, if you please, go gather up some more fodder and feed before dark. I'll be back about ten."

As Will started down the steps, Betty admonished him to be careful.

Will looked over his shoulder at Betty's dazzling blue eyes that fairly smoldered in the failing light. Behind her, Nathan stood smiling and Ellen stood in the doorway, smiling.

"You bet I will," he said. He laid his hand over hers and let it linger a moment, then he was gone.

Betty spoke to Ellen. "Momma, doesn't Will realize that Polly is in love with him?"

"I am sure he does, but he was raised to believe that she is his sister and that is how he feels. He chose you as his soul mate. I have talked to Polly about it, just so you two don't compete over him."

CHAPTER 13

Arriving at the Powell farm, Will arranged with Lucas and Little James to work two days hence. He was home by ten and found momma in the kitchen, nursing a cup of coffee. He sat down beside her and poured himself a cup from the old enameled pot.

"I know Betty is in love with me and I suspect Polly has feelings that run contrary to brother and sister. To be honest there were times at the end of the war my thoughts of Polly ran to marriage.

Then God had Betty cross my path and she is so much like you momma, I feel like I maybe marrying my mother. Rest assured I am only interested in Betty and Polly only as a sister. She will make some fortunate man a real helpmate."

The next morning Will rode to see Grandsir to talk about the wedding and his need for some good pasture for the cattle they were herding to Mobile.

"Go see Joseph Dykes about that, and while you're there, get the stud horse and bring him home to your place."

"I'll do that, sir," said Will. He stood motionless, looking as if he wanted to speak, but his mouth couldn't form the words. "Grandsir, I have been meaning to thank you for praying for Betty and me, in our special situation that has ended in a good fashion for us. I think Betty's moments of sorrow of the way Stephen's life ended are in the past. Thank God for all things, I would like to have a real wedding, so she could fashion her mind on a real new start. I am so in love with her, she fits in with everyone in the family, like fingers in a glove. It has been amazing. She isn't a horsewoman, but she is not afraid of them or riding after cattle. I have her taking riding lessons from Polly and I. She is also a good homemaker and has taken over cooking, cleaning and washing freeing momma from those chores. Betty and momma both mother hen Jason and he has latched onto big brother Nathan, like a wart. Where Nate is Jason is not out of his shadow. We would like to have a wedding at the church. I don't know how the congregation would accept the idea of her not being a member of the church. I don't want a big party to celebrate our wedding, just the friends and family. I will get Uncle Tootsie to pit a steer, and I will buy lots of food so no one will need to spend any hard-earned cash. Momma and Polly love to cook and are lookin' forward to makin' everything special, Aunt Winnie will help. We will haul the food to the church, so no one will have to come to our place."

"Don't worry about the acceptance from the church, I will put the bug in Nanny's ear and she will have all the women behind it."

"Thank you, Grandsir!" he cried, hugging the older man.

"Rest assured the families will provide liquid refreshments, there a lot of whisky makers in the clan and I will buy lots of real coffee for the non imbibers." chuckled Will.

"Will I would like a private meeting with you and Betty before we go much further with the wedding, I have some important things to say."

"Fine Grandsir, whenever you want to."

"How about this evening in the church office, Nanny and I will be there about 6:30?"

"Betty and I will be glad to hear whatever you and Nanny have to say," said Will.

Upon returning home he broached the plan to Betty and she pondered on what Grandsir wanted to say to them.

Knowing he was a Godly man she was confident that he had biblical principles to share with them.

Later that day when they arrived at the church office Grandsir and Nanny greeted them with hugs and kisses.

"Children, I have asked Nanny to sit in because she has been married to me since movin' from Georgia, endurin' Indian problems here in Alabama and in the hard pressed days of my Circuit riding to preach the gospel and buildin' this church. We have been together since 1831 and have some grasp of what love is."

"You both have said that outside of a hug and a kiss there has been no physical contact which is good. I would like to refer both of you to The Song of Solomon it is a love story from touching to the consummation of love. God used the word know. Adam and Eve knew each other, a physical and emotional deepness, giving and receiving pleasure from each other. I suggest you two rent a room in Enterprise for your wedding night and learn to enjoy knowing one another."

"Will, God says it is a husband's responsibility to care for his wife's physical, emotional, and daily needs and his family when God gives them children. Marriage is a big responsibility, but undoubtedly you are ready for the new chapter in your lives, always love one another."

"Nanny, did I leave anything out," questioned, Grandsir?

"No, said Nanny, that should just about cover it. Will, if you and Betty pray always asking God's direction in every situation through thick and thin it will be awright."

Will, spoke up "now we need to set a date for the wedding! Betty and I were thinkin' about Saturday the 2nd of July. How will that work out for you, Grandsir?"

"Nanny and I will be waitin' at the church for you"

"Then the date is set and we have two weeks to get stuff ready for the big day," said Betty.

"Grandsir and Nanny, thank you, for all the love you shared with us tonight, we will be headin' home as we got lots to ponder on."

Early the next morning Will saddled up Cat and trotted up to the Dykes' farm. He was riding around the buildings when he saw the stallion. Lord, what a magnificent creature Dan is. With that beautiful buckskin color the black dorsal stripe, mane and tail and the black up to his knees and hocks with white socks on two feet and a small star on his forehead. The men were trying to put shoes on him without much success. Nostrils flaring, he whistled piercingly into the air and his feet began to dance. Just holding the halter rope became a colossal chore as the stallion showed his mettle for Cat's benefit.

Will wheeled Cat back around the edge of the building, tied her up, and went back around to where the action was.

"Where is Mr. Dykes, my name is Will Cain, I need to collect the stud and take him home."

A burly white-haired man wearing bib overalls came around the corner, "Did I hear that Will Cain had come to collect that stud horse?"

"Young Mr. Will, we were going to shoe him, but I guess Old Tootsie will get that job. Tell Pastor David I owe him for some stud fees and I will settle up at a later time just tell him Mr. Dykes would rather owe them stud fees to him, than to beat him out of them." The old man laughed at his own wisecrack, his cotton white beard jumping up and down following the old man's mouth. "You look a lot like Bob did when he were young. He was a rascal if there ever was one, handy with his fist, but a real man of his word. Tell David I ain't forgot where the church is.

"It would be nice to see you in church someday, Mr. Dykes."

"By the way, would you know where we could pasture some cattle for a while?"

"Well, I got some grassland that was in cotton until the war messed up the market," said Dykes. "It's got a real good fence around it, horse high and bull stout it is. You have cash money, or you are aiming to trade pasture rent?"

"Sir, I got green Yankee dollar bills to pay with."

"That's mighty fine. Well, son, that field is full of weeds and grass. There is a creek branch that runs through it. Might help me out to have it et down. What you offerin' fer rent money?"

"I can offer twenty dollars for thirty days pasture rent and I will add another two dollars and fifty cents, 'cause it is watered."

"Mm-hmm, mm-hmm," said Dykes, mulling over the deal. "Sheriff Sloan says yore leavin' town, could you pay in advance?"

"Certainly can, sir. Here is twenty-two-fifty, there will be more later if I have more cows to pasture."

Will put Cat's saddle on Dan and rode away from the farm leading the mare, it had been a long time since he had ridden the stallion. Excited by Cat, Dan reared up and whistled profusely through his nose until Will cracked him over the head with the lead rope, and then he settled down for the ride home. Will knew he was riding something that was all horse. What an animal, responsive, quick as a cat and well-trained, his papa had done an excellent job of breaking Dan. The stallion was broken to the plow, giving Dan a chance to use all of his muscles.

With the specter of Will's departure hanging over their heads, the remaining time of his allotted three months was passing too quickly, but Will had things to do as the wedding was tomorrow.

Momma and Polly were busy in the kitchen fixin' ham, sweet taters, turnip and collard greens, green beans, gravy, biskits, corn bread. Uncle Tootsie had the spit turning and Aunt Winnie was making pecan and pumpkin pies and Nanny was churning the butter for the biskits and cornbread. Nanny was bringing some of that yummy mayhaw jelly she made earlier.

The sun was shining brightly as Betty woke up, this was her wedding day. Full of excitement and filled with expectation she reached into her closet and got her beautiful wedding dress out. It had lots of lace and pearl buttons and she laid it on the bed to get a good look. Polly would be up later to help her dress and fix her hair but for now she wanted to reminisce on the day that Will came into her life. Tears of joy were running down her cheeks, she was not going to allow Will's leavin' to dampen' the happiness she felt at the moment. This was her wedding day!

Will loaded the wagon with all the fixens for the wedding party and headed to the church with Nathan and Jason. They unloaded the food with Nanny's guidance. Once that was done they headed home to get dressed in their Sunday best and pick up the women.

Betty looked beautiful in her wedding gown and Will was awestruck by her beauty. Grandsir started the wedding ceremony with a prayer over the couple and then the wedding vows. "You may kiss the bride said Grandsir". Will smiled from ear to ear and kissed Betty passionately.

The party was a huge success with Will playing Mary Morrison and Aye Fond Kiss on papa's bagpipes. The food was outstanding and everyone had a grand time.

Time flew by as preparations were made to go to Mobile.

“According to Betty and Polly’s figures, we’ve got 131 head of cattle to market,” said Will with a mouthful of ham and biskit. Betty’s influence had improved Will’s manners a lot—he still ate with all the gusto but without the messiness of a hog at trough. “Eighty-one are ours and the other fifty belong to Grandsir. That should make all our pockets bulge! I think we should get ready to take this first draft of cattle to Mobile in the next few days. Today is the 25th of July, and my time for leaving is just a little over thirty days hence.”

“It’s better than a hundred and fifty miles to Mobile from here. I think we can make twelve to fifteen miles a day. We will have to graze the cattle all along so that they don't gant up real bad and be worth less money once we get there. I know Mr. McAtee will resell them to someone else, and our best bet is to keep the cows as full of feed as possible."

"How are we going to manage the cattle on the way to Mobile?" asked Polly. "And how will we travel?"

"I think I've got it thought out," said Will. "Jason can ride in the big wagon with momma. I think the dogs will keep the cattle following the wagon. Betty, Nathan, you and I will ride herd, with two horsemen behind and the other two on each side of the cattle keeping them from scattering across the country. The two cattle dogs will follow along and help when and where they will be the most needed and Butch can look and learn from Nailer. We will have to take along some feed for the cows to keep them following the wagon till they get trail broke."

Ellen said," We need to put the bows up on the wagon for shelter while we travel, too. The old wagon sheet should be in the barn. May have a rip or two, but nothing a big needle and thread won't cure. We'll take the grate from the fireplace to cook on and a washtub for cleaning up. Reckon we could use a new barrel for drinking water and some other supplies."

"Those ideas are excellent," said Will. "Nathan can go into town tomorrow for the barrel and stuff."

After supper was over, Ellen and Nathan retired for the night. Knowing how Will liked his evening coffee, Polly brewed a big pot. Will, Betty and Polly took it outside and sat on the pine bench under the whispering leaves of the spreading oak. He brought his cup of Old Crow to sip on along with the coffee. This bench had long been one of Will's favorite haunts, and never more so than in recent weeks. "Now I feel like a man that doesn't have a country." He murmured to both women. "I don't know where I'm gonna go or what I'm gonna do, as I still haven't gotten a letter back from Grandpa Cain. I may not be welcomed there for too long, for they may be havin' a real hard time, 'count of the war."

“We are doing better than most because Will has that Federal money,” Betty said.

“Yes, that is true. Most folks across the South are poor as church mice these days and we’re just gonna have to pull ourselves up by our own bootstraps. The Yankees sure as hell ain’t gonna help. What worries me is all the talk about carpetbaggers and scalawags running things. They got a lot of black folks in the office where they don’t belong. Not ’cause they are black, mind you, but ’cause they have never been educated. I don’t blame the black folk for wanting to get ahead, it is only natural. Look at Uncle Tootsie. Why, he is gonna prosper ’cause he has been taught differently. He is more than a plantation slave, for he has a vision. The Bible says, ‘My people perish for the lack of vision,’ and most folk, white or black, don’t have a vision or a dream.”

“Will,” said Polly, “I have a vision for this whole family and I am praying it comes true.”

Will looked off in the distance. The night bugs had grown silent, as if waiting for his answer.

“Polly, I have a dream also, but for a dream to be good, it has to be something obtainable that could actually happen. No dang sense in chasin’ an ole will-o’-the-wisp. Yes, I have a dream, and we are all in it: Momma, Betty, you, little Jace and Nathan and your future husband and anyone else that wants to partner up with us. What we’ve all accomplished these last few months by the sweat of our brows is just the beginning of the dream.”

CHAPTER 14

The next morning, Nathan hitched up the wagon and left for Elba before daylight, promising to return by mid-afternoon with the necessary provisions. Will took that time to ride over to Uncle Tootsie's to hire him to take care of the cows and other livestock while they were gone.

"Be glad to chore fo y'all while yo is gone, Mr. Will," said Uncle Tootsie in his deep musical voice. "If ah can't, my oldest nephew can, and he could sleep in de barn."

"No need for that, Uncle. He or you can sleep in the house and cook and eat there, too, and I will still pay you the same wages."

"That is mighty fine, Mr. Will. Dey sho is a lot of yo daddy and Jesus in you, just in the way you treat ole Tootsie and Winnie" He paused a moment and added deferentially, "Mr. Will, ah wants to say sumthin to you. I can scarcely think how wonderful it would be if everybody treated each other like y'all treats Winnie and me."

"Uncle, you and Aunt Winnie are family to us."

Nathan got in just at twilight. He and Will filled the water barrels while the women packed the wagon. After returning from Uncle Tootsie's, Will had reset the shoes on all the horses and the oxen. Throwing the oxen to nail on shoes was a real chore, but Betty and Polly pitched in like men and they got shoes on them all. Everything was in readiness for pulling out at daybreak. The last order of business was the cleaning and oiling of the firearms, which included the various pistols and the shotgun that Ellen would keep in the wagon.

Will was up early but not before Ellen. She had the coffee going and was making biskits and frying bacon long before dawn. Will went to the pen, caught the two oxen and fed them, along with the horses, and then he roped the milk heifer and put her with the oxen. Polly would be riding Smoky. Will was riding Cat, of course, and Nathan would take the gelding that Will had acquired in the Aberdeen skirmish. Nathan had grown quite fond of the horse, which had served him so well in the roundups, and had given him the ironic name of Yank.

Before they set out, Ellen stood up in the wagon and prayed for the trip and a good market. The sun was just coming up when they moved out. Will figured it would take them two or three days to get the cattle completely trail-broke and the first several miles were a complete disaster. The cattle didn't want to follow the wagon, but with the combination of Polly, Nathan, the two dogs, and the sting of Will's blacksnake whip, they finally got them strung out in a line they could manage. Polly was brilliant at anticipating where the restive cattle would try to go. Riding came naturally to Polly, and Will greatly admired the lissome figure she cut atop Smoky. Betty was not the stockperson Polly was but she was a valuable hand and she looked good in tight pants.

About noon of the second day, they were set on by a pack of four dogs. Will was not about to let them run off his stock. He rode up on the biggest dog and cut him good with the whip. The dog took off in a howling fit, and the others tucked tail and followed.

They were just thinking about stopping for a while when two men rode up.

"You the jackass who cut up my dog?" said the older of the two.

"I do not appreciate that language in front of women and children. Yes, I cut yore dog with my whip. Your dogs were trying to stampede my cattle and we couldn't chase them away. My advice to you is to settle down and take your mutts and ride off."

"Mister, I aim to be paid for my hurt dog."

"Well, sir, your aim is way wrong, Will said, you are lucky I didn't shoot him. Now accept my apology or don't, but we are goin' down this road and not you nor nobody else is gonna stop us, understand that?"

The younger of the two spoke up. "If you didn't have that gray coat on, we wouldn't let you get away with this."

Anger was rising quickly in Will. "Don't let this gray coat tie your butt to a tree, your yellow stripe is showing."

"I made a promise to myself on the way back from being surrendered in North Carolina that I was not gonna take any guff from any man or beast. Now I see you got a pistol stuck in your pants, if you want to use it, now is the time to root, hog, or die!"

The older man turned white, "I swan, mister, you don't need to be so harsh, guess you didn't mean no harm. That dog ain't worth spilling our blood over."

"Smartest thing you've said today, mister. Like I said, we're just taking' care of our stock as we mosey along to Mobile, not lookin' for no trouble. Good day to you!"

"Good day!" said the men and rode on.

"Will, I never knew you to be so brash and downright hard," said Ellen tearfully. "You weren't raised that way. Hasn't the judge's sentence taught you a thing?"

"I respect the way you and papa raised me," said Will, "but I ain't gonna take any lip from any man, regardless of what the judge and that fancy pants lawyer said. Maybe I was rough on that man, but he will remember that and not be so stupid next time."

Ellen sat stonily, brooding over the son she didn't recognize.

They stopped just before dark and gathered up some wood. Ellen commenced to cook up some meat and to go with the corn dodgers she had made before leaving home. Betty had become Will's coffee maker and she brewed up a fresh pot. They supped under a thumbnail moon with a slight breeze in the air.

Will got up and mounted Cat. "We are gonna have to take turns riding herd on the cattle every night," he said. "I will take the first three-hour watch, then Nathan, then Polly, then Betty. That should get us to daybreak. The dogs will go with us on our rounds. Y'all go to sleep now, 'cause we all need to rest up for tomorrow. It's eight o'clock now. See you at eleven or so, Nathan."

They had no trouble with the cattle that night. Will extended his rounds until midnight before he awakened Nathan. Nathan put in his shift, waking Polly at four. Ellen was on the go around five and they hit the trail by six. Will let the dogs take turns riding in the wagon, as they were both exhausted from the drive and the night watch. With few variations, this was the Cain's nightly routine for the rest of the drive.

Will had Betty practice riding in the dark for several weeks just on a surcingle pad, so that she could feel the horse move under her, thereby giving her a good balance for riding. When he gave her the surcingle, he said it would protect her and she would be comfortable as she rode. The trip proved blessedly uneventful and they made excellent time. Eleven days out, they came to the outskirts of Mobile. Five miles outside of town, Will rented a field for the cows from a man who was more than pleased to draw water for the herd, too, when Will showed him hard Yankee cash. Leaving Nathan in charge, he loped off on Cat in search of Sam McAtee.

He soon reached the town and, after asking directions at the livery to First Street, he came to the McLain Boarding House. The landlady directed him to the saloon across the street, where the barkeeper pointed out a pudgy man, prosperous looking and rather nattily dressed, with an immaculately trimmed salt and pepper goatee. He sat alone at a table, sipping a mug of beer and poring over a financial ledger.

Will walked up and extended his hand. "Mr. McAtee, I am Will Cain from up by Elba, Alabama."

"Well, good for you," muttered McAtee without looking up.

Will frowned. "You quoted me a price on my cows and I sent you a telegram a few weeks ago. I was drivin' 'em here. Of course, if you ain't interested—"

"Cows, why didn't you say so?" said McAtee, standing up and pumping Will's hand. "Certainly, I am interested in purchasing slaughter cattle. How big and how many do you have?"

"Sir, we have 131 slaughter animals about five miles north of town that will come in about 750-850 pounds apiece."

"Well, sir, let's just go see your cows. I'll go down to the livery stable and get a buggy. You wait for me here. I'll be back in about fifteen minutes."

Will walked to the bar and ordered a glass of whiskey and laying his money down, he went to the back table and sat down. Land sakes, he mused, 131 head at ten dollars each would bring $1310.00, which would keep the family on its feet while he took a look at Texas. Grandsir could sure use the $500.00 he stood to make.

McAtee returned promptly. Will tied the mare to the back of the buggy and directed the businessman to the field outside of town where the cattle were lying down, chewing their cud in peace. Will rousted them up on their feet so McAtee could drive through and around them. Will was pleased with the stock's robust appearance. They had taken on water, but not enough to look water-bellied. McAtee inspected the herd thoroughly and then drove around them again before approaching Will.

"Mr. Cain, they are acceptable to me, if you and I can agree on terms," said McAtee, hooking his thumbs in his suspenders. "I don't remember what price range I quoted you," he added cagily.

Will doubt that was the truth. He started to feel he was going to be offered a much lower price than the original quote and his hands started to sweat.

"Here is what I will do, and it is a fair price, I believe," said McAtee. "I am willing to give you nine dollars per head, no cut back. That comes to $1,179.00 cash on the barrel head."

Will reached down to snap off a grass shoot and chewed it thoughtfully. "That your final and only offer?"

McAtee glanced at the cows and then turned back to Will. "It is," he said evenly.

"Mr. McAtee, we drove them cows down here to sell," said Will. "Somebody here in Mobile is gonna get themselves some prime beef stock. Might be you, might be somebody else."

McAtee now had his own sweaty palms. Seeing the cattle in the flesh, he knew they were indeed prime some of the best he'd seen recently. He stood to make a tidy profit from shipping the cattle to Cuba. This Cain boy was young but wily, and he knew he had better watch his step.

"I can go to ten dollars a head," McAtee, a slightly nervous note creeping into his voice. "Cash on the barrel head."

Will made no response. He fiddled with the saddle strings and flank strap for a few moments, just for effect.

"Well, Mr. McAtee," said Will, acting like he was going to mount Cat, "I'm sorry, but if that's the best you can do—"

"Twelve dollars a head and that's as high as I can go!"

Will stuck out his hand. "Mr. McAtee, you just bought yourself 131 head of stock. Let's go back to town and draw up the bill of sale."

"You had me going there for a minute, young fellow," said McAtee breathlessly. "Tell your folks the happy news and we'll be off."

Will loped over to Ellen and whispered conspiratorially. "I sold the herd for two dollars more a head than originally quoted! That's $972.00 for us and $600.00 for Grandsir and Nanny."

"That's fine, son," said Ellen. Polly and Nathan beamed at him.

"I am going to town to get the money and a bill of sale, and then we will deliver the stock," said Will. "Y'all lay around here till I get back. Momma, you, Betty and Polly get up a list of things y'all need that are hard to find back home. Y'all can go on a regular shopping spree tomorrow before we leave town!"

Will cantered along behind McAtee's buggy, letting his mind wander hither and yon. His impending exile was foremost on his mind.

Texas was a long ways off and he would have to make a living doing something, but what? All he knew was farming, chasing cattle, and soldiering. Praise the Lord, there was no call for the latter at the present time. Besides, he had had his fill of it and cared not to make it his life's work. A hand to mouth existence was the farmer's lot—again, not for him but a cattleman, now, there was a way a man could make some serious money.

Arriving at the bank Will tied Cat to the buggy and followed McAtee inside with some trepidation. He couldn't remember ever having been in a bank before. It was a big, fine, bustling place with dutiful little tellers seated behind wooden counters that had little iron bars in front and small openings at the bottom. Will thought, they looked like they were in jail. There was an air of coldness in the bank no one smiling behind the metal grates.

McAtee walked into the bank manager's office, had a word with him, and then waved Will over.

"Mr. Cain, this is Mr. Wulff, the bank manager," said McAtee. "He will pay you as soon as we get a bill of sale ready."

Wulff extended his hand and smiled decorously. Will eyed the prim, tidy man with a pencil mustache and heavily pomaded hair with open distrust. He noted how soft the man's palm was and reckoned he could get a firmer and friendlier handshake from a fish.

Presently, a clerk came in with a paper and pen and presented it to Wulff, who scanned it briefly. "Very good, now, Mr.

Cain, I require your signature on the bill of sale, please sir."

"I need to see the money first, please," Will said in a no-nonsense voice.

"Of course, of course!" said Wulff nervously. He snapped his finger at the clerk, who scurried off and returned quickly with a handful of paper notes, which the manager began to count out in front of Will.

"I only want specie," said Will plainly. "I want no paper unless they are Yankee greenbacks."

McAtee cleared his throat. "Mr. Cain, it will take some time to gather that much hard cash."

"That's all right by me," said Will. "I can wait or I can go find another buyer."

Wulff shot McAtee a questioning glance. McAtee nodded.

"Your patience is appreciated, Mr. Cain," said Wulff flatteringly. "Make yourself comfortable and the clerk will summon you when we are ready."

"Tell you what," said Will. "I'd rather use the time to do some shopping. You got any fine stores in this town? Better than a mercantile, I mean."

"Many fine stores, Mr. Cain," said Wulff, "especially on Broad and Main streets."

Will rose and started for the door. "Good. I'll be back directly."

An hour later, Will returned from his errand and stowed his purchases in a tow sack on Cat's back before entering the bank. A clerk promptly escorted him to the bank manager's office.

"Mr. Cain," said Wulff, "here is the coin you requested. For your benefit, I will count it out. Do you know numbers, sir?"

Will looked indignant, "not my strong suit, but I know some algebra and lesser numbers very well, frontards and backards."

"Very good," said the bank manager. "You will be so kind as to correct me, then, should I err."

"Don't worry, I will."

Will watched closely as the bank manager counted out the greenbacks and placed the coin in stacks. The process took quite some time.

"That comes to $1,572.00," said Wulff. "Is that what you got, Mr. Cain?"

"Correct to the penny."

The clerk put the money in a strong cotton sack. Will signed the bill of sale, shook hands all around, and left as fast as his feet would take him.

McAtee caught him out by the buggy. "I apologize for the delay, Mr. Cain," he spluttered. "Next time, I will be better prepared. When do you think you could bring another herd down? I could certainly use another 150 or so head."

"Don't rightly know, sir," said Will. "I've got to go out of state on, er, business, but somebody from the family will be in touch with you at the boarding house. Now, you never did say where you wanted them cows delivered."

"You're so right, guess I got a little flustered. Take them down to the corrals by the dock."

"Well, then, follow me back to the field and we'll be on our way."

Arriving back at the rented field, Will mustered his troops. They had an easy time of it, with Polly and Betty in front with the lead oxen and Nailer and Sally ranging out on both sides of the herd. Will and Nathan brought up the rear.

The briny tang of the Gulf waters filled their noses, as they got closer to the docks. Ellen and Will had seen the ocean before, but to Nathan, Betty and Polly it was a new and awe-inspiring sight. McAtee looked on proudly as the cows filed into the corrals without protest and filled them up nicely.

"Thank you again, Mr. Cain," said McAtee, extending his hand. "If I were you, I would keep a close watch on that money sack—you never know who may know you have it."

"Thank you for the advice, but that's the last thing I'm worried about," replied Will. "No one comes near our camp without the dogs cutting loose. Besides that, my pistols are cocked and primed at all times and it would do my heart good to drill a few holes in some varmint's hide. If you come across anybody with larceny in their hearts, let them know I don't fire any warning shots. I shoot to kill and I don't take no prisoners. Mr. McAtee, take a good look at my brother and don't forget him. If we bring any more cattle down here, Mr. Nathan Cain here will deliver them."

McAtee gulped. “Yes, I can see you are a no-nonsense sort and you mean exactly what you say. Don’t forget, if you have more cattle for sale, I’m your man.”

The crew moseyed back to the wagon and lazed around for an hour or so. Everyone, including Ellen, oohed and ahhed at the cotton sack of money Will had to show for his bargaining skills. Nathan, Polly, and Betty all marveled at the heft of the sack, reckoning it must weigh close to five pounds. To satisfy their curiosity, he finally opened up the sack and let them run their fingers through the bright coins $972.00 for us and $600.00 for Grandsir.

“Why don’t y’all take the wagon and go into town and buy the things you need,” Will suggested after a while.

“Don’t you want to come?” said Polly hopefully.

“No, I want to stay here and think a while,” he said drowsily. “Here, take a few of these coins. Get me a couple shirts and some britches, please Betty."

After they had gone, Will went to his saddle, took out his secret whiskey bottle, and sat underneath the shade of a big oak that stood in the middle of the field. Spying her master, Cat whinnied and trotted over to Will with Smoky not far behind. He got up and gave them both a good rubbing with a sack, then sat down and filled his tin cup again. As was his habit, he confided in the mare about his future, about God, and the subject that most preyed on his mind, Texas.

"What's your opinion on Texas, old girl? 'Cause when I go, you are goin' too."

Cat shook her head vigorously, by coincidence only perhaps, but Will took it to mean she was in favor of the idea.

Nathan and the women came back late in the afternoon with a wagon stuffed to overflowing with all manner of goods.

Will whistled. "I swan, guess we needed to bring more stock so y'all could have bought the whole blamed town out!"

"We tried, Will," Ellen chuckled. "Reckon poor ole Nathan's growed a few muscles carrying our stuff to the wagon. Let's eat and be ready to leave at first light, for I feel the need to get home."

"Me too," Will agreed. "We need to get home quicker than we come down. I kindly wish the oxen were mules—sure would speed us up."

Nathan spoke up. "Boy, Will, you should have seen the way the men followed Polly around town just to look at her. They whistled and bowed at her like she was a princess or something!"

"Long as they didn't bother her, I reckon it's awright." He went to check on the horses. Cat whickered in delirious pleasure as he scratched her poll and neck. He heard footsteps behind him and turned around just in time to welcome Betty in his arms.

Betty tilted her head up and he kissed her sweet lips hungrily. There had been no time on the trail for romance, only stolen moments for them to talk and laugh about the adventures they had experienced as they traveled, along with the frustration of not being able to be completely and totally physical with each other. Waiting for private moments was hard.

The next morning, they treated themselves to breakfast in one of Mobile's fine restaurants. Nathan and Polly wanted to see the seashore again, so the family spent several happy hours on the beach at

Mobile Bay, picking up shells and frolicking in the surf. By noon, they were on their way home. Nathan rode ahead of the wagon, which Ellen guided at a leisurely pace, with Will and Betty riding behind, savoring each other's company. Without the cattle to tend to, they made good time while still enjoying the sights along the way. They pulled into the farm on September 15 at around three in the afternoon. No one said anything, but everyone was aware Will's exile would begin in exactly two weeks.

Will curried all the horses, paying special attention to Polly's beloved Smoky, and everyone helped unload the bulging wagon. Ellen and Polly had indeed had themselves a spree and the task took the better part of an hour. Will kept to himself the fact he had done some shopping of his own.

Ellen started supper and put on a big pot of real coffee, the way Will liked it. They were just sitting down to supper when Nailer and Sally cut loose. Will went to the door cautiously, but his scowl turned to a grin when he saw whom the caller was.

“Come on in, Uncle Tootsie! Sit down and have a plate of food.”

“Thank you kindly, Mistah Will. Ah gotta be gettin’ back home real soon. Ah jest come ova to feed the stock and heah y’all is back awready, if dat don’t beat all!”

“Have a cup of coffee, Uncle,” Will insisted. “No need to go back so quick. Tell us what happened while we were gone.” The family welcomed Tootsie. He sat down and accepted a piping hot cup of coffee.

“Well, Mistah Will, didn’t nuthin’ happen that was any different than a reglar day. I did have a fellow come by wants to breed two mares to that Chickasaw stud o’ yorn. He is willin’ to pay top dollar. He took a look at that stud colt what Star has an’ he wants one just like it” He paused and added quietly, “Pains me t’ brang dis up, but Sheriff Sloan come out to remember me that yo time to leave are real close.”

The grim reminder shattered the festive air as Tootsie prepared to take his leave.

“Just a minute, Uncle,” said Will. He got up and went to his room. When he came back, he had a jackknife in his hand. It was a handsome thing with the picture of a tall sailing ship scrimshaw on the whalebone handle. Will held another item behind his back.

"Cain't give this to you, Uncle," Will teased. "You gonna have to buy it."

Tootsie laughed his deep, rumbling laugh. "Yas suh, Ize know ah gotta buy that knife and ah gots a penny rat cher in my pocket."

"It is yours, Uncle!" laughed Will. "And here are your wages for taking care of the place while we were gone." He brought out the other gift. "I noticed how you needed a new pair of galluses. These here come all the way from Europe."

"Thankee kindly, Mistah Will! It sho a pleasure havin' y'all fo frens and naybos. Ah really must be goin' now."

Ellen halted him. "Before you go, Tootsie, here is some dress goods I got for Aunt Winnie. Lord Almighty, it is good to have someone trustable to look after stuff."

"My pleasure, Miz Ellen," said Tootsie, bowing low. "Good night, awl."

When Tootsie was gone, the Cain's finished their supper and spent the rest of the evening reliving the trip and discussing the future. To their equal delight and surprise, Grandsir and Nanny Garrison came to the door a short time later. Following a round of hugs, Will presented his grandfather with a beautiful red velvet bookmark for his Bible with a silver cross on one end. For Nanny, he had a delicate lace shawl. Will also paid Grandsir his share of the herd money $600.00 for fifty head.

"Praise God for the bountiful harvest he has given me and Nanny!" Grandsir whooped. "Thank you kindly son for your gifts and wheeling and dealin' on my behalf, I've got something for you, too. Sheriff Sloan came out yesterday with a letter from your Grandpa Cain. I knew you would want to see it."

Will opened the envelope and read aloud

"Dear William,

What a pleasure to hear from you. Times are hard here, but you are welcome to come see us and may stay as long as you want. We are out near the county seat of Jasper. You will have no trouble getting directions to our farm from anyone in town. We will be expecting you.

With affection from your grandfather,

William T. Cain.

P.S. Your Grandma Susan wrote this for me as my letters are not too good."

Will folded up the letter and put it in his pocket.

"Well, guess that about seals it," he said. "Jasper, Texas, and here I come!"

The next two weeks flew by and, too soon, the dreaded time came. Aside from Cat, Will had decided to take Star for a packhorse and her stud colt, which he knew would grow up to be a fine stallion. He put a lead rope from the colt to Star's tail, knowing this was a great way to break a colt to lead. His last advice to Nathan was to stud Dan often and enlist Uncle Tootsie's help as needed.

On the morning of his departure, he rode over to say good-bye to Aunt Winnie and Uncle Tootsie. Predictably, they shed a river of tears at his going and Aunt

Winnie favored him with a sack of her toothsome muffins. “Uncle, I told Nathan to be sure Socks and Chickasaw get bred to Dan. You are the stud horse man.

“Mistah Will, I thank Dan and Chickasaw is too close related. My nephew has a young stalyun that is by Dan out of a race buckskin hoss. It would maybe better to use him. He are the spittin image of Dan only shows mo race hoss.

“Uncle, you are the stud horse man, so do it. By the way, when I get settled up in Texas, I would like you to consider moving with us, providing I can offer you something better than you and Aunty have here. You may be a different color, but our hearts are alike.”

“We will pray on dat, Mistah Will.”

At Grandsir and Nanny’s place, the farewell scene was much the same. Grandsir hugged Will with all his might and said a prayer for him, and Nanny presented him with a long tartan scarf, in the pattern of Bob’s clans, which she had woven herself. Will wondered what use he would have for such a warm garment out west, but he accepted the gift with enthusiasm.

Later, Will and Betty strolled hand in hand to the pine bench and sat without talking for some time. At last, Will broke the silence with the words neither of them wanted to hear.

"I hate to leave all of you, but it seems I don't have any say in the matter. I made a choice to set them Yankee soldiers down a peg. No doubt in my mind that it was the right and only choice but I would have never predicted this sad outcome. I will write as often as possible and send for you Betty, as soon as I can. Everything's so uncertain now. I wish I could say how long that will be, but there's just no predicting it. Sometimes the right way is the hardest.

He swung up onto Cat's back.

"Well, folks, I'd better head on outta here afore Sheriff Sloan has to chase me out," he said. "Y'all be good, and may God bless you. I love you all."

"Just a minute, son," said Ellen. She took his hand between both of hers and bowed her head in prayer. Will thought she prayed for an awful long time. "Godspeed, my son and may the good Lord protect you on your journey." She paused and added, "Son, do you have to wear that gray jacket? It's brought you nothing but trouble so far."

"I have to," said Will.

"Will, no don't do it."

"If anybody asks where I'm bound, just tell 'em I've gone to Texas, like many a good Southern man before me."

They waved him down the long clay approach that connected the farm to the rest of the wide, wide world, and they didn't look away until his figure was a gray smudge on the horizon.

Betty Cain broke into a crying sobbing spell, comforted by momma and Polly. Only Betty and momma knew the realization of watching your man ride off to only God knew what.

As Will rode away there was a deep yearning in his heart. He wished he could turn back the pages of his life, beginning with his childhood and start over again. Will knew this was not possible. He wanted to express more of the Christ like attitude he had in his youth but had lost during the war. Being a compassionate and understanding man was his new quest as his intentions were to leave the rebel spirit behind.

His love for Betty was the only good thing to have risen in his life in the last few years since the joining the cause. Will, rode on towards Texas asking God to help him do right in the future.

ON TO TEXAS AND THE NUECES RIVER

ACKNOWLEDGEMENTS

First of all to Jesus, my Savior, who has poured out His blessings upon me and placed this book in my heart, I thank you.

I wish to thank the following family and friends that helped make Will Cain a reality. I could not have done this without each and every one of you.

Pat my faithful wife of 60 years who has stood by my side in all my endeavors and through many circumstances. *He who finds a wife finds a good thing and obtains favor from the Lord.* Proverbs 12:22

Elizabeth Ann Parker Gregg for her computer expertise, kindness and undying love for me, her Mom and family. You are so special to me and I love you so much. Your character is the mirror image of your Mother.

Ian Andrew Parker our youngest son, for his perseverance in seeking Jesus and for giving life to our precious Hannah Mishel Parker who is such a joy to me. I love you both!

Fred Fluker, who did a fantastic eye catching design on the cover of this novel.

Pamela Guerrieri and Kevin Cook, your guidance and long hours are greatly appreciated.

George Hayes, Pie Town, NM a solid friend who helped his friend when he needed to begin this journey.

The Parker clan and many friends, who encouraged and prayed for me during the writing of Will Cain.

My ancestors who left the British Isles and pioneered America making her what she is, who knew freedom was not free and paid the full price.

And to the band of my brother Marines, many lay at peace now the battles o'er.

There are many things in my life that stand out, two of them being a real cowboy and knowing that my enemies missed when they shot at me during the Forgotten Korean War.

BIOGRAPHY OF WILLIAM "BILL" B. PARKER

Born in Jasper County Texas on January 11, 1935 to Brantley and Jewel Parker. Being raised by a logger and rancher, cattle and horses naturally became part of my life. One of my first pets was given to me by my Grandfather, an orphaned calf named Bully who turned out to be an ornery critter but tasted real good. Toward the end of World War II, my Dad moved the family to Devils Garden located between Klamath Falls and Ashland Oregon where wild horses roamed in the big timber. Several years later we moved to Umatilla County in Eastern Oregon. In

1952 I graduated from Umatilla High and immediately joined a fine group of men in the U.S. Marines. A year later I married my high school sweetheart, Patricia Lane. In the 1st Marines I gained education and maturity with thirteen unforgettable months in Korea. Being honorably discharged as a Sgt, I enrolled at Portland State College with the intention of becoming a history teacher and a football coach. After 2 years I left college and began my career in the construction field in Hawaii, Oregon, Texas, and Washington. The background led me to rehabilitation of apartments and property management. While living in Hawaii my coaching dream became a reality as the school my son attended did not have a wrestling program. My buddy John Hay and I began Konawaena High Schools first wrestling team. My son Tom, along with numerous other young men who I hold dear till today, were coached by me in Wrestling and Jr. Varsity Football. Extremely memorable years!! We relocated to Arizona where I became a rancher with my partner, Nate Spencer on 27,000 acres we leased from the Bureau of

Land Management. We spent numerous hours on horseback, branding, moving and working cattle. I thank God that he allowed my dream of being a cowboy to come true as there is nothing compared to riding a good horse in good cow country. With our children and their families located in Hawaii we returned to be with them. Today we have a small coffee farm and are raising our precious granddaughter who has a love for horses as I. This is my first novel which is another dream come true. Thank you Jesus!